MISTRESS OF WYNDVIEW

The Wynd Brothers
Book 1

Jane Charles

ARE YOU SIGNED UP FOR DRAGONBLADE'S BLOG?

You'll get the latest news and information on exclusive giveaways, exclusive excerpts, coming releases, sales, free books, cover reveals and more.

Check out our complete list of authors, too!

No spam, no junk. That's a promise!

Sign Up Here

www.dragonbladepublishing.com

Dearest Reader;

Thank you for your support of a small press. At Dragonblade Publishing, we strive to bring you the highest quality Historical Romance from some of the best authors in the business. Without your support, there is no 'us', so we sincerely hope you adore these stories and find some new favorite authors along the way.

Happy Reading!

CEO, Dragonblade Publishing

CHAPTER ONE

Cape Colony, January, 1817

T REPIDATION FILLED HIS entire being as the coastline and port grew closer in view. Sterling Wynd, Earl of Wyndham, had not suffered such discomfort when he boarded the ship in Southampton, nor when he traveled the length of France and Italy, sailed to Greece, and then back to Spain, where he trekked across land again and through Portugal. His unease only began when he boarded this last ship—the one bound for Cape Town. Now, seeing the lush, green landscape, beaches without end, bright flora and fauna, and Table Mountain in the distance, he should have been awed and amazed. Instead, his stomach knotted. He knew who waited, but was uncertain of the reception he would receive, or how he would greet her.

Once he disembarked the ship, Sterling hired a man with a wagon to take him to Wyndview Farm, the place of his birth.

As they rumbled along the dirt road, he looked out over the landscape, once familiar and hardly changed, and considered what he would say when he saw her again. Sterling had rehearsed speeches in his head several times over, but none of the words were ever right. He had but one question. Whatever answer she gave would not suffice.

As the wagon pulled up to the stately whitewashed mansion, rising two stories with long ornate gables and a high thatched roof, memories flooded him from a time when he had been happy here.

Sterling closed his eyes and took a deep breath as he prepared for the meeting before he marched forward and knocked. He was as prepared as he was ever going to be.

A moment later, it was opened by the same butler who had served the family for decades. "Hello, George."

The man's eyes widened as some of the color fled his cheeks. "Lord Wyndham?"

"Yes," Sterling answered simply.

George stepped back and opened the door wider so that he could enter.

"We… well…we were not expecting you."

That had been Sterling's intention, but he had not anticipated the distress or perhaps panic in the old butler. George practically stammered. *Odd!*

Sterling stepped into the white, plastered entry, marble floors beneath his boots and glanced around. It was just as he remembered. "Where is she?"

"At the back of the house in the lavender sitting room."

Sterling remembered it as the place she missed the most after they moved to England. She had longed for the sunlight that often filled the room, and how it caught the ocean breeze when the windows were opened and the sweet scents from the gardens set out and away from the house.

With determination, Sterling strode down the corridor, turned left and stopped just inside the door to the sitting room.

She was as he had remembered. Hair, still golden, pulled away, braided and with curls appropriate for her age, high cheekbones, narrow nose, blue eyes intelligent and questioning even as they widened in surprise at the sight of him. She had always been beautiful and a day did not go by that Sterling had not glanced at her portrait. It was nearly impossible not to since it hung over the large fireplace in the library at Wyndview Hall in Southampton.

Sterling's heart constricted with the pain of betrayal, which he pushed aside. She was the one who had left him.

"Sterling?"

"Hello, Mother."

"LORD STERLING WYND, the Earl of Wyndham, has arrived," George quietly informed her.

Caroline Sutcliffe paused in her writing. She could not have heard correctly.

She prayed that she had not.

She slowly looked up from the ledger where she had been calculating the costs and income for Wyndview Farm to finalize the quarterly report to be sent to Lord Wyndham at the end of the week. "What did you say?"

"Lord Sterling Wynd, the Earl of Wyndham," he repeated.

Her heart started to pound against her chest as a tightness developed in her throat. A Wynd had not visited the property in years. Not since her family had arrived with the former Earl of Wyndham in 1806. Well, other than Lady Wyndham, who had remained behind, making Wyndview Farm her home instead of returning to England with her husband.

"Why?" Her question came out in a whispered breath.

"I do not yet know," George answered, equally quiet.

His response only increased her anxiety.

"Where is he now?"

"With Lady Wyndham."

Caroline nodded as her mind raced with what this could mean and what she must do.

"I am certain that he will want to be shown to his set of rooms and freshen from his voyage before asking to see your father," George said.

Yes, of course. He was an earl, at the end of a long journey. He likely wanted nothing more than brandy and a place to relax and not be bothered by anyone while he visited with his mother. At least that gave her some time to…

Caroline groaned. No matter the amount of time to prepare, it would not be enough, especially since they did not know why he was here. "Are my father and brother still inspecting the grapes?"

"I believe so," he answered.

"Thank you, George." Caroline rose from the desk and quickly closed the ledgers before she put them away, then made certain that everything on the desk was put to rights and organized to her father's preference.

Why is Wyndham here now? she asked herself as she hurried to the stables.

"I need a horse saddled," she told the stable hand, who rushed to do her bidding. She needed to find her father and prayed that he would not be difficult and that her brother, William, would remain by his side through all interviews with the earl.

After the man brought her the horse, Caroline mounted it and took off out of the stable yard. She wasn't dressed for riding, but time was of the essence; she did not have the luxury to return to her chamber and change into a proper riding habit.

Wyndham could not have picked a worse time to visit. They did not have time to coddle, entertain, or answer questions of a pampered lord, even if he was the owner and her father's employer.

Of course, Caroline was assuming much, but ever since the British took over the Cape Colony in 1806, and especially after formally acquiring it in 1814, English settlers came here to buy property as well as establish businesses, which caused several of the Dutch colonists to move away. England was more interested in expanding and protecting their trade routes and didn't even bother to learn anything about those who had made their home at the southern tip of Africa for centuries.

Was Wyndham here for a similar reason—for the benefit of Trade Wynd? Wyndview Farm, where she lived, was only a small part of the Wynd family import and export empire since they only grew grapes and made wine to be exported.

Maybe he was only here to visit with his mother, and perhaps meet with Governor Lord Charles Somerset, as all other titled visitors and those who were a part of English Society did when they visited the area. It really did not matter to Caroline so long as he stayed out of the way.

As her horse crested a small hill, Caroline looked over the vineyard, rows of grapes that would soon be harvested for wine. The farm workers were walking down those rows and inspecting the grapes and the vines, but she could find neither her father nor brother, so Caroline rode closer. She wished she would have brought her bonnet because the bright sun was in her eyes and sweat trickled down her neck and back.

"Caroline?" her brother called from three rows over. "Is all well?"

"The Earl of Wyndham is here!" she yelled back.

His brown eyes widened with alarm. "Bloody hell!"

"I agree with your assessment," she answered, neither shocked nor disturbed by her brother's language. "Find Father and return to the house. Wyndham is likely getting settled but I am certain he will want to speak with the estate manager."

"What are you going to do?"

"What is there for me to do?" she asked innocently. "I am simply a widow who returned to her father and family home."

William snorted. "If Wyndham believes you are nothing more than described, then he is a bigger fool than I ever imagined."

She could only hope that he was, otherwise, there was a risk that her father would lose his position, and they would all lose their home.

The Earl of Wyndham needed to believe that she was nothing more than an unassuming daughter of his estate manager. An estate manager who only cared about growing and harvesting grapes and making wine while she managed all other aspects of Wyndview Farm.

✦

CHAPTER TWO

"IT IS SO good to see you, Sterling." His mother smiled brightly as she started forward, arms out as if she were going to embrace him. "What brings you to Wyndview Farm?"

Did he let her enfold him in her arms? Sterling had not seen the woman in over ten years, not since she had sailed from England with Father, never to return.

"I intend to make a tour of our properties. I have already visited the wineries and quarries where we have business relationships." It was important that she know that this was not a holiday, visit, or reunion, but rather a trip to further the interest of Trade Wynd.

She reached his side, put her arms around Sterling, went on her toes, and pressed her cool lips to his cheek.

He simply stood stiff and unyielding. Bitterness at her abandonment, which had accompanied him these many years, nearly choked him.

"Did you visit Madeira and your brother?" she asked after she stepped away, not appearing at all flustered that he hadn't returned her affection.

"I will stop and visit Elliot on my return to England."

"He seems to enjoy his life there." She turned and glided across the room to stand near the window that looked out over her favored gardens.

How could she know what Elliot or any of them enjoyed?

Movement outside, beyond his mother, caught his attention. Straining, he noted a lone woman with dark hair ride toward the fields. Even though she was using sidesaddle, she was not wearing a riding habit, which left a good portion of her leg exposed.

Were hoydens common in the Cape Colony or just at Wyndview Farm? If it were only here, then who was she?

"Where did you visit?"

His mother's question pulled him away from his wondering about the mysterious woman, and he returned his attention to her.

"Vineyards in France, Italy, Spain, and Portugal as well as quarries in Italy and Greece."

She arched a brow. "Goodness! How long have you been traveling?"

"I left home nearly a year ago."

"That is a good deal of time to be away from Trade Wynd," she mentioned in a curious tone.

"Damian has Trade Wynd well in hand. My presence is not necessary." His younger brother had overseen the docks, warehouses, and scheduling ships for Trade Wynd since their father died and Sterling's presence truly was not needed.

Her lips thinned as she nodded. If she wanted a conversation about his travels or family, she would be disappointed.

"And you are here because we are in a business relationship and for no other reason."

"I am here because I own the vineyard and it is necessary that I tour the estate and see where we make wine."

"You were born and raised here. I find it difficult to believe you do not remember."

"As you know, I was ten and two when we moved to England, therefore, I was quite unaware of the details involved in the management of Wyndview Farm. I intend to rectify that failing."

She nodded again. "I suppose you want to review the books as well."

"Of course."

At least she now understood that this was not to be a friendly visit and perhaps he would not need to remain very long.

"Where is the estate manager?" The man should be able to provide him with all the information he required and allow Sterling to limit any interaction with his mother.

"Hallaway is not available to you, but away." His mother smiled as if she didn't have a care in the world. Perhaps she did not. She lived here alone, by choice, with financial support previously provided by his father and now him.

"Besides, you just arrived, therefore, we will have tea. Then you will rest. Tonight, we will dine and tomorrow you can begin your inspection."

If she thought to manage him or his time while he was at Wyndview Farm, his mother was mistaken.

Sterling stared into her pale-blue eyes and for the first time noticed a hint of sadness in contrast to her smile and warm welcome. His mother portrayed happiness that might not exist, which if that were the case, it was of her own making.

He was also about to tell her that he had no interest in taking tea and intended to find Hallaway when something, or someone, ran headlong into the back of his legs almost knocking him off balance.

Sterling slowly turned and looked down to find a little girl of no more than five or six, brown eyes wide with fear, backing away from him. Had she not seen him standing there or had she been running without looking at where she was going?

She was dressed far better than the child of a servant and in delicate yellow muslin trimmed in lace and her hair was neatly pulled back and braided with ribbons at the end.

Who did she belong to?

He glanced back at his mother. Was the girl hers?

It was possible, he supposed. Had she remarried after his father had died or was the child a bastard?

"Livia, come here." His mother held her hand out to the child, who did her bidding, but gave a wide berth as she maneuvered around Sterling, clearly frightened of him.

"Who is this?" he demanded.

His tone must have been sharp because Livia ran the rest of the distance to his mother who placed a protective arm around her slight shoulders.

"Miss Livia Sutcliffe," his mother answered.

"Where did she come from?"

Sterling nearly held his breath as he waited to find out if he had a younger half sister that nobody had told him about.

"She is the daughter of Mrs. Sutcliffe."

"Who is that?" he demanded, but assumed there were guests in the household.

"Your estate manager's daughter."

Sterling frowned. Hallaway had a son, William, and a daughter, Caroline. The entire Hallaway family had moved here from England in 1806 when Hallaway had been hired as the estate manager by his father. That was one of the reasons his father and mother had made the trip to the Cape. Clearly the child belonged to Caroline, who was now Mrs. Sutcliffe, but that did not explain why the child was running around this home.

"They are visiting?" he asked.

"Who?"

"Mr. and Mrs. Sutcliffe."

His mother frowned. "My dear, Caroline is a widow."

That still did not explain why a servant's child was running about the house, and he intended to find out exactly what kind of home his mother managed.

"WHERE IS HE?" Caroline asked quietly as she slipped into the kitchens, which had been built separately from the house because of the heat that could build during the day, to keep it from invading the house, and to protect against the risk of fire that could erupt when cooking on open flames. The two buildings were separated by a short, covered walkway.

She'd been nervous since George announced that Lord Wyndham had arrived. What would he think of the estate? What changes would he make?

More importantly, what might he discover that he should not? Her greatest fear.

"He is with Lady Wyndham," a senior maid answered.

This was good. The longer he remained occupied, the more time her father and William had to prepare. "My father and brother have come in from the fields and are repairing their appearance so that they can meet with Lord Wyndham."

"How is your father?" Cook asked with concern.

"He is well and I made certain to explain the importance of this meeting." Whether he did understand and took her warning to heart was another matter. "Also, William will be by his side." At least her brother did know how vital it was that this meeting went well so that Wyndham was satisfied with the state of Wyndham Farm.

"And you?" Cook asked.

"I will be near, but I also do not want to draw attention to myself."

"We will also be careful in what we say," the maid assured her.

"Thank you," she returned.

Oh, she hated that the servants might need to lie about how the estate was managed, but they also feared that if the knowledge became known to Wyndham that he might sack her father and hire a new estate manager which would alter the security of their positions.

"I am off to make certain that everything is put to rights in the office." She had left so quickly that she feared that something of importance may have been overlooked despite how careful she had been.

As she started to leave the kitchen, Caroline glanced at a

corner table and stopped. Her daughter was not at her usual place for this time of day, which was having a small repast following her lessons. "Where is Livia?"

A maid blinked. "She was just here. I did not see her leave."

Caroline's heart pounded. If Livia needed her, she would have gone directly to the office and she must warn her daughter that she could not go there any longer, at least not until Lord Wyndham had sailed back to England. In fact, her daughter needed to refrain from wandering anywhere in the house even though Lady Wyndham always welcomed her to do so because she enjoyed having a child around.

"Livia, where have you gone?" Caroline quietly called as she hurried past the sitting room that Lady Wyndham enjoyed and headed toward the office near the front of the house.

"I am in here, Mama," she called, her voice coming from behind.

Oh dear. If she was with Lady Wyndham, did that mean that the earl was somewhere else?

Caroline hurried back to the lavender sitting room but was brought up short at the sight of the Earl of Wyndham.

Goodness, he was handsome and tall. Blond hair streaked by the sun, deep-blue eyes, and bronzed skin likely from being at sea and in the sun for hours at a time. More handsome than he had been when she had spied him across a ballroom seven years ago during her one and only Season.

"Lord Wyndham," she greeted as she bobbed a curtsey.

"I take it that you are Mrs. Sutcliffe," he returned.

"Yes. I am. My father should be with you shortly," she offered. "I rode to the vineyard to alert him of your arrival." William's presence would be explained when the two arrived.

One golden eyebrow rose over his left eye. "I had wondered who the hoyden was who rode past the window not long ago."

Her face burned. It had not been her best moment given that she had difficulty adjusting her skirt and therefore her legs were not properly covered, something that would have been shocking in London, but not here. "I apologize if you were scandalized, Lord Wyndham, but I thought it more crucial that my father be alerted to your arrival."

"Should not a stableboy or other servant been given that task?"

Oh, dear, he was correct, but Caroline had a habit of doing things herself. "I did not want to disturb them when it was something that I could easily accomplish."

He nodded to indicate he accepted her explanation, though his tight expression spoke of disapproval that did not aid in putting her at ease.

"It is not necessary for Mr. Hallaway to rush on the account of my son being here," Lady Wyndham announced. "After tea, Sterling will be getting settled into his chamber, hopefully bathe, and then we shall dine."

He stiffened at the order or perhaps he'd been insulted, but Caroline was not close enough to him to know if a bath was necessary or if he simply resented Lady Wyndham ordering him about.

"I am certain that it is not necessary for your father to meet with him before tomorrow morning," Lady Wyndham concluded.

"If he will see me now…" Lord Wyndham began but his mother held up one finger, her thumb closed over the others as she pointed at her son.

"I understand that you have not been here in nearly seventeen years, but it is our summer and Mr. Hallaway has been in the fields most of the day, in the heat and under the bright sun. Days such as these, especially this time of year, leave everyone exhausted. It is bad enough that you have disrupted his schedule, but your demands can wait until tomorrow."

"He has already returned from the fields. Mrs. Sutcliffe said as much," Wyndham argued.

"He will need to wash, change into proper clothes then prepare the documents to discuss Wyndview Farm," she responded.

"He may be your employee but certainly, Sterling, you must also be cognizant. Your demands are rather burdensome when there is nothing urgent about your request, unless you intend to board a ship and leave tomorrow morning."

Caroline blinked and backed away, shocked at how Lady Wyndham had talked to her son.

"Very well, Mother," her son bit out, obviously irritated.

"George," Lady Wyndham called.

"Yes, Your Ladyship," George responded almost immediately, which meant he must have been just outside the door, eavesdropping. Caroline hoped he continued to do so and report to her anything he learned about the Earl of Wyndham and why he was here.

"Send word to Hallaway and his son that they are not required to meet with Wyndham until tomorrow."

"Very good, Lady Wyndham." George nodded and left quietly.

"Livia and I should be going as well." She held out a hand to her daughter.

"May I inquire, do you live with your father or are you visiting?"

"We live here," Livia answered happily as she skipped toward Caroline.

"I found it necessary to return to my father after my husband was killed in the Battle of Dresden," she added.

Wyndham frowned. "You have been a widow for over three years?"

Why did he seem surprised? There were women younger than she who were widows.

"Have you lived here since?" Wyndham asked.

Oh dear, he was going to ask her to leave. "Yes. My mother also died not long after and my father needed my assistance while my brother, William, was still in school."

Wyndham frowned. "Assist how?"

"His household, Lord Wyndham," she answered tightly.

"Further, I was without financial support and had no choice of where I might live."

She hoped he would allow her to remain and ask no further questions.

"If there is nothing further, I shall take my daughter home." Caroline grasped tightly to Livia's hand and slipped out of the room before any further questions could be asked.

Her pulse pounded and her hands shook as she returned to the kitchens, where the servants were preparing the evening meal.

There was no warmth to Lord Wyndham and she wasn't certain he possessed kindness either.

What could happen if he found displeasure with the estate, her father or…Caroline groaned. She must make certain that nothing went amiss while he was here.

"Have you seen His Lordship?" a maid asked quietly after she entered the kitchen.

"Yes, he is with Lady Wyndham."

"What of your father and brother?" another maid asked.

"They will meet with him tomorrow morning."

"Lord have mercy," a maid whispered.

The situation was not so dire. "All will be well. I am certain of that," Caroline said even though she lacked confidence. Perhaps a few prayers to see them through this situation would not be remiss.

CHAPTER THREE

AT LEAST HE now had a name to the woman who had exposed a good portion of her leg when she rode by the window, but Sterling had not expected her to be old enough to be a mother either. He'd really only glimpsed the leg and long dark hair. What had been missed was that she was nicely formed with a full bosom, long neck, plump red lips, and large expressive brown eyes framed in thick dark lashes.

Did she have a purpose in the household or were her duties limited to her father's home, and did she make it a habit to allow her daughter to go where she wished?

"I do insist that you join me to tea." His mother's voice broke into his thoughts.

Sterling had intended to remind his mother that she had no right to insist on anything from him, nor did he want to sit and force pleasantries with his mother, but when the service was delivered by a footman and he noticed the small sandwiches of ham, cucumber, and cheese, scones with clotted cream and jam, and small cakes, his stomach grumbled. He'd not eaten in hours and meals on the ship were not always appetizing, especially after being at sea for nearly three months, and reluctantly he took a seat across from her.

It was only because this would satisfy his hunger until dinner.

As his mother poured, he filled a small plate with one of each item provided.

"What stories did your father fill your head with to make you hate me so?"

He looked up and into her blue eyes. "He did not need to tell me anything. You abandoned your family." And he did not hate her. Just resented her decisions.

"Is that how you saw it?"

"There was no other way. Father returned to England; you remained here."

She nodded and took a sip of tea.

Perhaps this was the end of what he feared would be a fractious conversation and he would be able to enjoy his tea and sandwiches in peace.

"Did he offer no explanation?" she inquired.

"We asked, of course, and he only said that you stayed behind."

His mother harrumphed. "Did he tell you that he was the one who left me here?"

The cup was halfway to his lip when Sterling stilled. Was she going to blame Father?

"Why would he do so?" Sterling could think of no reasonable explanation for why his father would leave his wife behind.

"He was eager to return to England and I will admit that I was not," she offered.

Even though he had always known that she had chosen the Cape Colony over Southampton, it still hurt to hear her admit it.

"I missed my sons, terribly, but not England. I also knew that the visit would likely be the last that I had with my family."

Yes, it took practically half a year to sail to and from Wyndview Farm to England, but that did not mean that his mother would not have another opportunity to visit.

"We argued, but I knew that despite my wanting another sennight with my family that I would be required to leave with my husband at the date and time dictated by his schedule." She set her cup aside. "We were packed and I was ready the day before the ship was to sail. That evening, I went to visit my parents in the home they had built down the road. Your father knew that I planned on sleeping over because I anticipated a late night as we said our goodbyes. He was not pleased, of course, because he feared that I was the cause of a delay."

That sounded very much like his father, who had liked to keep an exact schedule.

"I woke the next morning before the sun and allotted myself more than enough time to return, said my tearful goodbyes and hurried home," she continued. "He had already left."

"Father was punctual," Sterling reminded her.

"Yes, and we had allowed for more than enough time to leave here and arrive at the ship before it was set to sail. However, he left earlier than he intended and informed the servants that if I did not arrive at the ship in time that he would leave without me."

"Why would he do so?" Sterling demanded.

"I assumed that it was because he was angry with me. He accused me of making decisions difficult for him when all I wanted was a little more time with my family."

Sterling's heart thawed, but only slightly. He understood and he would have been sympathetic to her reasons, but the fact that she never returned to England was inexcusable.

"By the time a footman found a wagon that could be used, and then had it loaded with my trunks, which your father also left behind, and drove to the port, the ship had sailed."

Sterling frowned. How long had she been delayed?

"After I returned here, hurt, upset, and uncertain as to what to do, I found a note from the captain on his desk stating that they intended to sail hours earlier than originally planned and gave a time that we should arrive at the port."

"Father cannot be faulted for you not being punctual."

"Yes, he can!" she nearly yelled. "That missive was received *after* I had gone to my parents. He knew what time I intended to return and he could have sent word but he never did. It was a test to see how punctual I would be."

Bloody tests!

Father had become fond of them after they moved to England. He had gone from being a gentleman farmer who laughed with his wife and enjoyed time with his children the Cape Colony to a strict task master of schedules and responsibilities to be adhered to by all in the household in England. That was when he began giving tests to see how prepared each of them were for the slightest shift in circumstances.

If he had intentionally not told Mother of the change in sailing time, then he intended for her to fail. Or had he expected her to arrive home earlier than she had because being early was better than being punctual, as it allowed for the slightest unexpected delays to be overcome? As she did not plan for such, she had failed.

However, that still did not change the fact that she never returned to England, and something he must remember despite the reason why she had not been on the same ship as his father.

"I waited for him to come back for me and truly thought that he would."

"You could have gone to him," Sterling reminded her.

"I feared that our ships would pass and he would arrive here as my ship docked in England, but after a year, I had to accept that he would not come for me."

"That is when you should have returned home," he insisted.

"I wrote and asked if I should or even could," she said quietly. "He never responded to any of my letters. Which, I suppose, was answer enough."

Her words momentarily halted all other thoughts until he started to doubt her words. Why would his father ignore her requests? Why wouldn't he want his wife home?

"I considered returning anyway, but your father no longer wanted me and I had served my purpose. Not only had I provided an heir and a spare, but an additional three sons."

"Who would have liked to have had their mother at home," Sterling insisted, his resentment returning. He could forgive her missing the ship for the reasons she claimed, but not for what came after, even if his father shared some of the fault. She should have boarded the next ship and returned to her family but she hadn't. Instead, she'd lived these past eleven years at Wyndview Farm while her husband and five sons lived in Southampton, England.

"For what purpose? It was not as if I were needed," she argued, much to his shock and dismay.

How could she say such a thing when five children had waited for her?

"When we were in England, everyone was away at school. I was lucky to spend any time with my sons when they returned home for the few weeks of holidays each year. And you, you stopped needing your mother long before your father and I sailed with Hallaway and his family. You were your father's first born, the heir, and he commanded your attention. I was given a kiss on the cheek when you returned home right before you disappeared into the library with your father to learn all there was to know about being the Earl of Wyndham and Trade Wynd, as did Damian and Elliot. If you weren't in the library, you were riding the estate or spending your days in the Trade Wynd offices near the harbor. I saw you at dinner and when the holiday was over, you kissed me on the cheek, said a goodbye and were on your way again."

Bitterness laced her tone.

"As for Jules, he could not wait to disappear into the former woodcutter's cottage at the back of the estate to sculpt and Avery, well, he preferred to read the latest scientific texts and check on his experiments in the conservatory and gardens. As for the rest of the year, it was spent living with a man who had no time to spare because his duties were too demanding and who thought so little of me that he left me behind."

Guilt churned and absorbed some of the bitterness created by her abandonment. Sterling had spent little time with his mother before she was gone because he had been at school and his father had demanded his time when he was home. Still, she was their mother and should have been there if one of them needed her.

"Your brothers have written. You are the only one who never did. I assumed you were too busy, now I believe it was because you hated me and I suppose you still do."

"My brothers wrote?" Was that how she knew that Elliot enjoyed living in Madeira?

"Not until they had completed their schooling, mind you, even though I sent regular letters to them."

He received letters as well but stopped reading after the first three because she never offered a reason for not living with them. He also never wrote her back because he'd been so angry.

Sterling did not like this at all. He had arrived bitter and determined. Now he experienced guilt for how he had ignored her and sympathy for what she had endured. However, she could also be trying to manipulate his emotions by providing a version of events that suited her better.

It did not matter because she was a mother who had abandoned her children and it did not matter what the circumstances. No, his father should not have left her behind, but that did not excuse her guilt for not returning home.

He set his tea aside and stood. "I think I will bathe and unpack." He then turned and marched from the sitting room, determined to remain defensive in further conversations because he was not so readily willing to forgive what she had done, nor was it easy to let go of an anger that had festered for eleven years simply because she offered an explanation, even if he was guilty of ignoring her.

"DO YOU UNDERSTAND the importance?" Caroline asked her father.

She took the reports that she had managed to retrieve from the office before coming home and spread them on the dining table. "Wyndham may question you and you must be able to recall what has been in the reports previously sent to him and the accounting."

"I am not concerned, Caro," her father responded.

That was the problem. Her father concerned himself with very little. All that mattered were the grapes and the wine. Not the cattle or the milk cows, nor the horses in the stable rarely ridden, nor their garden, which while not vast, fed the family and servants, as did the grove of fruit trees that needed to be cared for, and the chickens and their eggs, and the ducks in the pond, nor even seeing that common repairs were made to an estate that was one hundred and fifty years old.

Sometimes she wondered if he even remembered what else needed his attention as the estate manager. "Please, Father. Read and memorize the reports. They are duplicates of what has been sent to Lord Wyndham."

"I will," he promised. "I will read each tonight."

She glanced at William.

"As will I," her brother promised.

At least William understood the importance of providing accurate information for the meeting scheduled.

William reached forward and picked up the most recent report and accounting. "These are three months old," he stated.

"The current quarterly reports and accounting are back at the house and in the office waiting to be completed. I could not risk taking them while Wyndham was meeting with his mother. These were already set aside and easy enough to retrieve," she explained. "I will return later tonight, after all the lights have been extinguished on the lower floors and make copies."

"I will make certain that we both rise early so that we have time to prepare," her brother assured her.

Caroline gave a nod and rose from the table. It was time to have another serious discussion, which was not always easy when that child was only five.

"Come along, Livia."

Her daughter hopped off the chair and followed Caroline into the kitchen where water had been warming on the stove. After she poured the pots of water into the large basin, Livia removed her clothing and got in the large basin.

"I need you to promise me that you will not go beyond the kitchens."

"Ever?" Livia questioned as she lathered soap over her body.

"Only when Lord Wyndham is here," Caroline clarified. "If you are not in this house with me, Grandpapa, William, or Beatrix, you need to sit quietly in the kitchens and wait for one of us."

Beatrix was the daughter of another local landowner who served as a governess to Livia by watching over her and giving her lessons in reading, math, and sciences.

"Why?" Livia asked.

Why was it that children always asked the most difficult questions to answer? Why couldn't she simply accept what Caroline told her and obey?

"Lord Wyndham may not appreciate you being underfoot as you were today when you visited Lady Wyndham."

"She does not mind," Livia reminded her.

"I know, but he will and since Lord Wyndham is the gentleman who employs Grandpapa and owns the land, we must remain quiet and out of his way." The instructions were not only for Livia but Caroline as well. She could not draw further attention to herself and hoped that Wyndham forgot they had even met. She could only hope that she found a way to avoid him from now until the time that he sailed.

Caroline looked into her daughter's brown eyes and made certain that her tone was grave. "Do you promise to stay here or in the kitchens?"

Livia stared back, grew serious, and then nodded.

"It will not be for long," she assured her daughter and hoped that she was correct.

After washing and clothing Livia again, Caroline had her

brother haul the water out, and then crossed the paved terrace that separated the kitchens and house from the cottage Caroline shared with her family. She hoped that Cook would offer something that they could eat for supper since there was nothing but bread, biscuits, and tea in her kitchen.

It wasn't that Caroline didn't know how to cook, there simply had been no reason to because Lady Wyndham insisted that her father, brother, and Caroline join her for meals while Livia ate with the servants or Beatrix, something that they would not be doing while Wyndham was in residence.

Caroline glanced around the kitchen and at the servants. Some were cutting vegetables, others rolling dough, while another checked the contents in an oven while Cook stirred a large pot on the stove. Now was not the time to interrupt them, but as she turned to leave, Cook called out, "Dinner will be delivered."

"That is not necessary."

Cook paused and anchored a hand on her hip. "Do you prefer to starve?"

"I was simply going to request items so that I may prepare a meal for my family."

At her words, Cook laughed. "Now is not the time to risk your father's health. A hamper of food will be delivered."

"I do know how to cook!" Caroline insisted.

"I am certain that you do," Cook returned. "Just not well. Now, go along."

Insulted and relieved, Caroline turned and left the kitchen.

Her cooking wasn't so bad.

As she crossed the terrace, Caroline glanced back at the house. Awareness trickled down her spine as goosepimples stood up on her arms and the hair rose on the back of her neck—a sixth sense of being watched or danger was near. Slowly, she turned and looked around, first for a poisons snake or scorpion, but saw nothing. She then looked up, and right at Lord Wyndam who stood staring out his window—at her.

Her stomach churned as their eyes met, and Caroline quickly turned around and retreated to the home she shared with her father.

Oh, she wished she could have seen the emotion in his eyes, but perhaps it was best that she hadn't since his eyebrows were drawn together and his mouth firm with disapproval.

CHAPTER FOUR

SILENCE SURROUNDED STERLING when he stepped from the sitting room. Not even whispers from servants could be heard. If he didn't know better, he would have assumed that he and his mother, along with the butler, were the only people in the house.

Where had the servants gone?

A few had been present at his arrival but they had quickly scattered when his name was announced. Was he truly so frightening or was it as simple as they were surprised by his arrival?

Sterling walked down the corridor and paused at the foot of the stairs. Why had he not met the housekeeper either?

"Is there something that you need, Lord Wyndham?" George asked as he approached from behind.

"A bath," he answered. "And where were my belongings delivered?"

"To the same room you occupied when you were younger. The maids have seen that it has been freshened and new bedding replaced the old."

"Thank you." He started up the stairs and paused. "Did any-one see to unpacking my trunks? I do not have a valet."

"I can have the highest-ranking footman act as one while you are here."

He shook his head. "That is not necessary. I only need someone to collect my laundry. I have been at sea for months."

"A maid will be sent to you right away."

Sterling nodded, climbed the stairs, and turned to enter the room that he had occupied for the first twelve years of his life. That was when his father had been the caretaker of Wyndview Farm. He'd been the third son of an earl and the position had been better than having to go into trade, even though managing a family estate could have been considered as such.

His sleeping chamber had not changed. The plastered walls remained light in color in contrast to the darkening orange-hued pine floors. Dark-blue curtains framed the windows and when closed, were thick enough to block out the sun, which sometimes became necessary when the days grew hot, though more relief could be found from the heat with the curtains pulled away and windows opened for fresh air and a hopeful breeze.

He turned to his trunks and opened them, placing the clothing that needed to be laundered in one stack and the items that were still clean in another to be put away, then wandered to the window to await his bath.

The landscape was just as he remembered, with vibrant flower gardens planted away from the house to take advantage of the sun and filled with orchids, lilies, heather, proteas, hibiscus, verbena, daises, and honeysuckle—the names his mother had taught him when he was a child.

Beyond and in the valley were neat rows of grapevines. The blood of this estate. Now, after fifteen years, Sterling was back, eager to tour Wyndview Farm and be reminded of how it was run and how wine was made. It was an export of Trade Wynd, one of the largest importers and exporters in England and owned by his family, thus it was necessary for him to understand all aspects of the business.

Yet, despite his purpose for being here, melancholy settled into his soul. He recalled how he and his brothers had played outside, when they were free of their tutors, and how they had swam in the lake his great-uncle had dug out of the ground that had filled with rainwater over time until it was always full. It was down in the valley where he had started to learn how to run the estate because one day he would take his father's place.

They always assumed that it would be here, not back in England.

He remembered visiting with his maternal grandparents, but they had passed away after his family had left the Cape Colony.

He had not thought about his grandmother's tight warm hugs in a very long time and suddenly missed them.

Sterling closed his eyes as memories swept over him and back to a time when he had been happy. When his entire family had been happy and when they had all lived together and loved.

The same happiness could have continued in England, but it hadn't. His mother had been miserable and then she was gone.

When he opened his eyes again, Sterling looked down to the stone terrace that separated this house from the one that had been built for a great-uncle who had decided to live here even though his brother had been the caretaker of Wyndview Farm. It was now the home reserved for the estate manager and his family.

Movement at the corner of the terrace caught his attention and he looked to note Caroline crossing the terrace from the kitchens.

She stopped in the center of the terrace and slowly looked around then turned back to the house before she looked up—directly at him, fear in her dark eyes.

Had she sensed that he was watching?

A moment later, she hurried across the terrace and entered her father's home.

Why was she afraid?

WHILE HER FATHER and William reviewed the reports and

accounting following their evening meal, Caroline prepared Livia for bed, tucked her under the coverlet and read to her from a favorite story. When her daughter finally drifted off, Caroline extinguished the lamp and returned downstairs, relieved to see that father and brother were still reading and made her way to her chamber, which had formerly been a small parlor at the side of the house. She used to sleep above-stairs in the room next to her daughter's smaller sleeping chamber, but she had given it to William on his return, because it had formerly been his bed-chamber. The one where Livia now slept had been Caroline's and was too small for both of them. Therefore, Caroline had made a parlor into her chamber. Their family was not so large that they needed a sitting room and a parlor. There were no visitors and if documents needed to be prepared or there was accounting that could not be done in Wyndham's home, they used the small office here or the dining table if a larger space was needed.

William had tried to insist that he be the one to sleep down-stairs, but Caroline would not allow it. Besides, she was the one who was up the earliest and went to sleep the latest, and she liked the separation from her family. Further, she also had a door that led outside and made it easy for her to cross the terrace whenever Lady Wyndham might have need of her.

It was at that very door that she now stood, watched and waited for all lights to be extinguished on the ground floor, then waited for the chambers above to also darken. Once they were, she waited a little longer, then lit a lamp and quietly crossed the terrace and entered the main house through the back door before she made her way to the office. Once inside, she lit another lamp and then closed the door.

Settling behind the desk, she retrieved the ledger that she had been writing in earlier and finished the calculations for the quarter before she set to copying the figures on a separate ledger to take to her father. There were always two copies. One that was sent to Wyndham in England and one that remained at the estate, just as there was one quarterly report sent while a copy of said report remained here.

Once the ledgers were totaled, she completed the quarterly report with the correct amounts and began to make a copy so that they would be ready for Wyndham.

It was tedious but necessary work.

Caroline had just retrieved another piece of parchment, ready to copy the fifth and final page when there was a creak of the floorboards outside the office. Every part of her being stilled as she held her breath and waited as she strained to hear if there was someone in the corridor or if she was alarmed for no reason.

CHAPTER FIVE

WHEN STERLING WOKE in the darkness, he lay in bed for a moment, rather disoriented as to where he was. Then he recalled that he was in his boyhood bedchamber and, if it was not for the moon's reflection through the window, he'd be in complete darkness.

How late was it?

Sterling pushed the covers aside and sat up in bed before he turned and placed his feet on the floor, his toes and heels cushioned by a thick, plush rug that he remembered as being woven into various shades of blue.

The last thing he recalled was being overcome with exhaustion after he had bathed. He had crawled into bed with the intention of taking a short nap.

His stomach rumbled and tightened.

Had he missed dinner?

Sterling rose and padded across the room to the dresser where he had left his pocket watch then returned to the window so that he might note the time.

"Bloody hell!" It was just past one-thirty in the morning, which meant he had been asleep for…when had he come up here?

They had tea at three, because that was the hour his mother had always taken tea.

They had spoken for nearly an hour and then he had bathed.

Even if he hadn't fallen asleep until six, he had still slumbered for seven and a half hours.

After his stomach grumbled again, Sterling pulled on some trousers, then his banyan, leaving it open because of the stifling warmth in his room. Besides, there was no reason to be properly dressed. First, he was in his own home and second, everyone was likely asleep.

Sterling lit a candle, slipped on the smoking shoes he'd left at the side of the bed, and exited his chamber with every intention of visiting the kitchens in hopes of finding something to eat, even if it was only some bread and jam, which would do until it was time to break his fast.

Except, once he reached the foot of the stairs and turned down the corridor, he stopped.

A very soft light brightened the floor beneath the door to his office.

Was Hallaway working in the middle of the night? Was there too much estate work for him to complete during the day? Or had he been neglectful of his duties and was hurrying to bring his records and accounting current before they met tomorrow?

Sterling lit the candle in the bronze wall sconce behind him and slowly walked toward the door, thankful that he was not in boots, but a softer sole so that he might surprise the person on the other side of the door, not giving them a chance to come up with an excuse to save a position. However, when the floorboard squeaked beneath his foot, Sterling paused and waited. He hoped that he had not been heard and in case he had, he waited to see if Hallaway would come to investigate.

When there was no movement beyond the door, nor did he hear anyone, Sterling then placed his hand on the round knob in the center of the door and pushed it open before he stepped inside and turned toward the desk.

Seated behind, a lamp illuminating the parchment before her, dark curls falling over one shoulder, and staring at him with wide eyes was Caroline. Not her father.

"Mrs. Sutcliffe, what are you doing in my house at this hour?"

CAROLINE COULDN'T THINK. She couldn't speak. It wasn't for the lack of a ready excuse. It was because Wyndham was barely dressed. The candle he held cast shadows upon his face and enhanced the definition and sharpness of his high cheekbones and the perfection of his straight, narrow and well-defined nose usually only seen on Greek statues.

He was far more handsome than he'd been earlier, with his thick hair tousled from what she assumed had been slumber and light scruff along his jaw and chin.

Wyndham also wasn't wearing a shirt and his banyan had come open revealing his muscular chest and flat, hard stomach.

Caroline blinked and her mouth went dry.

"Mrs. Sutcliffe," he prompted when she had failed to answer his question.

"I..." She looked at the parchment before her, the quill, and ink stains on her fingertips. What could she tell him?

"I did not expect you to be awake so early, Lord Wyndham," she said.

"Is that your way of claiming that you would not be here if you thought anyone was about?" he inquired with an edge to his tone.

Yes, she wanted to answer. "I am just surprised, that is all."

"You still have not answered my question, Mrs. Sutcliffe."

He was every bit the employer, though her father's, demanding an explanation, which she had ready. "I was preparing the reports for my father," she answered as she looked at him again. "His handwriting is no longer neat because of pains in his fingers." That part was true. "However, as I can still read what he has written, I recopy the reports and accounting into a neater hand for presentation to you. I had not had an opportunity to do so before you arrived today. I intended to have them finished by the end of the week when they were to be sent on a packet to England."

Wyndham frowned and she feared that he might doubt her excuse. She hadn't told a complete falsehood; she just had not been completely honest.

"I had noticed the change in penmanship a few years back. I assumed your father had hired a secretary, though found it odd that there were no wages paid to one."

"I do this as a favor to him and so that you have legible documents to review." She smiled in hopes that he would accept her response without further questions.

Wyndham studied her, his blue eyes slightly narrowed as if he were trying to decide if he were going to believe her.

"Why are you awake so early, Lord Wyndham?" she asked in hope that a change in topic would cause him to abandon his current line of inquiry.

"I am hungry." He pushed his fingers through his already disheveled hair. "I had not meant to sleep so long when I took a rest earlier and find I missed dinner completely. Given that I have already slept longer than I usually do, it is unlikely that I will be able to return to slumber."

Her heart pounded. He must go back to bed. She had work to finish, even though she was near the end.

Wyndham placed a hand against his stomach. Was he in pain? Had he gone too long without food? From what she viewed beneath his open banyan, it appeared that Wyndham ate exactly what he needed. While there was no extra flesh, he certainly was not emaciated either. Not overly muscled and finely formed.

Goodness!

The room had suddenly grown warm and her body heated with a desire she had thought died along with her husband. Instead, it had only gone dormant and now her body tingled with awareness. She truly believed such pleasures were behind her, as they should be, but apparently, they were not.

Lust!

She hadn't lusted after anyone, except for her husband. Back then, he had introduced her to the delights of the marriage bed and Caroline had assumed those desires were only for him.

Apparently, that was not accurate because she was currently lusting after the Earl of Wyndham and she must stop immediately.

"I am certain that you will be able to find something in the kitchen or perhaps the larder." Caroline smiled. "Please, do not let me keep you." She needed him to go. Not only because she had work to finish, but them being alone in a darkened room with only a few candles lit to chase the shadows while Wyndham was only partially dressed, was rather intimate. She needed her concentration to be on the report and not his chest, and flat abdomen where a line of hair disappeared into his trousers, leading to…

Caroline blinked and tried to focus on his face and not think about his partially clad body.

"Yes, well, I will leave you to your work."

Yet, he stood there, studying her.

And she could not look away from him.

CHAPTER SIX

WHY WAS HE simply standing there when he should leave? Caroline had explained her purpose, and he appreciated the fact that she wanted him to have clearly written documents for his meeting with her father in the morning, and he was hungry, but he could not make his feet move.

He also should have closed and secured his banyan to shield his chest and abdomen, as would have been proper, but he did not and only because of the high color in Caroline's cheeks when she first viewed him. Though she first looked at the papers before her and then at his face, her eyes did eventually stray below his chin. That was when her eyes darkened and if he was not mistaken, her breaths grew a little shallow as her plump lips parted.

While she might project being the proper daughter of an estate manager, and only wanted to assist her father, she was also a woman who had known intimacy, and perhaps she missed what a husband and wife shared in the privacy of their sleeping chamber. And, given she was a widow, it was acceptable for her to take a lover, if she wished.

Did Caroline want or need a lover?

The appreciation in her dark eyes also had an effect on him and Sterling was grateful that he was wearing trousers and that he was shadowed, shielding the stirring of his own desire for Caroline.

How long had it been since he engaged a mistress?

Good God! It had been over a year. He had last seen his mistress a month before he sailed from England, the same day he had terminated their agreement as he did not know how long he would be gone. No wonder the need for intimacy and release rose so quickly.

It wasn't that he hadn't had the opportunity to bed various women during his travels, but Sterling had always shied away from unfamiliar women and certainly avoided courtesans and light-skirts. After all, he did not want to be afflicted with an uncomfortable consequence of coupling.

"Lord Wyndham, did you have further questions?"

Her inquiry penetrated the fog in his mind and Sterling cleared his throat. "No. That is all. I will now leave you to your work." This time he did leave the office and made his way to the kitchens.

He should not be thinking about taking a lover, especially not Caroline. It was improper! He was the employer of her father; therefore, she was his responsibility much like a servant would be and he would never seduce a maid, therefore, he could not seduce Caroline.

He first set a pot of water over a flame so that he could brew tea, then rummaged through the larder and came away with jam, then found the bread that remained from the day before. As he cut a slice, his mind wandered to his encounter with Caroline.

If she needed time to prepare the reports, her father could have asked for a later meeting.

Were they afraid of his reaction if he had?

Did Hallaway think that he would refuse and demand an immediate meeting?

Or maybe Hallaway didn't want him to know that his daughter assisted him.

If that were the case and given that most men were proud and tried to hide that they relied on the assistance of a female, Sterling decided that he would not mention the matter to

Hallaway.

As he slathered the jam on the bread then prepared a cup of tea, Sterling recalled how enticing Caroline had looked bent over the desk with her full breasts pressed against the bodice of her gown, nearly spilling over. Yes, it was the fashion and, on most women, it would not be something he spent much time thinking about, yet his eyes had been drawn to her bosom.

Except, Caroline wasn't dressed fashionably. Her dresses were light cotton, likely due to the oppressive heat, and without any decoration of ribbons or lace. Simple and practical, which he supposed was appropriate for her rank.

He swiped the crumbs from the counter and set his empty cup in the sink before he snuffed out the candles in the kitchen.

There was no need for Caroline to keep working. He could reschedule the meeting with Hallaway to later in the day tomorrow, which was what Sterling intended to tell her, except when he returned to the office, Caroline was gone and the lights had been extinguished.

He entered slowly and stopped at the desk. In the center and to the right was the report. To the left were the ledger pages for the last quarter.

As it was unlikely he could sleep again, Sterling lit candles and settled in the chair to begin his review of the report written in Caroline's neat penmanship. He had not reviewed any reports or accounting for nearly a year because he had been traveling and wondered if anything of import had been contained in them.

Sterling shook his head. He could simply ask tomorrow what those reports had contained.

With those thoughts, he opened the drawers in search of parchment, but instead found a ledger labeled in his father's hand. Why would anything from when his father lived her still be kept in the desk?

He withdrew it only to realize that the estate accounting had been added to the back providing a history of accounting from when his father was the estate manager through last year.

His father had changed so much once they moved to England. All of them had, but one thing that his mother had said that still bothered him about his mother wanting to return to England. *I wrote and asked if I should or even could. He never responded to any of my letters.*

Why hadn't Father written her back?

In that instant, he remembered. When the post arrived, his father tossed any letter from her into the waste receptacle. He did not even bother to read them. Sterling knew this for certain because he had looked, but because they had been written to his father, he did not read them either.

How could he have forgotten? No wonder she hadn't come home. She was waiting for permission or to be asked but his father never read her damn letters to know that she wanted to come home.

When you have erred, the mistake is yours and you must make the proper correction on your own, without consultation, so that you learn and so that it is not repeated in the future.

He could still hear the voice in his father's head when Sterling had failed to plan properly.

His father had waited for her to make that proper correction, without consulting him. No doubt, she was to have taken the next ship available next ship. As she had not, again she had failed.

Sterling wasn't even certain that his mother had been aware that was one of his father's rules because he had instructed his sons to make them better and responsible men.

Bloody hell!

His father was more at fault than his mother. Far more at fault. He hated that he may have been wrong about his mother for nearly eleven years. Then again, she still hadn't come home. Despite her reasons, some of the blame still lay with her.

CAROLINE STARTLED AWAKE to a room bright with sunshine.

How could she have slept so late? Yes, she had not gotten to sleep until sometime around three in the morning, partly because she had worked so late and partly because she had been thinking about Wyndham's chest, abdomen, and imagined what had been shielded by his trousers as a longing and ache that she had not experienced in years made it difficult for her to fall asleep quickly. Still, she always woke with the sun. Always! But by the amount of light flooding her room from a side window, she was certain that the sun had risen hours ago.

"Are you sick?"

She turned her head to find Livia standing by her bed. "No, darling. Why do you ask?"

"Because you are still in bed."

Her daughter was already dressed, her hair brushed and there was a bit of jam in the corner of her mouth.

"Where is Beatrix?" Caroline asked as she pulled herself from the bed.

"She is still drinking her tea and told me not to disturb you."

Caroline chuckled. "Then why did you?"

"Because I was afraid you were sick."

"I was up very late, that is all," Caroline assured her daughter. "Are Grandpapa and William still at the breakfast table."

"No. They have already gone to the fields."

She truly had slept late if they were already gone and now her entire day would be off schedule. "Return to Beatrix and I will be along shortly."

Livia skipped out of the room and closed the door behind her.

That morning, Caroline did not take time at her toilet but rushed it. She brushed and pulled her hair back and knotted it at the back of her head then chose a simple, light gown to wear. One that was also durable and already stained because her work today would likely leave her dirty. She just hoped that she did not encounter Wyndham. Not that it should matter. She was the daughter of a servant and her appearance should not even be noticed.

She then hurried to the small dining room where her family shared their meals, and her heart sank. The documents that she had brought back early that morning and set on the table so that her father and brother could review them did not even appear disturbed. She had told them how important it was that they were familiar with the information within those documents before their meeting with Wyndham, which was to take place later that morning.

When she glanced at the clock her panic increased, likely because she was already suffering from some anxiety from having slept late.

"I will return shortly and will break my fast then. If someone returns for the hamper of food, please set aside some bread and butter for me," Caroline instructed Beatrix before she marched from the house and once again had a horse saddled and rode out to the fields lined with grapevines.

"Why are you out here?" she demanded of William once she found him.

"Father wanted to check the ripeness of the grapes."

"Did you even bother to read the reports and accounting?"

"I tried, but Father insisted on leaving early this morning and I did not dare let him go off alone."

If they lost sight of their father, he would likely disappear into the test fields, or anywhere grapes grew, instead of seeing to the rest of the estate as he was supposed to.

"You are to meet with Wyndham in two hours. We must return to the house."

"I will bring Father back right away," William promised.

"See that you do!"

Caroline turned her horse and rode back to the stables. Once she had dismounted, she stomped to her home, prepared a cup of tea, and hoped that it calmed her irritation. She then slathered butter on a piece of bread even though she was no longer hungry, then waited.

She even went so far as to arrange the papers so that she

could remind them of what was most important so that time was not wasted reviewing the state and health of the grape crop because her father had that information memorized. It was the rest that he didn't retain.

It was nearly a half hour before she heard her father and William enter at the back of the house.

"Have you even looked at the reports?" she demanded when they joined her.

"You worry too much, Caro," her father dismissed her.

"I must since you do not seem to have any concern."

"I will read them," William said as he settled at the table.

"I will wash and prepare for my meeting with Wyndham." Her father mounted the stairs that led to his chamber.

Caroline sighed with aggravation. Her father was so certain that all would go well and that his position was secure. He likely assumed that he could charm Lord Wyndham as well as he did Lady Wyndham, which he did to hide his faults. Caroline would need to warn her father again when he returned. Lord Wyndham did not appear to be the type of lord anyone could charm.

Whether her father would heed her advice was another matter.

CHAPTER SEVEN

S TERLING HAD REVIEWED the reports and the accounting. All seemed to be in order, but he also had a list of questions. They were the same matters that he had wondered about in England before he had left and would now be able to discuss directly with Mr. Hallaway.

He was also more invigorated and not at all tired, despite the hour that he woke, and it was because he had gotten some work done. Idleness did not suit him and had set him on edge whenever he was sailing because there was little for him to do. Even though he had only been settled behind a desk, his mind had been engaged.

He was also hungry again. The bread had only satisfied the emptiness of his stomach for so long and Sterling made his way to the dining room where he found his mother already seated.

"I missed you at supper," she said as he entered. "I thought perhaps it was because you still hated me and would rather starve than share a table."

Now she was being dramatic. "I do not hate you."

In fact, much of his opinion had been altered after the revelations of yesterday, and early this morning. Yet, a part of him still resented that she hadn't returned to her sons on her own. That would take the longest to reconcile, if he ever could.

"But George advised that when a footman called you to supper and finally entered your chamber when there was no answer, he found you sound asleep. I insisted that they not disturb you because I know how exhausting travel can be."

How could she know such? She hadn't left the Cape Colony in ten years. Unless she traveled to other places, just not home—where her husband and sons waited.

Sterling pushed his anger aside as he filled a plate from the selection of dishes which included eggs, cold meats, bread, and fruit on the table.

"My brothers never told me that they corresponded with you." Not that it should be a surprise. After his father had returned without her, and when she never came home, he had insisted that her name never be mentioned. Sterling and his brothers even stopped mentioning her when their father was not around. His father only mumbled her name when he was deep in his cups and would stare at her portrait.

"Jules wrote when he was on the Continent. Even though he was with his closest friend, he missed home and wanted to be back at Wyndview Hall. He was also at war, which I am certain had much to do with his longing for England."

Battles that had affected his brother deeply. There had been a profound change in Jules between the time he left for the Continent and returned without his closest friend. Sterling had tried to question him, but Jules refused to talk about the war and took himself off to the cottage where he spent much of his time sculpting.

"Elliot visited me, before he took up residence in Madeira."

Sterling startled in surprise. He had been under the impression that none of his brothers had seen their mother. Then again, he had not seen Elliot since he left England some five years ago, but he could have mentioned the meeting in a letter.

"We visited for a fortnight and spent hours talking about the time when we all lived here and how it had changed. He also wondered if he might miss England after he lived in Madeira for a while, knowing he had little choice of where he could make his home because of what was expected of him."

Elliot had moved to Madeira to learn from their Uncle David and then take over their vineyard. It was his destiny—a dictate by their father. Each son was to do their part for Trade Wynd so that it didn't fall to one person, as it had to Sterling's father.

"As for Avery, he plans to visit, and eventually move here, but wants to further his studies in botany before he does so."

"He knows that Jules will never leave Southampton, and since the responsibility had been assigned to him, Avery plans to take his place," Sterling clarified.

His mother frowned. "Avery never fully explained, but I assume that it is because of Jules's art and that his sculpting is too important. Given Avery's interest in botany, he is probably better suited to manage this estate."

Sterling wasn't going to tell her the reason why Jules would likely never come to the Wyndview Farm. If Jules had not confided in her, not that he confided in anyone, Sterling was not going to be the one to talk out of turn, even if it was to their mother.

"If Father were still alive, I am certain that he would have forced Jules here and forbidden him from becoming a footguard. I, for one, am glad that he is pursuing his passion for sculpting. Everyone should be allowed to follow a course they prefer and not one forced upon them by an overbearing parent."

Sterling did not voice whether he agreed with her or not because he had done what was expected. He had no choice because he had been the heir. He had a duty. Had he been a younger brother, perhaps he would have explored other options and opportunities not dictated by their father. But, as his situation would not change, there was no reason to wonder what he might have done if circumstances had been different.

AFTER GAINING A promise from her father that he would read the reports and once again become familiar with the accounts and all other aspects of the estate, Caroline left him to see that her daughter was at her lessons with Beatrix and then made her way to the main house in search of Lady Wyndham.

She should have finished breaking her fast and would likely be in the lavender sitting room where she preferred to spend her time.

Except, Lady Wyndham was not there.

It truly wasn't necessary that Caroline inform Lady Wyndham of the change in duties or the schedule, it was only out of respect.

With that thought, Caroline stepped back out into the corridor, prepared to leave when she turned right into Lord Wyndham—her breasts pressing against his chest and his hands on her upper arms to steady her produced a sizzle of awareness that swept through her being.

Goodness!

She quickly stepped away. "I beg your pardon. I should have…" The words died on her lips as she looked up at his face, tight and unforgiving, his blue eyes darkening.

So much for trying to stay out of his way and go unnoticed.

"Might I have a moment of your time?"

"Yes, of course," she answered dutifully.

"Come with me."

Caroline took a deep breath and followed him to the office.

The report and accounting that she had left on his desk early this morning was in place, but disturbed and there was another parchment with handwriting. Did he have questions for her father? Could she hope that he asked her instead?

"How may I be of assistance?"

"It is a curiosity," he answered. "Your copied report is here, but not the pages written by your father. Not even in the waste receptacle."

Because they did not exist.

"Where might they be?"

Oh, she hated to lie, but it was a necessity. "I took them back to Father. He likes them destroyed after they are copied."

"Does he not keep a copy for himself?"

"Yes," Caroline answered. "I make two copies, which you saw me do last evening. One to remain with my father's records and one to send to you."

"I would like copies of the reports from the past year. As I was traveling, they did not reach me."

"Yes, of course," she answered. Those had been read, at least by William, and could easily be returned.

Wyndham nodded, accepting her answer.

He then looked at her and frowned. No doubt because of the stains on this dress. He was also probably too much of a gentleman to ask.

"I apologize for my appearance. I only came to see your mother to tell her that I would be working in the gardens today."

Wyndham frowned further. "Why? You are not an employee of Wyndview Farm."

"As a favor to your mother," Caroline answered. "She does adore the gardens but the weeds do need to be tended to." When Caroline had arrived, it was Lady Wyndham who spent her time in the gardens, but it had become too painful for her knees and back so Caroline had taken over the duties.

"Do I not employ a gardener?" he demanded.

If he had read the reports, and accounting, then he would know already that no wages were paid to one. "There is no one who can see to the task so I took it upon myself."

"There is no one else?" It was partially a demand as if he did not approve.

There would probably be much that he would find fault with, which was why they all needed to be very careful in what they said and did.

"Ah, Lord Wyndham," her father greeted boisterously as he entered the office, William following.

Caroline prayed that this meeting went well.

"I have not seen you since I left England." Her father stopped before Wyndham and bowed. Her brother did the same.

"My son, William," her father introduced.

"Father has been teaching him since he returned from England so that he might be an estate manager one day," Caroline offered so that Wyndham did not question William's presence. It was imperative that her brother be allowed to remain for the meeting.

"Please have a seat." Wyndham indicated to the two chairs before his desk. "I have reviewed the report and accounting and have a few questions."

Caroline was certain that her heart was caught in her throat. So long as the questions were about grapes and wine, she had no concern, but if Wyndham asked about any other aspect of the estate, they could be doomed.

"I am certain that you would rather have tea, or brandy, or perhaps a glass of Wynd Wine, before we begin," Mr. Hallaway suggested.

"After being on a ship for so long, you must want to rest. We can always discuss the estate tomorrow," William offered. "You only arrived yesterday."

"I am well and rested, thank you," Wyndham answered curtly. "Nor do I believe brandy or wine is appropriate for this hour. If you require tea, I will have it served."

Caroline winced as she backed toward the door.

Her father had attempted charm and failed.

Wyndham looked in her direction and arched a brow.

He clearly wanted her to be gone. "If you will excuse me," Caroline offered then ducked out of the room. However, she left the door ajar and found a position where she could hear what was being said without being seen or her shadow being cast into the room.

"I am certain you are eager to learn about the grapes, harvest, and wine making," her father began. "We have an excellent crop this year..."

"Tobacco."

Caroline nearly groaned. Why couldn't Wyndham ask about the wine?

"Tobacco?" her father asked as if he had never heard the term before.

"You started growing tobacco two years ago, but you no longer do as of this year. May I ask why?"

"Mr. Avery," William sounded rushed in his answer, likely to keep their father from blurting out anything that may cause Wyndham to become alarmed.

"My brother gave you the instruction?" Wyndham's tone was one more of confusion than curiosity.

"Yes," her father answered.

"I will ask him for his reasons when I return home, unless they are already contained in the reports that I have yet to read," he responded. "You now recommend that we grow more wheat, barley, oats, or rye and increase the household garden of vegetables and herbs."

"What?" her father asked. "That is not…"

"Did Mrs. Sutcliffe misinterpret what you suggested?"

"Yes…I will speak with her. Wheat and barley!" He grunted and then harrumphed.

Maybe if Wyndham just let her father talk about his precious grapes, he would be happy and William could answer the rest of the questions.

"How is it going?"

Caroline nearly jumped when Lady Wyndham whispered in her ear.

"Not well, I am afraid," Caroline answered quietly.

Lady Wyndham looked her over from head to toe. "Why are you wearing that dress?"

"I was going to tend to your gardens today."

"You will do no such thing," she insisted. "Change into an appropriate dress and I expect you to take tea with me this afternoon."

It was not an unusual request because she often took tea with Lady Wyndham. "Do you think it is wise with your son here?"

"The only crop that matters are those that include grapes," her father insisted in a raised voice.

"Oh dear!" Lady Wyndham exclaimed. "I believe it is time that I interfere."

As she never answered Caroline's question pertaining to tea, she supposed that she must make an appearance and hope that Wyndham had other plans.

CHAPTER EIGHT

S TERLING LOOKED BETWEEN the two men. Why were they anxious and why did Hallaway only want to talk about grapes? Was there another reason William had wanted to put this meeting off for another day, besides his assumption that Sterling needed rest?

It was all very strange, especially when Hallaway seemed surprised that they had grown tobacco. As the estate manager, should he not have already been aware?

"No business today," his mother announced as she entered the office.

Hallaway and William came to their feet instantly, but Sterling did not stand for his mother.

"There is no harm in waiting to discuss the crops, the estate, vineyard, and wine for another day. After all, you became the owner nearly seven years ago and you are just now getting around to visiting."

"I am here for the purpose to ask specific questions about the estate before I tour it," Sterling insisted.

"Then you should have considered the time of year for your visit. Your appearance brings disruption to my household regardless of your title."

Sterling pulled back at her rebuke. He had not heard that tone since he was much younger, recently returned from completing his first term at Eton and filled with self-importance. She had quickly put him in his place as she had done just now.

"William and Mr. Hallaway should be preparing for the harvest."

It was rather humiliating for her to censure him in front of the estate manager and son, so Sterling simply shook his head and chuckled. "Yes, Mother." He hoped that, by his dry tone, Hallaway would realize that Sterling was only humoring her when he intended to remind his mother that he was the owner of Wyndview Farm and that he would make decisions on when he took meetings. Except he would do so in private.

"Mr. Hallaway, William, you are free to return to your duties," his mother instructed.

While William hesitated, not certain what to do, Hallaway marched out of the office without a word or acknowledgment.

There was something odd about his estate manager, but he also increased the profits of Wyndview Farm yearly, so perhaps Sterling could overlook his eccentricity.

"You may go," Sterling finally said to William, who hurried after his father.

Why were they so reluctant to meet with him? It wasn't as if Sterling had any complaints as to how the estate was being managed. He simply had questions that he hoped would offer more clarification as to why decisions had been made, such as he now knew that the decision to plant tobacco had been at the suggestion of his younger brother.

"What other advice has Avery given for the estate?" Sterling asked his mother.

"Oh, I would not know dear," his mother answered innocently.

Sterling narrowed his eyes. Yes, she did. She just didn't want to tell him, but why?

"Does that mean that he writes directly to Hallaway and you are told nothing?"

"Suggestions get mentioned occasionally but as I am not the one who makes the decisions for the estate and I simply live here,

I am rarely consulted."

Sterling practically snorted. His mother was knowledgeable about everything that happened at Wyndview Farm and likely managed those around her. Or, she had when his entire family had lived here.

"When do you plan on leaving?" she asked abruptly.

He tried to ignore the sudden stab of pain at her words. He had only just begun to consider what she had told him about Father's part in their separation, but maybe it had been a lie and she really did not want to be around her children. "Do you want me gone soon, Mother?"

Her eyes widened. "No. Of course not," she insisted. "In fact, I hope that you remain through March."

It was only the end of January, but at least she wasn't sending him away immediately, not that she had the power to do so. "Why is that?"

"So that you can be present for the grape harvest and making of the wine. Only then will Mr. Hallaway have the time to properly meet with you."

"A month?" Sterling nearly yelled. More than a month.

"Yes, at least," she answered calmly.

Sterling gaped at her. One would think they were discussing an afternoon tea, not an extended delay in his travels before he sailed to Maderia.

"Certainly, you recall from your childhood that you rarely saw your father during the months of January, February, and March."

Sterling tried to remember, but the months flowed together...except, that last year when they were here. He had begged his father to let him help and had been taken along to watch the workers cut the bunches of grapes from the vines and start to destem them before he had been sent back to the house. That had been not long after Twelfth Night and they rarely saw his father until early April, just as his mother said. His father had promised that the following year Sterling would be old enough to take part, but they were forced to sail for London before the next harvest arrived.

Hallaway now had the same duties as his father and very likely had little time for an audience with Sterling.

"Very well, Mother. I will wait until a more convenient time to meet with Mr. Hallaway, but I am not promising a month. I have been away from England too long already."

This also meant that he would likely not be able to return to England before the Season came to an end thus making it impossible for him to settle on a bride. One of the reasons he had intended for this visit to be short was because he needed to get back home. He had a duty to wed and produce an heir and a spare, which he should have put his attention to before now, but he'd also wanted to see the world, or the part of it that made his family wealthy, so his plan had been to travel, then settle on a bride. That would likely now be put off for yet another year.

He could insist that Hallaway meet with him in the evenings, after the sun had gone down because it was unlikely he would be working in the fields then. Except, the man might be too exhausted. His father had been, with little time for his sons or wife.

Yes, Sterling was beginning to recall the harvest months when he and his brothers had sat on the hill and looked down at the servants cutting the grapes and how he couldn't wait to fully participate.

Blast!

He really hadn't wanted to remain in the Cape beyond a fortnight. What could he possibly do to occupy his time between now and then, if he could not meet with his estate manager, other than walk the farm, which would only take a day, at the most?

CAROLINE HAD FOLLOWED her father and brother from the house

and to their own.

"Did you read anything I had written?" she demanded.

"Yes," her father answered.

"Did you remember any of it?"

"I remembered what was necessary," her father answered. "Lord Wyndham will be satisfied after he sees the grapes and observes the harvest and will then leave. That is all that matters. Now, I must change and return to the vineyard."

He marched up the stairs and Caroline glanced at her brother helplessly.

"He could be sacked for not taking his position seriously. Then where would we be?"

"I will see that he is better prepared and remind him that if he fails in his meetings that he might never work in the vineyard again or be near his precious grapes."

"Thank you."

Her brother left and climbed the stairs as Caroline wandered into the parlor she used as a sleeping chamber and sank down on the bed.

William's suggestion may be the only thing that brought her father into line—his grapes. If he was removed from them…Caroline did not even want to think what he would be reduced to.

The problem was, would they be able to convince their father that there was an entire estate that he may have forgotten.

She fell back on her bed. They may not even start to harvest the grapes for a few more weeks and then it would be another week, though more likely a fortnight, before they were all cut, destemmed, stomped, and the juice poured into barrels. She closed her eyes and groaned. It was far too long to have the Earl of Wyndham underfoot disrupting their life and duties and asking questions.

"Something must be done about my son!" Lady Wyndham announced when Caroline arrived to join her for tea.

Caroline glanced around to make certain there was no one

else in the room, nor outside the window that may have heard Lady Wyndham.

"Do you fear he will discover the truth about my father?" she asked quietly as she settled across from her.

Lady Wyndham waved a hand in dismissal, the jewels on her fingers sparkling in the sunlight that came through the windows. "If he has complaints, he can take them up with me and I will remind him that this estate is doing very well. If he were truly concerned, he would have voiced that immediately and would not have allowed me to delay the meeting."

"Then what worries you?"

"He is just like his father, which is my fault, I suppose, since I was not there...except, by the time I left England he was eight and ten and his father was already had the greatest influence on his life."

Caroline said nothing as it certainly was not her place to criticize any of them.

"Sterling needs to learn what is important, what his father forgot, and I am going to see to it that he does or he will never be happy."

As she had no idea what Lady Wyndham meant, Caroline simply nodded.

"And you are going to help me."

Caroline blinked and pulled back in surprise. "Me?"

"Yes. I have not fully formulated a plan, but when I do, it may require your assistance, especially if we want him away from the estate."

She paused when a footman entered with an elaborate tea service of purple and gold that Lady Wyndham enjoyed. Caroline's stomach grumbled at the sight of the finger sandwiches and delicacies. She had barely eaten this morning and was now starving.

"But I cannot be away," Caroline reminded her once the servant was gone.

Lady Wyndham leaned forward to pour the tea. "You must.

Otherwise, Sterling might discover what you have been about," she said as she handed Caroline her tea.

Caroline bit her bottom lip. As William was here, he could see to those duties that her father no longer found time for. "Very well, but only because you asked." She would do nearly anything for Lady Wyndham but secretly hoped that whatever distractions she planned for her son would not take too long or take them too far from the estate.

"Ah, Mother," Lord Wyndham announced at his arrival. "I had not anticipated that we would have a guest at tea."

Caroline's appetite quickly diminished and she set her tea aside. "I should go."

"Nonsense! I invited you and you will stay," Lady Wyndham ordered.

"Yes, please stay, Mrs. Sutcliffe," Wyndham insisted as he took a seat between Caroline and his mother.

Though his invitation should be comforting, it only made her stomach tighten, which was probably from the guilt of keeping secrets.

"Do you often join my mother in the afternoon?" he asked after Lady Wyndham gave him a cup of tea.

"On occasion, when she extends an invitation," Caroline answered quietly. In reality, they had become nearly friends and confidants despite their separation in stations and ages.

"Caroline is a companion," Lady Wyndham announced. "And Livia brings me joy. I like having a child about. Do you have an objection, Sterling?"

CHAPTER NINE

"Of course not, Mother," he answered tightly.

"Good!" She gave a nod. "As it appears that you will have time in which to enjoy a holiday until Mr. Hallaway is free from the vineyards, I suggest that you explore not only the estate but the surrounding area include the Cape of Good Hope. Cape Colony has changed since you were a child and there are sites that you had not been old enough to enjoy."

Did she want him gone even though she hoped that he stayed? Or did she simply want him out of the way?

"What would you suggest?" he asked. It was only to humor her because he had no intention of leaving Wyndview Farm.

"The first that comes to mind is a visit to Table Mountain. Cook can pack a picnic and Mrs. Sutcliffe could accompany you and point out anything else of interest."

At her suggestion, Caroline choked on her tea. At least the companion had not been aware of his mother's intentions, which made Sterling wonder if his mother wasn't also playing matchmaker. But certainly, she understood that the daughter of an estate manager was not suited for an earl.

Except, no gentleman in his family had ever married the daughter of a peer because they found love. As Sterling did not expect the same to ever happen to him, or it would have by now, he would settle for marrying a woman of equal rank to his own. A woman who understood the sacrifices a wife must make when her husband was an earl and managed an import and export business. Something his own mother had not grasped.

"As much as climbing Table Mountain is a pleasure, I fear that it is impossible for me to be gone from morning until evening," Caroline answered with a smile. "I am certain Lord Wyndham could find a guide or maybe another servant can show him the way."

His mother arched her brow. "You need to take a holiday as well, Mrs. Sutcliffe, as I was just saying."

What was she about?

"Therefore, you will accompany my son."

"Yes, of course," Caroline murmured before sipping her tea.

"Which day would be convenient, Caroline?" his mother inquired pleasantly.

Why did his mother consult her instead of him?

"I will need to check with my father and brother. Then I will let you know."

"I will expect your answer soon."

"Yes, of course," Caroline answered without enthusiasm.

Did she not want to go to Table Mountain or did she object to his presence?

It was a rather intriguing question that he might ponder later.

"Now, as for tomorrow night, I expect you both to accompany me."

Caroline's eyes grew wide as some color faded from her sun-kissed cheeks.

"I do not think that is proper, which I have explained on previous occasions," Caroline insisted.

What could his mother have planned now?

"Nonsense," his mother dismissed. "You are the granddaughter of a baron and you were welcomed into Society in London, therefore you will accompany me. Besides, I already responded to expect us both and sent a missive this morning that my son will be joining us."

"Where?" Sterling asked warily.

"To a ball, dear."

Of all the entertainments he could imagine his mother might enjoy, a ball was not on that list. He wasn't even aware that there was a Society here to participate in such an activity.

"Yes. Governor Lord Charles Somerset is hosting a ball and we will be in attendance."

THIS WAS NOT the first ball that had been held since Somerset arrived, nor was it the first time that Lady Wyndham had wanted Caroline to accompany her. In the past, Lady Wyndham had always accepted when she declined the invitation because it was not her place, the daughter of an estate manager, to attend a ball at the Governor's residence.

That is, until today.

The ballgowns she had packed away from years earlier were certainly now out of fashion and had been designed for an innocent debutante. Caroline was seven years older, a mother, and no doubt the gowns no longer fit.

She also had no choice which was why as soon as she returned to her home, she pulled out the trunk that had been hidden away after her arrival. Inside was the clothing of her past. From a time when she had been hopeful of a happy life and marriage. She'd had a happy marriage; it had just ended too soon.

As she shook out each carefully folded gown then stood in front of the mirror and held them to her body, Caroline's mind drifted back to her one and only London Season.

That spring had been magical and she remembered the first time that she had glimpsed the Earl of Wyndham across the ballroom. She hadn't known who he was, but she had noticed that he was one of the most handsome gentlemen in the room. It was only after she asked a friend that she realized he was her father's employer.

Any interest in Wyndham disappeared because even if her father hadn't worked for him, she was still beneath an earl, though she still could not help but notice him whenever they were at the same entertainment.

It wasn't long after that she had met Peter. He was handsome, gallant, kind, and wonderful. She fell deeply in love, or so it seemed at the time, and married him at the end of the Season and looked forward to a promising future.

A future she was denied when her husband was killed in war.

Now she was a widow and living on Wyndham's estate. And tomorrow, she would be attending a ball with him and not simply watching him from across the room.

Whatever was his mother thinking?

She did not belong, regardless of who her grandfather happened to be. Surely Wyndham would agree but would remain polite because that was how those in Society behaved—most of the time.

CHAPTER TEN

STERLING WOKE IN a restless frame of mind. He hated having to wait for anything or anyone, yet he had been told by his mother to cool his heels because the estate manager did not have time to meet with him.

Not only was it inconvenient, but nobody had ever told him to wait before. He understood why Hallaway could not be pulled away, but that did not mean that he could not go to Hallaway or begin his own tour of Wyndview Farm. Therefore, after breaking his fast, Sterling used a well-worn path to make his way to the vineyard.

It was a familiar sight from his youth when he used to stand on this very hill and look down into the valley and watch the growers tend to the grapevines, planted in neat rows and supported by wooden trellises so that they grew up and not along the ground. Today men walked the paths and would occasionally stop, stoop, and sometimes inspect a vine.

His father had been able to tell if the grapes were ready almost by sight and only tasting when he was certain that it was time to cut the bunches from the vine. It was a skill that Sterling had been eager to learn but never had, and even now, he wanted to be down there and be a part of the harvest.

Would he remember anything that his father had taught him?

Tomorrow! He would walk the rows of grapes with Hallaway. He wanted to do so now, but he couldn't see his estate manager among the men in the vineyard.

Instead, he turned and strolled down to the large barn. Unless wine production had changed, this would be where the grapes were brought, crushed, and poured into oak barrels.

When he stepped inside, grateful for the shade, he was brought back to his childhood once again. This area used to be huge, and it still was, with two wagons waiting at the end of one opening and between them, men stacked baskets inside so that they could be taken to the fields to be filled with grapes. The men were preparing for a harvest and excitement filled Sterling's veins, much like it had when he was a boy, forced to watch from a distance and dreaming about the day he would be a part of making wine.

Beyond that was the wide ramp that led to a large cellar that had been dug out of the ground and lined with stone to keep the wine cool and away from the tropical sun. But as the grape production grew, tunnels were built to accommodate the volume of barrels produced each year before they were loaded onto ships. Usually, the large doors remained closed to keep animals, and more importantly, snakes from going down there for relief from the heat. Was there a reason they were open now?

Curiosity brought him further into the barn and then down the ramp where the voices below reached him.

"Do we now have enough oak barrels?"

Sterling frowned. Was that Caroline? Why was she inquiring about barrels?

"More will be delivered tomorrow," a man answered.

"How many more are you expecting?"

"Twenty," the man answered as Sterling reached the foot of the ramp.

"I will add that to the total of what we have. I do not antici-pate that more will be needed, but when the barrels are delivered tomorrow, order ten more. If we do not use them, they can be stored down here until needed."

Sterling frowned. Why was Caroline directing the purchase of barrels? Was that not her father's job as the estate manager?

They had not seen him yet and Sterling took in the vast cellar, not surprised that there were several barrels stacked that nearly took up the entire area and waiting to be filled, but a few barrels remained where some full wine casts were stored. They grew three types of grapes that became three different types of wine. Each type was segregated to their own wall and tunnel off each wall. There was only one barrel on each side—each with a spigot. On the fourth wall were smaller casks, also with spigots.

"Where is all the wine?" he asked, startling both Caroline and the man she was speaking with, who Sterling did not know. "Lord Sterling Wynd," he introduced himself.

"Johan Theron," he responded.

The surname was familiar because members of the Theron family had worked at Wyndview Farm for decades.

Theron then nodded to Caroline. "If you will excuse me," he then turned and climbed the ramp leaving the two of them alone.

"Where is the wine if we produce so much?"

"Shipped," she answered. "Very little stays at Wyndview Farm. What remains is one barrel of each kind from last year's harvest."

That explained the near empty walls not the smaller casks.

"A few barrels remain local and are taken into town while the rest are loaded onto Trade Wynd ships and taken to ports around the world."

"Not so far," he corrected with a smile. "Only to America, England, and the Caribbean."

"Not to countries on the Continent?"

"They produce their own wine and are of the opinion that theirs is superior to ours."

"Is it?" she asked with a smile.

"I suppose that would depend on the person you ask." He chuckled.

She started to walk up the ramp and Sterling assumed they were done in the cellar, which he supposed they were. Instead, he watched her back and the movement of her dress and how it pulled gently against her backside each time she stepped until they emerged back into the large barn.

"Why are there smaller barrels separate from the others?"

"Those are Father's experiments," she answered. "He has been grafting grape roots in an effort to create a better grape for a better wine."

"Has he been successful?"

"I can ask a servant to bring you a glass and take you below so that you can taste for yourself." She smiled as her brown eyes lit up with humor.

"Would you join me in that tasting?" he asked.

"I have already sampled the wine and prefer not to do so again."

"Is it truly so awful?"

"It is drinkable, but the quality is not what one would expect from Wyndview Farm. I believe Father is hoping that it will still age well and become superior." She strolled for the entry to the barn. "I am not so optimistic."

"Then I will also forgo a sampling," he decided with a chuckle as they stepped into the sun. But he could not fault Hallaway for attempting to improve their wine and perhaps one day he might be successful.

Caroline did not wear a hat, and he wondered if she ever did due to the delicate spattering of freckles across her nose and the golden bronze of her skin. It really should not be a surprise. Even during the colder months, it was still warm enough to spend out of doors without too much extra clothing, unlike England, which could be cold, damp, dreary, and chill a person to their bones during the winter.

Caroline did not possess the pale and porcelain complexion that Society adored. Instead, she appeared healthier with her tanned skin. The debutantes in England would look sickly next to her.

"What is it that you do around here, Mrs. Sutcliffe?" She

seemed to be everywhere he went.

"I assist my father when I can."

"Such as inquiring about barrels."

"He needed to know if there would be enough as he expects a larger grape harvest than in the past," she answered. "I can now tell him that there will be a sufficient supply as he requested."

Perhaps that is all there was to it, but when she had been below, she had spoken with authority. Sterling had a gnawing feeling that she was more than an assistant to her father, but with no proof or explanation for feeling in such a way.

It was very odd.

Caroline stood in front of the mirror, surprised by her reflection.

The rose dress with delicate white lace fit well and even though it had been designed for an innocent debutante, it was not girlish. In fact, she had not worn it during her only Season because her mother thought the modiste had erred in cutting the bodice too low. It may have been inappropriate for a miss of nine and ten, but it was not for a widow of four and twenty.

She slowly turned and tried to get a glimpse of the back of her head the best that she could. It had been so long since she had taken the time to curl and pin her hair and wondered if she shouldn't arrange it in a more moderate chignon given her status. Except, she liked the cascade of curls brushing her neck. It made her feel feminine, pretty, just like she had so long ago, instead of a widow with a young daughter and aging, forgetful father to take care of.

Maybe if Lord Wyndham saw her dressed as the granddaughter of a baron, he would forget that he found her standing in the wine cellar discussing the purchase of barrels. It was also a reminder that she needed to be more careful because he could wander anywhere at any time. He did own the property.

But she would not think about that tonight. She was going to her first ball in years.

With a lightness and anticipation almost foreign to her, Caroline bid goodnight to her daughter and made her way to the main house where Lady Wyndham was waiting for her in the lavender sitting room, but her son was not present.

Caroline would be more comfortable if he remained at the estate. Except, then she would worry about who he was talking to and what he was being told, or if he went in search of her father.

"I do hope that Sterling does not keep us waiting long."

"I will not."

Caroline turned at his voice and nearly sucked in a breath. Dressed in finery of black with a gold waistcoat and simple cravat, was enough to speed up her pulse, especially since she remembered what his chest looked like beneath the white linen.

Goodness! What was wrong with her? Just because she looked forward to the evening did not mean that she should allow attraction for her father's employer to muddle her mind. Yet, she could not help but admire Lord Wyndham because he was indeed the most handsome gentleman she had ever met. It was a shame that he was not always as pleasant as his appearance.

"Well, then, come along," Lady Wyndham called as she came to her feet.

Lord Wyndham approached his mother and offered his arm.

"Not me, you will escort Caroline. I am past the age of needing or wanting one." She then marched past him, out of the room and down the corridor.

"Mrs. Sutcliffe," he said holding out his arm.

Caroline wanted to tell him that it was not necessary, but she couldn't speak the words. Unconsciously, she placed her hand on his sleeve to be led to the carriage.

❧ ❧

CHAPTER ELEVEN

S TERLING'S MOUTH NEARLY went dry when Caroline turned to face him. When her back was to him, he had admired her mahogany hair, the gentle curls falling from the back of her head, brushing her bare shoulders, drawing attention to her long, delicate neck. Then she had turned and he had nearly forgotten to breathe. The rose gown complemented her dark eyes and hair, and tanned skin. But that was not what truly drew his attention but the fit of her bodice, which only emphasized the fullness of her breasts and the paler, creamy skin that had been sheltered from the sun teasing and hinting at what was concealed.

She was put together in a manner that filled a man with desire, longing, a need…

Sterling cut off the thoughts before they became any more improper. She may be a widow and in any other circumstance he would pursue her for a night of mutual pleasure. But because she was also the daughter of his employee, a companion to his mother, Sterling would not.

Though, he would like to paint her, just as she was, sitting across from him with a gentle smile on her full lips, brown eyes bright with happiness, and her rounded cheeks kissed by the sun.

Paint, or sketch, two things he had not thought about in a very long time. He could spend hours sitting on a hill, looking out over the horizon and sketching the mountains, the fields, the wildlife, whatever drew his eye and sometimes he painted. It was a hobby that he had enjoyed as a boy. A sketchbook and pencils were always with him while they sailed from Cape Colony to Southampton. When he had grown tired of the sky and sea, he had sketched the ship and the sailors, his parents and brothers. As for painting, he gave that up once he went to school, only because he'd been teased that it was a girlish hobby, but he didn't stop sketching. Not until he returned home and found his mother gone. By that time, he no longer had time for such foolish activities and his sketchbook and pencils had been put away forever.

He had been at peace in a way that he could not explain when he drew, and something he had not experienced since.

"What are you thinking, Sterling?"

His mother's voice intruded on his thoughts and he looked at her. "What did you say?"

"I asked what you were thinking? You are very quiet and staring out the window. It is rather rude. You may not want to speak to me, but we do have a guest."

Caroline gasped. "I am your companion, Lady Wyndham, not your guest."

"Rubbish! You are a guest tonight. You can be a companion tomorrow." His mother chuckled. "You are so many things to me, dear Caroline, that I do not know what I would do without you."

Caroline was a companion and a gardener on occasion, but what else did his mother mean by *so many things*?

Except, she was not truly an employee either.

"We do not pay her wages for being a companion or your gardener," he said. "Are you taking advantage of her kindness?"

"No, your mother is not," Caroline assured him.

Sterling wanted to make certain and question her further but the carriage came to a stop before the Governor's residence. However, the conversation was not over.

He first assisted his mother to the ground and then Caroline. When he offered his arm to his mother, she glared at him and nodded to Caroline. He truly hoped that his mother did not have it in mind to play matchmaker. If so, he would quickly discourage her from doing so.

OH, WHY HAD Lady Wyndham mentioned that she acted as her companion? But at least she had not elaborated on the many things Caroline was.

After Lord Wyndham assisted her to the ground, they followed his mother and passed between columns with classical embellishments before entering the residence. They then proceeded into a long drawing room that would serve as the ballroom.

"Governor Somerset had the ballroom built because he thought the residence too small," Lady Wyndham whispered to her son and Caroline before she walked away while waving to a friend.

The two of them stepped away and moved close to a wall.

"Do you know anyone in attendance?" he asked quietly.

"I recognize faces from residents who have visited your mother on occasion, but I do not know them." Caroline answered. "Nor should the daughter of the estate manager."

"You are also a companion, which puts you in their company," he reminded her.

"Far below them in station."

Lord Wyndham looked down at her with humor in his blue eyes. "And gardener, apparently."

It nearly took her aback because this was the first time he did not have the air of disapproval about him.

No, that was not correct. Yesterday when they were in the cellar, he had chuckled a few times, but she had been too concerned that he had been wandering about and came upon her that she hadn't noted the change in his disposition.

Perhaps he could be a pleasant gentleman after all. Maybe he had simply been ill-tempered because of being months at sea and now that he was rested, he would be in a better frame of mind.

"A woman of many skills." He chuckled.

Her smile tightened because Caroline doubted that he would be pleased, nor would he be chuckling if he knew the extent of her duties at Wyndview Farm.

"Would you care for a refreshment, something to drink?"

She was rather parched. "Yes please."

He gave a nod then disappeared into the crowd.

Oh, it had been so long since she had been in a ballroom and did not like the insecurity of being inadequately prepared or dressed.

What had once been exciting now brought nerves as others glanced at her out of curiosity.

And, while many of the guests had met Caroline previously or at least recognized her, no doubt they were wondering about the handsome man who had escorted her into the ball. Once they learned, no doubt mothers and fathers with daughters ready to wed would soon be begging for an introduction.

The very idea was suddenly depressing, which was ridiculous, of course. He was an earl and she was a companion, among other things. She did not even know him, at least not well. They had only met three days ago! Though she had lusted after him, which should also never happen again.

Chapter Twelve

MUCH TO HIS surprise, Sterling had managed to make it to the refreshment table without being stopped, unlike a ball in London. But, then again, he was a stranger here. Unfortunately, such was not the case when he attempted to return as word had spread that he was the Earl of Wyndham, owner of Wyndview Farm, and an eligible bachelor of eight and twenty. At least, that is what he assumed given the number of misses and unmarried ladies he was introduced to as he tried to make his way back to Caroline while carrying two glasses of wine.

However, when he finally drew near, his stomach tightened with jealousy upon seeing her speak with a handsome major in the army.

Was the major special to her?

Why did he have such an unpleasant reaction?

Bloody hell! Was the summer heat affecting his mind and making him irrational? Or had he been away from Society and formal gatherings for so long that he forgot how to behave? Just because he had escorted Caroline into the ball did not mean she must speak to only him. Besides, he'd barely been here three days, and certainly had no claim to her, yet every instinct insisted that he remain by her side so that nobody else could enjoy her attention.

What the blazes was wrong with him? This was certainly out of character because he had never reacted in such a manner with regard to any woman of his acquaintance, not even those he had briefly considered courting.

And, as he did not want to leave her too long alone in a conversation with major, Sterling marched forward with every intention of introducing himself, possibly in a manner that might warn the major away. Yet he was halted when his mother stepped in his path to introduce him to an acquaintance. Sterling was polite but made his escape quickly and once again started for Caroline.

"Mrs. Sutcliffe, your wine." he pressed it into her hand.

"Thank you," she murmured, taking in from him before she sipped.

"Lord Sterling Wynd, Earl of Wyndham," he introduced himself.

The man drew himself up and frowned. "Major David Cooper."

"Were you and Mrs. Sutcliffe previously acquainted?" He needed to know if the man was courting her, even though it was none of his concern.

"Her husband was a close friend," the major answered.

Ah, so they did know one another, which he did not like.

"I have recently been posted here and I hope to renew our acquaintance," the major finished looking into Caroline's eyes. "If she would allow me to call on her."

Caroline's jaw tightened even though she smiled. "That is not possible, Major Cooper. I am needed by my father and daughter and have duties at Wyndview Farm."

Her duties were not such that she did not have time to be courted, but Sterling rather liked that she was rejecting the man.

Major Cooper glanced at Sterling, a question in his eyes, and since she had rejected the major, Sterling stepped closer to Caroline.

Bloody hell! Why was he suddenly possessive and protective of a woman he barely knew?

"Perhaps after the harvest." Cooper nodded and walked away.

"You do not care for Major Cooper?" Sterling asked.

"I have no time for gentlemen callers," she answered simply, except it did not truly answer his question.

"Several people stopped for introductions as you made your way back," Caroline noted.

Sterling groaned just before he sipped his wine.

"I assume the same happens every Season."

"Except I will not be in attendance at the upcoming one."

"Had you hoped to return home in time to attend?"

"Yes," he answered. "I only planned on being here a fortnight at the most then sail to Madeira, visit with my brother, Elliot, then return to England, which would have me arriving in London in May."

"Do you enjoy the Season so much?" she asked in surprise.

"No, I do not, but it is a necessity since it is time that I must settle on a wife. I thought to pick one from those available in the ballrooms of London." He hadn't meant for his tone to be so disparaging, but he truly dreaded the process of what was to come.

"Then I hope that we can begin the harvest soon so that you are not delayed in your quest," she offered with humor.

"Do you find my discomfort amusing, Mrs. Sutcliffe?"

"Not at all, Lord Wyndham. I am just humored to see that how a bachelor lord approaches a Season filled with misses ready to wed never changes."

It likely never would.

"Perhaps I am no longer in a hurry," he offered before he took a sip of wine. "Maybe my mother was correct in that I need to take a holiday."

Caroline's brown eyes widened in alarm. Did she not want him here?

And what of the major? Why would she discourage a potential courtship? Which brought another question to his mind—how could she know how bachelors approach a Season?

"You said that your husband died at the Battle of Dresden. I assume he was English."

"Yes, he was."

"Did you meet him here? Was his regiment first here then sent to the Continent?"

"No. I met him in London," Caroline answered.

Sterling frowned. "When were you in London?"

"The year I turned eighteen. Mother insisted that I have a Season so we returned to England and my grandfather, Baron Hallaway, provided one."

How was that possible? Not that she had a Season, but that he hadn't known. "I have not missed a Season since I returned from university. One would think that we would have been introduced."

"We were often at the same ball, Lord Wyndham," Caroline answered.

He frowned even deeper. "Please do not tell me that we were introduced and I have failed to recall." He couldn't imagine he would have forgotten someone as attractive as Caroline.

"No, we were not. I did know who you were, however. Your name was on the lips of several debutantes who hoped that you would settle on a bride," she explained in a whisper. "A friend pointed you out to me."

Did Caroline just tease him? She seemed so reserved and unassuming previously. Was there more to his mother's companion gardener than he realized? "I wish you would have asked for an introduction."

"I would not have been so bold. Your father was my father's employer and it would not have been proper."

"There would have been nothing improper. You were the granddaughter of a baron and attending the same Season as I."

"I felt that it may have made you uncomfortable in a social setting."

"Then you misjudged me, Mrs. Sutcliff. I would have liked to have met you back then."

What had she been like as a girl fresh from the school room?

She was likely just as beautiful as she was now though he found that impossible or he would have noticed her. If she had been in England long enough, maybe her tan had faded and she blended in with all the other dark-haired debutantes. Except he still found it difficult to believe that Caroline could have gone unnoticed among even the loveliest gathering.

How had he not noticed her?

CAROLINE WAS TAKEN aback by his statement.

Perhaps she had misjudged him when he first arrived. Maybe he wasn't as rigid and disapproving as she believed.

And what did he mean that he was no longer in a hurry and that maybe he did need a holiday?

The idea of him lingering around Wyndview Farm was rather disconcerting given…well…everything.

Then Caroline looked around the ballroom, and particularly at the guests. Some were English and some were ancestors of the Dutch who had settled in the area during the 1600s. The first to plant grapes that created a wine empire.

And, among the English and Dutch were pretty daughters of marriageable age.

Why should Wyndham hurry his return to London when the wife he sought might be in this very room?

He was rather callous about the away he was going to decide on who he would marry by picking one *from those available in the ballrooms of London.* What were his requirements? That she be pretty enough or have the right connections, daughter of a peer?

What about love?

Except, English lords rarely considered love when choosing a wife. At least, that was what she had observed during her one and only Season.

It also bothered her that she did not want to witness any

courtship that he might engage in and told herself that it was only because she pitied the woman that he chose for reasons other than the heart. Yet, she was already jealous of the woman for reasons that she could not fathom. Yes, she may have had a moment of lust, but that was all.

Was he the type of gentleman who gravitated toward the blushing and simpering misses who would obey without question or someone who showed more confidence—a challenge? Or perhaps he wanted one with more maturity than a miss fresh from the schoolroom. Who he chose to dance with and perhaps walk about the room with would tell her what type of mate he sought.

As the musicians took their seats and tuned their instruments, Caroline glanced around the room as the women nervously smoothed their skirts and cast shy smiles at the bachelors, many of them aiming their attention at Wyndham.

Quietly, she waited for him to leave her side and approach a lovely miss and ask her to dance. But, as partners were claimed and the first country dance began, he remained by her side.

She knew he danced. She had seen him do so in England, but he showed no interest here. At least, not yet.

"I brought the two of you here so that you could enjoy yourselves, not stand off to the side like wallflowers hoping to go unnoticed," Lady Wyndham chided as she joined them.

"I was not asked," Caroline answered. "Nor do I expect to be."

"Of course you will not."

Lady Wyndham proclamation rather stung, even if it was the truth.

"Not while you are standing with my son, as if he has a claim on your heart," Lady Wyndham continued. "No bachelor will approach."

"I hardly think that is the case," Caroline returned.

"And you, Sterling, you need a bride."

With that, Lady Wyndham turned and marched away from her son.

⁕

CHAPTER THIRTEEN

STERLING NEEDED TO stop his mother from playing at match-making. He could choose his own bride when the time came and needed no help in doing so.

Besides, he would not be here long enough to determine if any of the local women would suit. A bride picked from a ballroom in London was much safer.

If there was one thing that he had learned from being in Society, wives liked to visit their families, which was not easily done when they lived on two separate continents.

Though, he could consider the English-born misses who had traveled here with their families. They may only be here on holiday, or if their family had taken up residence, might wish to return to the country they were familiar with.

As he glanced around the room, noting the different guests, Sterling allowed himself to consider the possibility, but grew concerned that there simply was not enough time to come to know a miss well enough to be certain that they would suit. Even if he were to remain at Wyndview Farm for two or three months, it would not be enough time. He was needed at the estate and to be available if Hallaway ever found time for him, not off courting someone.

He glanced down at Caroline, who quietly sipped her wine and said nothing. Simply observed those around her.

If he was going to spend any time with an available woman,

he preferred her. Not only was she beautiful and nicely put together, but she had an air of maturity and did understand sacrifices. Afterall, she had lost her husband and was left with a daughter to raise and was forced to return to her father for support.

"Would you have wanted to remain in England if given the opportunity, or were you eager to return to Wyndview Farm?" For some reason, her answer was very important even though it mattered little to his future.

"It is a difficult question to answer," Caroline offered. "When we first moved here, I was with my family, as you know, but I still missed my grandparents in England, as well as my friends, but then I came to love it here. My heart ached when Mother took me away so that I could be presented and I thought I would miss the Wyndview Farm tremendously, and my father and friends, and be miserable in England. But I was not." She smiled. "Yes, I missed my father while I was away, but England was a separate adventure and I embraced London, the Season, and enjoyed all forms of entertainment that cannot be found here. I was content, happy even when I married then settled into my grandfather's home."

"Why your grandfather?"

"Peter owned no property, nor did he have family, and since he was with the footguards and would soon be going off to war, he thought it best and safest if I lived with my grandfather."

Sterling nodded because it had been the best solution.

"I was looking forward to Peter's return and settling into our own home in England. Grandfather was going to find him a position so that he could support a wife and children. Then he was killed, which left me questioning what I should do next, especially since I had an infant daughter." She glanced up. "It was then that I decided to return to Wyndview Farm where my child would know her grandparents only to arrive and learn that my mother had died while I was sailing home." She sighed. "And, as you know, I did not leave again."

"Do you miss it?" he asked quietly.

"England?"

"Yes."

"At times." She smiled.

"If given the choice, where would you choose to live?"

The question was suddenly very important. Then again, she had information that those in this room likely did not, and that was a comparison of having spent time, years even, living in both places. Maybe it would help him understand his mother better.

"If it meant that I would not need to be at sea half of the year going between the two, I think I would live in both places and never suffer another cold winter." She chuckled. "I honestly do not think that I could choose between the two because they are both different and wonderful."

"Does that mean you would be content to live in one place so long as you could visit the other occasionally?"

Caroline tipped her chin. Her smile faded as if she were giving his question serious consideration. "I do believe I would," she finally answered. "I want to return to England one day. I want my daughter to experience England when she is older but I do not think that I could leave here knowing that I would never return, nor do I believe that I could be content here if I knew that I would never see England again." Then she laughed. "Of course, this is a silly conversation because I truly do not know when or if I will ever go back. It all depends on the whims of fate, though I do hope that I am given the opportunity."

Whims of fate! They had brought her to London once, gave her a husband, then took him. Sterling wasn't so certain he would be as content to wait for what may happen next but that was because he intended to have complete control over his destiny.

IT WAS SUCH an odd conversation that she was having with

Wyndham, and she had to carefully consider her answers. Rarely had Caroline thought about what she wanted or what she would even like to do. Her mother and father had been the ones to bring her and her brother to Wyndview Farm when she was a child. It was her parents who decided she needed a Season. She accepted Peter's marriage proposal because she did love him and it was expected that she married. She hadn't wanted to keep returning Season after Season until she wed. That would be unfair to her mother, and costly for her father, even though Grandfather had paid for gowns and had given them a home.

When Peter died, she really had no choice but to accept her fate and do the best by her daughter.

A sense of melancholy washed over Caroline with the realization that she could very likely spend the rest of her life at Wyndview Farm and never experience London or even visit England again.

Soon, she would not even have a purpose here, other than raising her daughter, because William would be taking over as estate manager if Wyndham approved.

Then what would she do? Keep her father's home? Do his and William's laundry? Cook and prepare meals and educate her daughter, and remain a companion to Lady Wyndham?

Would there ever come a time when she would be able to decide for herself or would those decisions always be made for her because of the circumstances in which she found herself?

It was a sobering thought that took away some of the joy she had experienced coming to the ball this evening. Most disturbing perhaps was the idea that she was a widow who would likely never wed again or even enjoy the company of a man.

"Is all well, Mrs. Sutcliffe?"

She blinked and looked up at Wyndham who watched her with concern.

"Woolgathering, I suppose," she offered as an excuse. Then she smiled as if all was right in the world when, in truth, her heart ached.

Lady Wyndham glanced back at them, frowned, and marched over, which was rather surprising because Caroline expected her not to speak with her son the rest of the evening, which would have also made for a very uncomfortable ride in the carriage back to the estate.

"The two of you are too serious for a ball," she chastised.

"Even if you are not going to dance, Sterling, do not occupy all of Caroline's time. There may be gentlemen here that want to dance with her."

"I hardly think that is the case," Caroline interjected.

"Nonsense," Lady Wyndham scolded. "You may be a widow, but you are still young so it stands to reason that you might wed again. But nobody is going to approach with my son constantly hovering at your side." She then stepped between Caroline and Lord Wyndham and raised an eyebrow. "The least you could do is greet our host." She nudged her son away.

Wyndham gave a barely discernable shake of his head and Caroline suspected that he would have liked to have rolled his eyes, then made his way to Governor Somerset.

"Now, let us not see if the gentlemen are more encouraged to approach now that Sterling is not glaring at everyone," Lady Wyndham whispered and before she barely finished her comment, a military man did start in their direction.

"Ah, Captain Rowling." Lady Wyndham smiled. "Caroline, may I introduce Captain Charles Rowling, recently arrived and the third son of Viscount Rutledge?"

She dipped into a slight curtsey.

"Captain Rowling, this is Mrs. Caroline Sutcliffe."

His smiled slipped slightly but he maintained his polite expression.

"A widow, who lost her husband three and a half years ago."

In other words, Lady Wyndham announced her availability.

"I am sorry for your loss," he murmured. "I had hoped to ask you to dance, but you may not wish…"

"Nonsense. Caroline would love to dance," Lady Wyndham

announced.

"Excellent." Captain Rowling held out his arm. "Shall we join a set forming for a country dance?"

She would rather not but since Lady Wyndham had already accepted on her behalf, to decline would be seen as a rejection, which Captain Rowling did not deserve. Therefore, Caroline allowed him to lead her to the dance floor, which was when she noticed Wyndham offer his arm to a pretty miss with blue eyes and blonde hair. The type of miss any earl would consider as a potential wife if he wanted a peaceful life without anyone questioning his decisions.

CHAPTER FOURTEEN

STERLING HAD NOT planned on dancing with anyone other than Caroline, but his mother's interference, which forced him away, had found him greeting the governor and then being introduced to Miss Harriet Smythe, who looked hopeful when couples began gathering for the next dance. He had intended to pretend like he was unaware of her silent plea, but then he saw Caroline with Captain Rowling and found himself asking Miss Harriet to partner him then navigated her through the crowd until they were in the same group as his mother's companion and the captain.

He told himself that he needed to protect Caroline because neither her brother nor father was here, but he was more concerned that she may be attracted to Rowling and wondered if she were interested in marrying again.

The thought gave him pause, but then Sterling reasoned that if Caroline was courted, then her father might become distracted from his duties at Wyndview Farm, which Sterling certainly wanted to avoid. Therefore, it was his duty to see that all was well with his estate manager's daughter.

He also knew that his excuses were just that—weak excuses when he really just wanted to be near her.

As the partners changed and he came face to face with Caroline, they clasped hands, danced in a circle, broke apart then went to opposite ends of facing lines.

By the time the dance had come to an end, he was once again parched and after returning Miss Harriet back to her parents turned to approach Caroline to ask if she would care for another beverage. Before he even got close, his mother raised a blonde eyebrow and with the tilt of her chin, sent him away.

However, the gentleman who approached next was welcomed.

Blast!

What was his mother up to?

Did she want Caroline to wed, or did she just not want Sterling to spend any time with Caroline?

But why would his mother want to keep them apart? Especially after she had insisted that he act as her escort earlier.

Sterling watched Caroline dance with one gentleman, soldier, or mister after another. She was flushed, laughing, smiling, and happy.

He did not dance. It was much too hot. Instead, he spoke to others, and walked the ballroom, not staying in one place too long or a miss would become hopeful. However, when he learned that there was to be a waltz, he made his way to Caroline and no subtle warning from his mother would keep him away.

In fact, he was the one who lifted a brow to warn her to cease interfering before he asked if Caroline would share the waltz with him.

Given how his mother pursed her lips and narrowed her eyes, he was convinced that she did not want him to pursue Caroline, which he had no intention of doing, but still wondered if there was another reason why he should not even speak to her. What did his mother hope to gain by keeping them apart?

CAROLINE WAS TIRED and overheated from dancing and would love to rest, but Lady Wyndham was so encouraging that

Caroline did not feel as if she could reject anyone who asked. However, when Lady Wyndham suggested that she sit out the waltz, Caroline had almost agreed until she noted that it was Lord Wyndham who approached.

Apparently, Caroline was good enough to be her companion but not worthy enough to waltz with her son, the earl, not that it mattered. It was simply a waltz.

She took his offered arm and allowed Wyndham to lead her to the dance floor then went through the motions of a curtsey and bow before she placed her hand in his and the other on his arm.

He was powerful in his steps and Caroline was left to simply follow. It was the first time she had waltzed since London, and it was so easy to get swept away by the music and enjoy the warmth of his hand on her back and the other in her gloved hand.

Never had she experienced a partner so perfectly matched to her. Not even her deceased husband.

"Are you enjoying your evening?" he asked as they turned at the end of the room.

"I am. Are you?"

"I have enjoyed a few conversations."

"Perhaps you should dance more," she suggested.

"It only offers encouragement when there is none," he ground out. "Miss Millicent has now watched me the entire night and it is rather disconcerting."

Whereas he had no fears that Caroline would be encouraged, and she was not.

"How often has my mother dragged you off to one of these entertainments?"

"This is the first that she has forced me to," Caroline answered.

"Why is this one so important?"

She shrugged. "I do not know."

"But she does ask?" he questioned.

"Yes, often, and I remind her that it is not my place and that I am far too busy to spend an evening in frivolity and she leaves me be."

"Until today."

"Until today," she returned and still wondered why this ball was so important. More important than the others.

Caroline could think of no reason.

She had forgotten how much she enjoyed dancing, but she especially enjoyed dancing with Wyndham. It was easy and there was no need for uncomfortable conversations, which so often occurred when the partner was a near stranger. With him, it was relaxed and she didn't feel the need to fill the silence.

It was more than simply comfortable. Wyndham was strong, powerful, in control and she couldn't help but remember how he looked that night when he came to the office, his banyan open and revealing his naked chest.

Goodness, it was warm.

So much dancing in a crowded room would make anyone lightheaded and she wished that was the true reason for the fluttering in her chest and the increased pulse, but Caroline couldn't even lie to herself.

Ever since Wyndham had arrived at Wyndview Farm, she had been experiencing desire for the first time since her husband marched off to war.

She suffered from an ache that only a man could relieve, but that wasn't all. How long had it been since she'd simply been held and comforted? She could barely recall the dark nights of quiet conversation, a gentle touch, a kiss on the cheek, friendship.

An ache of loneliness grew within, smothering the desire that had stirred.

Her life may be full with her duties at Wyndview Farm, and with taking care of her daughter, who was the light of her world, but there was nobody just for her with which she could share her thoughts or even comfortable silence.

Goodness, her emotions had changed in the space of a dance and Caroline would like to push everything away and return to being content with her life but wondered if that would ever be possible again and if she would be haunted by what would never be.

"Is all well, Mrs. Sutcliffe," Wyndham asked quietly. "You seem suddenly disturbed. I did not tread upon a toe, did I?"

Caroline chuckled, thankful for his humor. Wyndham was an excellent dancer, as he likely knew. "It is warm in here," she answered, not willing to discuss what was on her mind.

"Aye, it is," he agreed. "When we are finished, I will retrieve some wine and we can step out into the gardens, though I wonder if they will be any cooler."

It was an excellent idea, but Caroline was not certain that it would be wise to be alone with him. Not because of her earlier desire, but because of a longing for so much more that would never come from him or anyone.

CHAPTER FIFTEEN

THERE HAD BEEN the strangest shift in Caroline's mood as they waltzed. had gone from being happy to nearly downhearted.

His dancing was not so bad but Sterling could not think of another reason.

The conversation had been of little importance other than learning that this was the first time his mother had forced her to a ball.

Was she worried that there was a particular reason?

As the song came to an end, he bowed again to her curtsey then led her away from the dance floor to the refreshment table where they selected a glass of wine, then he turned her to the open doors leading to the gardens.

While it wasn't as hot outside, it was not cool either, but there was a relief from the noise and conversation of the crowds.

"Would you like to sit?" he asked after spying a bench set off and away from the entrance.

"Please," she answered with a grateful smile. "It has been years since I have worn dancing slippers and stood for so long."

Sterling led her to a bench and joined her after she was seated.

"Is all well with you, Mrs. Sutcliffe?" He asked the same question he had inside because he was not certain her answer had been fully truthful.

"I grow tired," she answered.

Tired did not explain sadness, which he noted in her eyes while they were still within the well-lit ballroom.

"That is all?"

Maybe he should not press for a full explanation, but Sterling could not help himself.

Caroline sighed. "I had forgotten what being at a ball could be like. It has been years. Not since…"

"Since your husband," he finished for her.

That was it. She missed her husband.

Had she been so deeply in love? Did that explain why after three and a half years she had not wed again and had been reduced to being a companion for his mother?

"Do you miss him so very much?"

Maybe he shouldn't have asked such a question but Sterling needed to know if she had been so in love that she was now married to a ghost.

"I miss the companionship," she answered quietly. "Not that we had much time for such since he was off to war within three months of our marriage…maybe I miss the promise of what could have been."

Ah, it was not so much a deep love as it was a future she was denied and for some reason he was glad that her heart had not been buried with Peter.

Caroline then shook her head and chuckled. "You must think me terribly silly. I am certain that I am only tired and not used to a night of standing, conversation, and dancing."

He may not know her well, but Sterling was convinced that there was nothing silly about Caroline and likely never had been.

"I am not used to this either," he offered. "There were no balls on the ships, and few entertainments during my travels." Except, there had been dinners and soirees, but he made excuses to leave each early because he was more intent on his purpose of continuing lucrative trade for Trade Wynd, not forming distant friendships or gaining temporary lovers.

Sterling was not bothered that he had not taken more opportunities to enjoy himself either but was disturbed by her words because they awoke something deep within him. He envied his friends who married well. Not only a woman they loved but also someone who was a friend and companion. He had hoped for the same, but as the years passed and when he had not met a woman who could be all those things, Sterling had accepted that his would simply be a marriage of common values, respect, and of similar ranks for the purpose of an heir and a spare. In fact, it is what he preferred because then he would not have to suffer through emotional upheaval.

How much of that had been a lie to himself so that he would be more accepting when he did enter a loveless marriage?

Not even the excuse that he didn't want to go through what his father experienced held any weight. He had witnessed that marriage from when he was a child, and how happy both had been. The changes only occurred when they were forced to give up their life at Wyndview Farm. His mother hadn't been the only one who would have preferred to remain at Wyndview Farm. His father had been happy here too, but duty had required him to return to England, and each day that passed after he took of the mantal of the earldom and running Trade Wynd a little more of his humor and happiness faded until it was gone completely.

Sterling glanced through the glass doors leading to the ballroom and at his mother. She was laughing with whomever she was speaking, happier than she had ever been in England.

He had judged her too harshly and he understood so much more now, not that he had discussed the matter further with her, but she also wasn't aware that Father ignored her letters and Sterling wasn't certain if he should even tell her.

Maybe, but she had also not returned to her children.

Except, she hadn't believed she was wanted any longer.

Sterling shook the thoughts away. It no longer mattered because the past could not be changed, and maybe he should try to better understand.

At least Caroline had been able to enjoy love and companionship for three months. More than he ever expected to have.

Blast! Now he was as maudlin as she had appeared at the end of their waltz.

But it also forced him to reevaluate the type of wife he would seek once he returned to England. Maybe she wasn't in a ballroom but in Southampton. He had failed to attend entertainments there because he made excuses for being too busy. That would need to change and he might just find the perfect wife for him at a local assembly, dinner in the home of a friend, or even in church, if he bothered to attend.

CAROLINE COULD NOT believe that she confessed her sadness to Wyndham. Those were private concerns and should not have been shared with a gentleman who was barely an acquaintance. Had she not been tired, or perhaps in a melancholy state, she likely would have pretended all was well.

"Tell me of your travels," she said to move away from their depressive discussion. "Where all have you gone since leaving England?"

He chuckled but then began to tell her of being in France, Italy, Greece, Portugal, and Spain. Caroline sighed with envy as she would have loved to have visited each of those places but it was not her lot in life. Therefore, she lived vicariously through his descriptions of all that he had seen and done in less than a year. More than she would in her lifetime.

Her wine was long gone, and she had cooled from being away from the ball, but Caroline kept asking questions, which he readily answered.

He even laughed when he described mishaps or when they were misdirected and at other times his blue eyes darkened with descriptions of the ruins in Greece and cathedrals in Italy. Caroline could almost see them herself.

Wyndham was not at all like the gentleman she judged him to be when they had first met. In fact, she liked this version very much. He was charming and witty, and painted pictures with his words.

"I have been looking everywhere for you two."

At Lady Wyndham's announcement they both straightened as if they'd just been caught misbehaving when all they had been doing was having a conversation.

"It was only when I heard whispers that the two of you had disappeared out here over an hour ago and not returned that I became alarmed."

An hour! Caroline could not believe they had been absent that length of time. Had this happened in London she would have been ruined or, at the very least, gossiped about. Thank goodness she did not make a habit of visiting the residents in Cape Colony and remained at Wyndview Farm.

"How can you ever meet someone worthy of courting you, Caroline, if you are out here with my son?"

Caroline blinked at her. *That* was the reason Lady Wyndham insisted that she attend! Had that been her plan when she first began asking Caroline to attend balls with her?

"And you, Sterling!" his mother scolded. "There are English misses and ladies inside who would like to make your acquaintance and possibly dance with you. They will not always live here and many want to return to England. And, as I said earlier, it is time you found a bride."

Caroline slid a look to the Earl of Wyndham to note that any humor or even happiness that he had just a few moments ago was gone and replaced with a firm set of his mouth and narrowing of his eyes—no different from the gentleman she had first met.

"I had hoped that you were above matchmaking, Mother, but hear me now, there is not one woman inside that I wish to come to know better."

"You have not even met everyone," she argued.

"Nor do I intend to. I will find my bride in my own time and in a place of my choosing."

"Did you ever consider that the nearly three-month voyage back to England might be more pleasant with a companion?"

"Yes, I have." He stood. "For that very reason, I will not be seeking a bride here because I will not be in the Cape Colony long enough to know if a woman would suit, which could make for a most unpleasant trip to England without an escape if she does not."

"You are the one who insists on leaving as soon as possible when there is no reason why you cannot remain long enough to make certain that your bride is not among the guests."

"I have already been gone too long and will not prolong my journey for courtship. I need to return to England as soon as it is convenient for me to meet with Mr. Hallaway."

Caroline wanted to shrink into herself and wished that she had not witnessed the argument between mother and son, but there was nowhere to hide and they did not seem to mind that she witnessed them.

"Oh, very well. You are as stubborn as your father," Lady Wyndham said right before she turned her attention to Caroline. "Come along, dear. Just because my son does not care if he has a happy future, I insist that you do. It took me long enough to get you to a ball and I do not want you wasting your time out here when there are prefect candidates for a courtship inside."

Why did the woman suddenly want her to wed? The topic had never been mentioned before but now it seemed extremely important. Did she even realize what could happen at Wyndview Farm if she wed and left the estate? Or did Lady Wyndham hope that by the time it happened William would have full control of the estate manager's duties and therefore Caroline was no longer needed?

No longer wanted!

Slowly she stood and joined Lady Wyndham and began their return to the ball.

"I know that there are several men who have land and estates here," she was saying. "I will not introduce you to those who might return to England because I am certain you would not want to be parted from your father and brother."

"That is very kind of you, Lady Wyndham, but I have no intention or desire to wed again."

"Nonsense. You are young and have a daughter to support, therefore, you need a husband."

Caroline glanced back at Wyndham, helpless and not certain how to make Lady Wyndham stop what she was doing, but he was too busy glaring at his mother to be of any assistance. Caroline was on her own and would have to do her best to discourage anyone who may want to call on her.

Well, unless there was someone of interest.

Maybe Lady Wyndham was correct in that she should marry again.

At least she would have a companion who could turn into more.

As Caroline stepped into the ballroom, she glanced around at the male guests and for the first time truly considered if she should remarry, after her brother was installed as the estate manager, of course.

CHAPTER SIXTEEN

HIS MOTHER WAS meddling where she should not!

Irritation burned in his gut that she would even attempt to organize his life after she had been absent for the past ten years.

He would not have put up with it even if they had never been separated and nothing irritated him more in London than gossiping woman and matchmakers who could not mind their own business. And now, she was managing Caroline's potential future.

Why was it now so important that Caroline find a husband?

His mother had accepted her declination of invitations before and he was curious as to why this ball was different.

It was not possible that it had anything to do with him since he had only arrived a few days ago, so why was it so important *now*?

Maybe she had forced Caroline to this ball because she thought it would be easier to manage him and he'd remain polite if her companion was present. If so, his mother had been mistaken because Sterling did not care who overheard them argue.

Irritated, Sterling found another glass of wine and a place where he could support the wall. He was only polite without encouraging whenever his mother brought someone over for an introduction. He had no intention of engaging in more meaningless and shallow conversations, especially since he had been having the most enjoyable one with Caroline. She had truly been interested in his travels and not just pretending as a miss in search of a husband would have. And she asked intelligent questions about marble, ruins, rose windows, and if what she had read of such places was correct. She had truly wanted to know and had an appreciation for the places he had visited.

His aggravation only increased as the evening continued all while watching Caroline dance with one man after another.

The color was high in her cheeks and the ringlets about her face and neck grew damp.

She had to be miserable in the heat but would not disobey his mother. She certainly could not have been interested in any of the men who asked to partner her, could she? There was no doubt that had probably been complimented and then asked how she found the weather enough times that she wanted to scream. Her smile was not even genuine, not like the one she had when they had been in the garden discussing his travels.

Blast!

She was going to faint if she did not rest. Therefore, he crossed the expanse of the room, retrieved a glass of lemonade and was waiting for the set to end when he approached and pressed it into her hand before leading her to an open window.

"Thank you," she murmured before taking a sip.

"You could decline the invitations to dance," he reminded her.

Caroline glanced over at his mother. "I do not want to disappoint Lady Wyndham."

"I believe that it is time that we leave." He did not ask. Instead, Sterling waited until Caroline finished her lemonade then escorted her to his mother.

"We are returning home!"

"The ball is not over," she objected.

"Then I will send the carriage back for you but Mrs. Sutcliffe and I are leaving."

"You cannot be alone with her. What of Caroline's reputation?"

She was a widow so there was little concern, except he did not want those at the Governor's ball to think she was the same kind of widow who attended functions in London and often left with a bachelor to share time in a more intimate manner. And while it may be acceptable in London, even if remarked upon, he was not so certain how such would be viewed here. Therefore, if his mother refused to leave, Sterling had two choices: Remain until she was ready or leave Caroline behind, except he was doing this for Caroline as well as himself, but more for her.

As he glanced around the ballroom, Sterling decided that he must remain because not only were there bachelors who watched Caroline with too much interest, it would not be safe for her and his mother to return to the estate alone. Though, he supposed his mother did so often.

"I am not certain my reputation matters," Caroline said quietly. "I am not an innocent miss new to the marriage mart, but a mature widow."

His mother snorted and Sterling nearly did as well. Mature indicated someone of his mother's age. While Caroline lacked the silliness of a debutante, she was still young enough to be desired as a lover or a wife.

"I would not mind returning to Wyndview Farm," she said after a moment.

"You do not wish to remain and dance more?" his mother asked in surprise.

"I am not used to such a late night or dancing or..." She glanced around the room. "And being around so many people for so long."

"It has been some years since you enjoyed a Season in London," his mother agreed with sympathy. "I supposed it might be overwhelming; therefore, we will take our leave, but only because I do not want you miserable." She then glanced at Sterling and raised an eyebrow. "Not because my son wishes to be gone."

He did not care what her reasons were. Sterling was simply glad they were leaving.

"This was a lovely evening and more successful than I anticipated," his mother said once they were settled in the carriage and on their way back to Wyndview Farm.

"Successful, how?" he asked, not certain he was prepared for the answer.

"Several gentlemen and military men asked after Caroline," she answered. "They asked if they might call on her."

Sterling forced himself to remain calm, though he was extremely irritated at his mother's interference and her attempt to take on a guardianship role. "It is not your place to grant permission," he reminded his mother.

"Of course not, dear." She dismissed with a wave of her hand. "That is why I told them that as soon as the harvest was complete that I would invite them to tea, which would give Caroline a better opportunity to know them and then decide for herself if she would welcome them calling on her."

Sterling glanced at his mother's companion just in time to see her brown eyes widen in horror, yet she did not voice an objection.

"Please inform me who you invite and when so that I can determine if I want to join you or not," she finally said and turned to look out the window.

Were there gentlemen that she would not mind meeting again? Were there some she did not want to encourage?

"We will have time to decide whom to invite after the harvest," his mother promised. "And you shall determine whom it will be."

Who did she want to call on her?

Sterling crossed his arms over his chest and sank into the corner of the bench.

He did not like this at all and feared that Caroline would be pushed into a courtship because she did not want to disappoint his mother.

CAROLINE DID NOT want to meet other men. She did not want to have tea with other men.

But, more disturbing, why was Lady Wyndham suddenly deciding that she wanted to be a matchmaker—for her?

Did she want her gone from Wyndview Farm?

Now that William was almost ready to take over his father's duties as the estate manager, did she believe there was no reason for Caroline to remain?

The thought was distressing and had kept her awake most of the night.

What would she do if it was decided that after William became the estate manager that she and her daughter could no longer remain in the home she now shared with her father and brother? The estate manager was allowed a wife and children, not siblings, or even a parent. At least that was what she had understood. And William would likely wed one day and there were no other bed chambers available if his wife provided a child.

Where would she and her father go? Furthermore, what would her father do without the grapes? They were his passion.

She thought she had more time before such decisions would need to be made.

At least she had until after the harvest before men were invited to tea, which gave her nearly two months to plan a different future for herself because Caroline could not imagine marrying again...

That wasn't correct. She would not mind having the security of a husband for her and Livia, but she had no intention of marrying without love and companionship. Not a single gentleman nor military man that she had met at the ball even interested her enough that she wanted to invite them to tea, well, other than Wyndham, but he was not a candidate for her future.

Caroline shook her head as she crossed the terrace to the main house.

In time, she would let her thoughts be known to Lady Wyndham, but there were other duties that required her attention today.

"Ah Caroline, I am glad you have arrived."

This was often the greeting she received from Lady Wyndham.

"Is there anything amiss?"

"Cook has asked me to discuss the menus for the coming sennight."

"As she does every week," Caroline reminded her, preparing herself for a familiar argument and already knowing how it would end. "Cook cannot plan properly if you do not tell her what you would like prepared for your meals."

"Because I do not know," Lady Wyndham argued. "How can I possibly know what I will want to eat three days from now?"

"If not for you, maybe you can plan a menu that will be pleasing to Lord Wyndham," she suggested.

Lady Wyndham frowned. "Yes, well, I can only speak to when he was a child. I have no idea what his preferences are as an adult."

"You could ask." It would not be so difficult a question.

Lady Wyndham waived her hand in dismissal. "You decide, Caroline. It is what I have told you to do every week for months but you still insist on asking."

"It is not my decision to make, Lady Wyndham."

"I have told you that it is, and you have never failed me. Now, go along and arrange the menus with Cook so that she can send someone to the market."

"Yes, Lady Wyndham," Caroline answered with a sigh.

"If you do not want to make a menu, Mother, why not ask the housekeeper instead of Mrs. Sutcliffe?" Wyndham asked as he entered the sitting room.

Caroline nearly groaned. Why did he always arrived at the most inopportune times and ask questions that she would rather he not.

"We do not have one," his mother answered.

Her son frowned. "Mrs. Nel was to have retired six months ago. The notification was provided to me in the last quarterly report received before I sailed. I had instructed Hallaway to hire a replacement immediately so that one could be trained before Mrs. Nel left. Did he not do so?"

"He was too preoccupied with the estate," his mother answered with little concern.

"That is one of his duties—to see that the estate is fully staffed." Wyndham's voice rose in irritation. "Since I have arrived, I have discovered that there is no gardener employed, when there should be if one has gardens and now, I am told that there is no housekeeper."

"You are making too much of the situation," Lady Wyndham dismissed his concern, much like Caroline's father dismissed matters that did not involve grapes and she well understood Wyndham's frustration with his mother.

"I interviewed candidates and did not like them so Caroline has agreed to fill the position until such time as we can once again begin interviewing." Her answer was so pleasant, a problem easily resolved, that Lady Wyndham likely believed that her son would simply accept her explanation while Caroline knew that it would not be so easy.

Wyndham stared at her, his blue eyes dark with lingering irritation. "Besides being your father's secretary, sometimes gardener, and my mother's companion, you are also the housekeeper?"

His voice was tight with disapproval.

"I am simply being of assistance and my father assured me that he would see to hiring a new housekeeper as soon as the harvest is complete." If he remembered, or maybe she would need to see to that duty, but Lord Wyndham did not need to know the extent of the difficulties they faced. "Besides, it is not a burden and I already know the servants and everyone who works at Wyndview Farm, and how the household is run so it is easier for me than for your mother or my father to train someone new."

"Then you will be compensated for the positions you now fill."

"No," Caroline insisted. "I am grateful for a home with my father for me and my daughter. This is a way for me to repay the kindness of allowing him to take me in when it might have been prohibited. Therefore, compensation is not necessary."

"You seem to be of the opinion that you have a choice," Wyndham returned.

Oh dear!

Where had the kind gentleman she enjoyed speaking with the evening before gone? Did Wyndham leave him behind at the ball? It was the only explanation because he was behaving very much as he had when he first arrived and she did not like this version nearly as well.

CHAPTER SEVENTEEN

WHEN STERLING HAD first awakened, his mood had been odd in that he was conflicted as to why he had been bothered by other gentlemen and military men showing Caroline attention. Why did he hate the idea of anyone calling on her? His time was limited at Wyndview Farm and soon he would be sailing to Madeira and then back to England, and Caroline would remain here with her family. Once he left, it was likely he would never see her again so why was he so bothered by potential suitors?

He tried to convince himself that it was because he did not want his mother forcing a match that Caroline did not want, but that was only part of the truth. The other was that he wanted her for himself. To what extent, he did not yet know, but he wanted to come to know her the best that any man could know a woman outside of a marriage before he did leave.

Sterling had never experienced such emotions when it came to any woman he did not know or what to make of them, nor how to respond.

Nor did he not have time to court her, to come to know her any more than he did any of the women he had met the evening before, except, he was able to visit with her far more frequently without having to leave the estate…but to what purpose? His life was in England and hers was here. There was no future.

"Do you miss it?" That was the question he had asked her last

evening.

"*England?*"

"*Yes.*"

"*At times.*" She smiled.

"*If given the choice, where would you choose to live?*"

That question was just as important now as it had been last evening.

"*If it meant that I would not need to be at sea half of the year going between the two, I think I would live in both places and never suffer another cold winter.*" She chuckled. "*I honestly do not think that I could choose between the two because they are both different and wonderful.*"

"*Does that mean you would be content to live in one place so long as you could visit the other occasionally?*"

"*I do believe I would,*" she answered. "*I want to return to England one day. I want my daughter to experience England when she is older but I do not think that I could leave here knowing that I would never return, nor do I believe that I could be content here if I knew that I would never see England again.*" Then she laughed. "*Of course, this is a silly conversation because I truly do not know when or if I will ever go back. It all depends on the whims of fate, though I do hope that I am given the opportunity.*"

There truly was no reason why he could not occasionally visit Wyndview Farm. Yes, it could be a three-month journey by ship to his home in Southampton, but little over two months from his home to Cape Town because of currents and prevailing winds. Yes, it might as well be half a year of sailing, but it could be done every few years, especially if the estate in Southampton was properly cared for while he was away. He had already been gone nearly a year and there had been no catastrophes, which was a reasonable belief since at each port he came in contact with captains of other Trade Wynd ships, the last being at Gibraltar before he sailed here and was assured all had been well a month earlier. Of course anything could have happened since that time, but it was doubtful.

Sterling shook his head as he approached the house from the fields. He had known Caroline not even a full four days, which was certainly not enough time to consider how she might fit into his future.

Perhaps he would revisit the question later, after he had spent more time with her, but it was far too soon to do so now.

He paused just inside the door leading to the terrace as the voices of his mother and Caroline drifted toward him and marched to his mother's sitting room where the topic of conversation brought a return of his irritation.

How could he have not realized that there was no housekeeper at Wyndview Farm, well, other than Caroline, apparently? He should have noted the absence of one within his first day of being in residence, yet he hadn't.

It angered Sterling that his family, no, his mother, had been taking advantage of Caroline. Unlike many vineyard owners in the Cape Colony, his family did not participate in the distasteful practice of using slaves for reasons that came to light back to the early seventeen hundreds, yet apparently his mother had no difficulty allowing Caroline to work positions without pay and it would stop now. Further, he knew of no person who would be willing to take a position and not ask for wages. With regard to her being a companion, he assumed it was more of a convenience and maybe Caroline enjoyed his mother's company, but to perform the duties of the housekeeper without compensation was beyond his understanding.

It was also suspicious. He had entire families of fathers, wives, sons, and daughters working on his estates in England, and they each received wages. So, why didn't Caroline want the same, especially since she had a daughter to support? If she had her own funds, she would never have returned to Wyndview Farm, therefore, why would she decline wages?

"Is there anything in particular you would like on the menu for the coming week, Lord Wyndham?" Caroline asked.

"Oddly, I cannot think of a thing and leave all menu plans to you, Mrs. Sutcliffe."

"Is there anything that you do not like. If so, I will make

certain that it is not served."

"There is not a food that I do not like…well, of what I have tasted to date, and will sample anything Cook decides to serve."

Caroline gave a nod. "Very good. Then I shall excuse myself to meet with Cook."

Sterling watched her leave, her dark hair pinned at the back of her head, styled for efficiency and to be out of the way, different than the dark curls that had brushed her neck the evening before.

Her mood and demeanor were also different. Last night, she'd been a widow at a ball, engaging in conversations not only with him, which he had enjoyed very much, but with gentlemen and military men and she had danced. However, today, she was restrained and respectful, much like his housekeeper in Southampton.

He frowned. Caroline was much like a chameleon who changed its colors depending on its environment. While he had enjoyed studying them when he was a boy, Sterling was certain that he did not like the shifts in Caroline and he couldn't help but wonder what else she hid from him and when that change would come about.

"A moment," Sterling called, hurrying after Caroline before he caught up to her as she neared the dining room. "I had hoped to speak with your father this morning. Do you know where he might be?"

She stiffened, her spine straightening, before she turned to face him.

Another shift. Was it fear or concern? And if so, why?

"I was to believe that you were going to wait to discuss the estate until after the harvest."

"That is my intention, however there is no reason why I cannot tour the estate now."

"I could show you, Lord Wyndham. I know it well and have spent many hours walking the land."

"I believe you have a menu to plan," he reminded her. "Therefore, please direct me to your father, if you know where he might be."

Caroline drew in a shaky breath.

He had asked a simple question and her answer should be either to tell him where her father was or say that she did not know, yet he sensed that she was reluctant to provide him with the information he requested.

"Is there something you are trying to keep from me, Mrs. Sutcliffe?"

She blinked and then her brown eyes grew wide. "I…um…no, of course not," she finally managed to answer. "I am simply not certain. My father is likely studying the grapes for ripeness, but as your vineyard is large, I do not know exactly where he might be."

Sterling suspected that she was not being fully truthful, but what could she possibly have to lie about?

In time he would determine the source of his concern, but other important matters required his attention.

"That is all you needed to say, Mrs. Sutcliffe. I will search for him myself."

AFTER CAROLINE MET with Cook and the menu was planned, more elaborate now that Wyndham was in residence, she sent a maid and footman into town so they could visit the market and shops to obtain the items Cook would need.

She then returned to her home to find Beatrix helping Livia with her reading.

Caroline did not interrupt, satisfied that all was well, then left again. This time she walked to the small rise that looked out over the rows of grapevines. Worry ate at her but there was little she could do, nor could she control what her father might say. She could only hope that William was near and could answer the more specific questions.

She strained and tried to locate them below, but could not, which did not calm her.

With a heavy sigh, she returned to Lady Wyndham to inform her of the meals to come.

"Why are you distressed?" Lady Wyndham demanded.

Caroline thought she hid her discomfort, but apparently, she had not. "Your son is looking for my father."

Lady Wyndham's blonde eyebrows drew together over the light-blue eyes. "Why?"

"He wanted to tour the estate. I offered to accompany him, but he reminded me that I had to meet with Cook." Caroline narrowed her eyes on Lady Wyndham because there was no reason why she could not plan menus herself.

"You worry too much, Caroline," Lady Wyndham dismissed her.

Her father was no different than Lady Wyndham and if he told her one more time, "You worry too much," Caroline would scream.

Did neither one of them realize the consequences of her and her father's duplicity being discovered by the owner of the estate?

"Would you please ring for tea?" Lady Wyndham requested then turned her gaze to the gardens.

"Of course." Caroline strode to the bellpull and tried not to sigh. It would do no good to force a confrontation with the older woman, because just like her father, Lady Wyndham was set in her ways.

The two were very specific in where their interests lay and had no desire to pay attention to anything they deemed tiresome.

While Lady Wyndham had that privilege, her father did not. He was paid to attend to certain details—many of which he ignored.

Lady Wyndham slowly turned to Caroline, her eyes grave. "My son needs to concern himself less with an estate that he will likely never visit again and put his mind to more serious matters."

Was she finally beginning to accept or at least understand the difficulties of Wyndham being underfoot and would no longer be dismissive of her concerns?

"Such as finding a wife." Was that not the reason she had claimed at the ball?

"I fear it is more serious," Lady Wyndham admitted. "I fear that when he learns what we know about Wyndview Farm, and what you truly do for us, that he will change everything and maybe make me return to England."

Caroline nearly sighed with relief that Lady Wyndham did understand the serious nature of their situation. "I cannot imagine he would do so," Caroline assured her. There would be no purpose in forcing his mother to abandon her home.

"I am afraid of what will happen if Sterling askes too many pointed questions."

Their eyes met in understanding.

"I need him distracted, even if it means sending him away."

If he were gone, then they could all relax, and she could see to the duties that have been neglected since his arrival, even if he was gone only a few days. "Yes, but to where?"

Lady Wyndham slowly smiled. "To a place he begged to visit when he was a child."

✦ ✦ ✦

CHAPTER EIGHTEEN

AFTER FINDING HALLAWAY on one of the paths that separated two rows of grapevines, Sterling had followed and tried to ask questions, but Hallaway was too intent on studying nearly every bunch of grapes and occasionally taking one to taste before moving on.

"Are they ready?" one of his employees asked.

"Not yet," Hallaway had answered.

The servant turned around and walked back to the large barn.

"When will they be?" Sterling had asked.

"Soon."

"How soon? A day? A week?"

Hallaway pulled back and looked at Sterling as if he asked an impossible question to answer. Gone was the jovial man who had met with him after he first arrived and had suggested they enjoy brandy and wine before discussing business. Before him was a man, aged from working in the sun, his gray hair in need of a trim and sticking out in different directions as if he hadn't bothered to brush it that morning. His brown eyes, intense beyond simple concern, as if Sterling had the audacity to question him.

"I do not know," he announced. "They will be ready when they are." Hallaway then turned around, dismissed him and marched down the path at the edge of the vineyard and repeated the same action of examining bunches of grapes and tasting a few.

Sterling studied Hallaway's expression as he pinched a grape, or bit into one and savored it as if it were already a fine wine. Sterling would be surprised if Hallaway even remembered that anyone was with him, which was rather concerning since Sterling was his employer and owner of the vineyard. Never had an employee or servant shown him so little respect. Was it simply because Sterling had been absent from the estate for so many years that Hallaway had forgotten how one treated an employer? He had been in charge of Wyndview Farm for nearly eleven years with instructions coming by way of correspondence and not in person.

Sterling was not certain what to make of the man's disrespect but held his tongue and simply observed while he wondered if Hallaway was simply an eccentric or had forgotten his place.

They were soon joined by William, who also quietly observed his father repeat the same examination and tasting, with his father explaining why the bunch was not yet ready to be cut, minus the dismissive attitude he had shown Sterling.

While father was educating son, he ignored Sterling.

Was Hallaway preparing his son to take over his position when he decided to retire? Caroline had mentioned that he was being trained to be an estate manager. Was it this estate that he was being trained for?

Hallaway was getting on in years and it would be good to know that when Hallaway retired that his son could take over.

"Are these ready?" Sterling asked when they reached the end of the row.

"No," Hallaway answered and walked away.

He looked at William. "Is he always like this?"

"As we near the harvest, yes. We are used to it."

Well, he certainly wasn't, but Sterling just shook his head and followed Hallaway, not certain where he might be going.

In ordinary circumstances Sterling might have sacked Hallaway for his impudence, but he managed a vineyard that produced wine that was coveted by many and helped increase the coffers of Trade Wynd. That was the only reason Sterling allowed him more latitude of behavior than he would anyone else.

It was only after he had followed Hallaway to a small piece of land set aside, that his employee took the time to explain to Sterling that he was grafting different grapevine roots for a better wine, just as Caroline had previously told him, that Sterling finally returned to the house. He was hot and thirsty. Of course, he was dressed as a gentleman from London when visiting his estate, including a suitcoat and cravat. Next time, he would dress as the employees in the vineyard, in cooler cotton shirts and trousers without any of the layers he was accustomed to.

He had also been intent on climbing to his chamber and requesting water so that he might wash the sweat from his neck only to pause outside of the parlor where his mother was visiting with Caroline—her companion and housekeeper.

For a moment, he thought of joining them for tea, but he was uncomfortable in his own clothing and wished to change. And so, he simply passed the door.

"Sterling do join us," his mother called out.

"I will return momentarily," he promised.

"Please do, because I have an adventure planned for you and me."

The words reached him as he neared the stairs.

Adventure? What could his mother have in mind this time?

His anger and resentment from the past had diminished since his arrival but that did not mean that he would allow her to manage him.

Sterling also considered ignoring her words and continue to his chamber, but he knew that he would not be able to relax and retraced his steps and returned to the sitting room, but only out of curiosity and concern, and found his mother seated by her favorite window. Across from her was Caroline, who looked lovely in a light, cotton gown of pale yellow, which was very complementary to her dark hair and eyes.

"What *adventure* do you have planned?" he asked, hoping that it was a sojourn into town.

"Tomorrow morning, if your ship is available, we will sail to Cape Agulhas."

He could only stare at her. Shock and surprise mingled with suspicion settled in his mind. Why did she want to venture there now?

"I remember how badly you wanted to visit as a child so that you could have one foot in the Indian Ocean and the other in the Atlantic Ocean, but your father was never able to get away for such a holiday." She smiled. "I see no reason why we cannot do so now. It is not as if you have anything to occupy your time until Hallaway has completed the harvest."

There were some duties that he could attend to, but they were few and he wanted questions answered before he decided to make changes.

"Please, Sterling. I have wanted to go myself, and now we can. You and I, to the one place you begged us to take you as a child."

His mother had always been spontaneous and he suspected that this was one of those moments. If she woke up and wanted to go on a picnic, she informed Cook, who packed a basket. She was not one to plan ahead, at least not until they arrived in England. There she became dull because Father no longer had time to indulge her whims. But today, apparently, she had awakened and decided to sail to the most southern point on South Africa. The question that lingered, however, was why? And perhaps, more importantly, why now?

It would also take at least a day and a half or two days to sail to Cape Agulhas and another day and a half or two back, which he remembered being told when he was younger. Did he want to be away from the estate for so long?

Sterling did want to go, but it was not nearly as pressing as it had been when he was twelve.

His eyes shifted to Caroline. If she were to join them, he might find the holiday more pleasant.

"Would your companion be joining us?"

"Oh, as much as I would like to have Caroline on our holiday, I fear that she cannot be away."

"Because she is your housekeeper and sometimes gardener," Sterling clarified.

"Yes, of course. What other reason could there be?" she asked vaguely before she sipped her tea.

Sterling sighed. "I will ride into town tomorrow and speak to the captain," he promised before he left them to their tea, his stomach churning with suspicion.

He was certain that his mother had something else planned for him, but could not imagine what it might be, and why did he suspect that she was hiding something from him?

It was in her manner and her vague answers.

Or could it be that this was nothing more than a hopeful request and a desire to spend time with her son?

He certainly did not know her well enough to gauge her unspoken intentions since they truly had not spent any time in the company of the other for eleven years. He had changed in that time so she certainly must have as well.

WHEN LADY WYNDHAM announced her plan yesterday, Caroline had grown envious. She had also wanted to visit Cape Agulhas as a child and for the same reasons.

Maybe one day she would be able to take Livia to the southern tip of Africa.

But that would not be now because once Lady Wyndham and her son were away, she could attend to matters that needed her attention before the harvest.

Matters that she put her mind to as she settled behind the desk in the office after Wyndham had ridden away from the farm.

Grapes were not the only harvest they need to concern themselves with, but their other crops as well. While half of their employees would see to the planting of wheat, followed by the planting of barley, oats, and rye as soon as the grape harvest was complete, the other half would be picking oranges and lemons. Pomegranates were being picked now, before everyone was required to attend to the grapes. Yet the household gardens and vegetable fields could not be forgotten either.

Managing each of the groups was a balance in timing and organization that could not be ignored, even if her father didn't believe they were important any longer. At least William understood and as soon as he was able, he would assist.

Caroline had just finished the schedule that needed to be followed, and concerns that needed to be address when the front door opened and George greeted Lord Wyndham.

"Were you successful in securing passage, Lord Wyndham?"

Caroline quickly dusted the ink on her schedule then slipped the document into the top drawer in hopes that it wasn't discovered then rose from the desk and walked to the corridor.

As Wyndham had not answered, she was curious as to why and made her way to the sitting room where she expected Lady Wyndham to be because she was rarely anywhere else when not sleeping or dining.

"The captain refuses to sail to Cape Agulhas unless I do not mind the potential loss of a ship and the lives of my crew and family," he announced.

"That is rather dramatic. He is a captain. Can he not sail a ship? If not, then perhaps you should dismiss him," Lady Wyndham returned as Caroline entered the sitting room.

"He is an excellent captain," Wyndham insisted. "He is just not foolish."

"You do know that ships sail the area nearly daily," Lady Wyndham reminded him.

Caroline edged further into the sitting room but did not want to draw attention to herself. She *needed* both mother and son to take this holiday, even if they would only be gone five days.

"Those are captains with experience in sailing through the

tumultuous waters caused when the warm Indian Ocean meets the cold currents from the Atlantic Ocean. The captain of my ship is not and as there are already dozens of shipwrecks along the coastline, he did not want to add to that number," Wyndham explained as he crossed to the sideboard and poured himself a brandy.

"Oh, very well," Lady Wyndham dismissed with a wave of her hand. "We will simply need to travel by carriage."

"Carriage!" he cried.

"Yes, or wagon, or horse…" Lady Wyndham frowned. "I am not certain of the terrain from here to there but we will see it done."

"How long is such a journey?" Caroline asked. She hoped that they would be gone at least a sennight.

Lord Wyndham whipped around to face her. "Mrs. Sutcliffe," he offered with a nod, as one addressed a servant, before he returned his attention to his mother. "We are not traveling there by carriage, wagon, or horse."

"Why not?" Lady Wyndham asked innocently.

"It would take a sennight alone to arrive at Cape Agulhas and then another sennight to return. I cannot be away from Wyndview Farm for so long, especially with the harvest so close."

No doubt that it was because he wanted to have the detailed meeting with his estate manager and then return to England where he'd find his wife and go about begetting an heir and a spare.

Anxiety and discomfort churned in Caroline's belly. Why did his intentions bother her so much? Not that he wanted a meeting with her father, though that was a concern, but that he would be gone. And that he would be sharing intimacies with the woman he chose to wed. Intimacies she would no longer experience. Intimacies that could relieve the aching need that had been awakened with Lord Wyndham's arrival.

"Why do you want to stay here when there is so much that you could be enjoying?" his mother asked.

"I want to be available for not only the harvest but to meet with Hallaway."

"Darling, that will not be for a least a sennight," his mother promised.

"How could you know when your estate manage does not?"

"Do you think the harvest takes only a day?" Lady Wyndham laughed.

"I know that it does not," he grumbled.

"Therefore, you should take time to explore." Lady Wyndham's eyes brightened. "I know. You shall accompany Caroline to Stellenbosch."

Panic seized Caroline's heart. She had no intention of traveling to Stellenbosch. There was no reason to. She needed to remain at Wyndview Farm and had hoped that he and his mother would be away, which they were no longer doing.

✦ ❧ ✦

CHAPTER NINETEEN

"Why Stellenbosch?" Sterling asked. He could think of no reason why Caroline would need to travel there. Then again, there was much he did not know about her.

"For one, it is where my family lives," his mother answered, seeming rather offended. "After my parents were gone, those in Stellenbosch are all I have left."

He had not meant to insult her and was certain his tone had not indicated such. He'd simply been surprised. But that was not a reason for Caroline to visit, was it? Had his mother thought of someone there who would make a fine husband for her companion?

"They are your family too," his mother reminded him.

He had not seen his cousins since he was a child and likely would not recognize anyone now or know their names, but he recalled traveling there regularly to visit with his great-grandparents, aunts, uncles, and cousins. How could he have forgotten something so important from his childhood?

"If it is to visit family, then the two of us should make the journey," he suggested.

"No, that is not possible," his mother answered.

"Why?"

"I do not feel up to making such a long trip. I am getting on in years."

"You just suggested that we travel a sennight to and from

Cape Agulhas." This time he meant for his voice to rise in exasperation. His mother was being rather aggravating and he was not certain what she was truly up to.

"Further, you also just claimed that Caroline was too busy to have accompanied us to Cape Agulhas." What mischief was she about?

"A visit to Stellenbosch should only take three days, whereas one to Cape Agulhas is much longer," his mother explained.

"And three days is too much for you?"

"Yes, well, I have reconsidered. It was a poor idea to suggest a visit Cape Agulhas to begin with and no doubt my health would have suffered from such travels."

His mother was going to drive him to madness! Yes, she may be getting on in years, but there was nothing fragile about her, nor was she in her dotage.

"Why is it that Mrs. Sutcliffe will be visiting Stellenbosch when it is your family, and mine, who lives there?" Sterling asked, quickly coming to the end of his patience.

"To chaperone, of course," she answered as if he should have already known. "Please ring for tea, Caroline."

"Chaperone?" Caroline asked as if she was as confused as him.

"Yes. Kaya cannot travel a full day, alone with two men. It simply is not done."

Caroline sighed and walked to the bellpull shaking her head.

Did he ask who Kaya was and why she was going to Stellenbosch with two men, one he assumed was him?

As her answer would likely frustrate him all the more, Sterling decided to offer a different argument. "I do not know anyone there any longer,"

"All the more reason to enjoy a reunion with your cousins."

"It will take too long," he insisted. He needed to remain at Wyndview Farm and not waste time on a holiday.

"It is one day there, you will spend the night, spend the day with your family, then return the following day. I expect you home at the end of three days. Therefore, do not dawdle."

Though in retrospect, why was he arguing with his mother? Was it simply because he did not like being manipulated or told what to do? Which was foolish on his part since he had not given any thought to the one advantage of this trip—he would be with Caroline, without his mother's interference. It would be a chance to know her better, learn what he could. It was what he had wanted, so why was he so quick to dismiss the opportunity?

Because his mother had exasperated him with first a trip to the coast then, suggesting Stellenbosch and becoming suddenly too fragile to leave her chair. Sterling did not know her reasons or what plan that she might have brewed in the back of her mind and found he did not care when he would be given three days, nearly alone, with Caroline.

CAROLINE STROLLED TO the bellpull and gave it a gentle tug.

She did not want to travel to Stellenbosch either yet feared that whatever objection she offered would be dismissed even though Lady Wyndham knew that she could not be gone from Wyndview Farm for three days.

"What of Livia? I cannot leave her."

"Livia will keep me company when not at her studies," Lady Wyndham insisted. "I do enjoy having her around and she is coming along very well with her stitches for one so young."

Lady Wyndham had begun to teach Livia needlework be-cause Caroline had no time to teach the finer arts, nor had she thought Livia old enough, but Lady Wyndham was eager to do so because she had never gotten the opportunity since she'd never had a daughter.

"What troubles you, Mrs. Sutcliffe?" Wyndham asked. "You have been frowning ever since my mother decided that the two of us shall travel together." The corner of his mouth tipped. "Is it because you do not wish to spend so much time in my presence?"

That certainly was not the reason, though it should be. Wyndham caused her to think of matters that a respectable widow should not and long for intimacies now missed.

"I believe you will find the travel tedious," she answered. "All day in a wagon, a night in uncomfortable quarters, though a day spent in Stellenbosch should be pleasant enough, but then you would need to spend another uncomfortable night before you start out again the following morning. The travel can be tiresome."

"Why not take a carriage?"

"For such a distance and difficult roads, a wagon is better. I can assure that you will find the trip most uncomfortable."

Maybe if she made the trip sound horribly inconvenient and wearying, Wyndham might reconsider and remain here, then she could as well and someone else could be sent along to chaperone Kaya, especially since Caroline suspected that Malik would also join the young woman, whom he wanted to wed.

"I begin to think that you see me as a pampered gentleman who could not cross a county without a cushioned seat in a well-sprung carriage."

If she agreed, it would be seen as an insult. Of that she was certain.

"It will not be comfortable travels, Lord Wyndham, and I simply wish to make you aware."

"I am made of sterner stuff, despite my title, Mrs. Sutcliffe."

Oh dear. Now he was going to go along simply to prove himself to her, which was the exact opposite of what she wanted.

"As I accept that the next few days may be grueling and the most unpleasant that I have ever experienced, I vow not to complain and now ask what time we shall depart?"

Caroline forced a smile. "At sunrise," she answered wondering how the conversation had gone so terribly wrong when she had intended that she not travel at all.

More concerning, however, was what Lady Wyndham had been thinking to send them both to Stellenbosch?

Though Caroline would wager that Lady Wyndham had just invented a reason to travel to Stellenbosch since they would not be traveling to Cape Agulhas. Caroline just didn't understand why she had to go anywhere.

She would have asked the older woman but Caroline never got the chance and when she arrived at the wagon the following morning, Lord Wyndham was already waiting.

"Good morning."

"Mrs. Sutcliffe," he greeted her boisterously.

It nearly took her aback because she had not expected him to be so…well…happy, especially at this time in the morning.

"Malik has gone inside to retrieve the basket of foodstuffs that Cook has prepared. Kaya is gathering what other necessities we might need," he informed her. "I am not certain what those items are but I have been assured that we will need them."

Caroline eyed him warily. Why was he so jovial?

"By the way the two were looking at each other, I would assume they are smitten. Are they?"

She also would not have expected someone of Wyndham's station to even notice such about servants. Then again, if it had been just the three of them before she arrived, the courtship would have been obvious since Kaya could not help but watch Malik whenever he was about and he did not miss an opportunity to brush her hand by *accident*. "Are there rules against courtships between servants?" She did not know of any but that did not mean they did not exist.

"Do they work in similar positions and encounter each other often?"

"Malik works in the stable and Kaya is a kitchen maid. They rarely see the other while they are at their duties."

"Do they tend to those duties without distraction or interruption? Do they perform at least adequately?"

"Each of your servants serve you well, Lord Wyndham, and are diligent in their tasks."

"Then I do not see why a courtship should not be allowed. Is that the reason you chose them to accompany us—because they are courting?"

"Your mother can be blamed. I believe the visit to Stellenbosch is more for them than you."

"She said you were traveling there," he reminded her.

"I can assure you that I only learned of my plans to do so when your mother announced them."

He frowned, blond brows drawing over his nose. Perhaps he was wondering what his mother was about because Caroline certainly was.

Malik came from the house, hamper in hand and placed it in the back of the wagon, then took Caroline's valise and placed it there as well. Kaya returned only moments later with blankets and pillows which offered some comfort while they traveled.

"Is all ready?" Caroline asked.

"It is," Malik answered then offered his hand to help Caroline into the back of the wagon. He then turned toward Kaya, smiled and held out his hand to assist her.

Wyndham stood there as if he were not certain what to do.

"Your place is on the bench next to Malik," Caroline advised. "He will drive the wagon."

Wyndham frowned at her. "Why should I not sit back here with you?"

That was a foolish question indeed, but Wyndham was acting rather strangely this morning. "For one, you are the Earl of Wyndham, therefore you should not be forced to ride in the back of a wagon. Second, it will be more comfortable for you."

"I shall ride back here, with you, and Kaya can sit beside Malik," Wyndham announced.

"No, no, Lord Wyndham," Caroline insisted. She could not spend an entire day alone with him. It did not matter that Malik and Kaya would be on the bench, driving the wagon and not far away.

Wyndham glanced at Caroline, Kaya, and then Malik. "Do I not have a say? I am the Earl of Wyndham and employ each of you."

Except, Caroline wasn't one of his servants, not that she reminded him of that since he had threatened to pay her wages.

"It is not right, Lord Wyndham," Kaya whispered.

"No, it is not," Caroline agreed as she arranged the blankets and pillows for comfort to keep from bruising her bottom and back during their travels. She had accompanied Lady Wyndham five times previously and knew that she would be stiff and sore once they arrived.

"Nor am I the pampered gentleman you believe me to be. I shall ride in the back of the wagon as you do, and as has my mother."

Kaya's eyes widened as she glanced over at Malik as if he could force the Lord of Wyndham from the wagon.

"Would you prefer to drive?" Malik quickly suggested.

"Is it more difficult than a phaeton or barouche?" Wyndham asked.

"What are those?" Malik questioned.

"Open carriages," Caroline answered. "You would do well driving a wagon, Lord Wyndham." Maybe he would change his mind about riding with her and take his place on the bench.

He stared at the trio, hands on hips, lips tilted in irritation, and then shook his head. "Perhaps later, if Malik does tired of driving." He stepped up and into the wagon.

Why would he, the Earl of Wyndham, want to ride in the back of a wagon?

It made no sense to her.

"You should ride next to Malik," Wyndham said to Kaya. "I am certain that he would enjoy your company."

"Yes…um…of course, Lord Wyndham but do let me know if you want to ride on the bench."

Malik held his hand up to Kaya then assisted her from the back of the wagon before escorting her to the front to be seated next to him.

Wyndam gathered the extra blankets, the ones that Kaya had planned to sit upon, offered one to the servant so that her bottom was cushioned against the hard bench then made himself comfortable with pillows to support his back and layers beneath his bum.

He had done this before. Perhaps Wyndham wasn't so pampered after all.

He grinned at her. "It is a fine day for a drive, is it not?"

Why was he so damned happy?

Except, he wasn't, not in the sense she originally believed. She had challenged him, and now Wyndham was going to prove that not only would he not suffer hardship but he was determined to be pleasant and enjoy himself even if he hid his misery from everyone else.

Well, she would see just how long that lasted, then smiled as she looked over his shoulder at the passing scenery.

CHAPTER TWENTY

WHEN CAROLINE BECAME comfortable in the back of the wagon, Sterling did the same. He was not a weak and pampered gentleman and for some reason, it was necessary to prove that to her.

Maybe it was his pride, but the need was strong.

"Why are we acting as chaperones? I understand that Kaya is a miss, but the two are also servants and not subject to the same rules as a miss in Society." Or at least that is what he believed since he had often seen servants of separate sexes alone and nobody thought anything untoward was happening. He glanced over at the couple.

"Why did you say that this trip was more for them than us?"

"They would like to wed but Malik has not had the opportunity to ask permission of Kaya's father. If granted, he would then need permission from your mother, though, I suppose that should now be you as his employer."

If the two were happy, he had no objection. It was better than losing two servants who might go somewhere else so that they could be together.

"That was the reason my mother insisted on this trip?" he asked shaking his head. "Why did she not just come out and say so instead of her veiled excuses?"

"I am assuming that she wanted your presence so that you could grant the permission as well."

This was all very unnecessary. All the couple had to do was ask. Instead, he was sitting in the back of a wagon, his arse likely bruised, all so a young man, his servant, could be granted permission to wed.

"Does my mother often go about playing matchmaker? She certainly attempted to do so at the ball." And he had not liked it at all.

"Yes, but until that night, she had not attempted it with me."

"Well, she better not think to interfere in my life."

As MUCH AS Caroline always believed that she would do anything that Lady Wyndham asked, she was beginning to reconsider.

This entire journey to Stellenbosch was because Lady Wyndham had decided that…how had she put it? *Something must be done about my son!* It was not so Malik could gain permission to wed Kaya. Those two were a convenient excuse to get Wyndham to do what she wished.

But why must she accompany him? This was not what Caroline had envisioned when Lady Wyndham informed Caroline that she was going to help.

Caroline studied Wyndham's profile as he looked out his side of the wagon and tried to reconcile the various versions of him. He had been arrogant, cold, and demanding when he first arrived. Then, at the ball he'd been witty, charming, and an excellent storyteller, and she came to like him very much. However, when he was with his mother, he was often irritated and the two bickered, but many mothers and sons did, so maybe that was not unusual. Today, he was jovial and, even though he wondered why they were even here, he did not seem to mind.

How many personalities did Wyndham have and which one was the true Earl of Wyndham, deep down inside?

This was all very strange.

Caroline leaned back and watched the birds soar overhead and to the horizon where wildlife could sometimes be seen.

There were dangers to being away from town and in the country, usually from cobras, puff adders, and wildlife predators, but all she noted was the beauty and peaceful tranquility and smiled at the antelope running in the distance.

"I had forgotten." There was nearly awe in Wyndham's tone.

"There is little wildlife in London," she chuckled.

"None unless you visit a menagerie," he grumbled.

Caroline shifted to look at him. "You do not approve?"

"No." He pointed to the antelope. "They are free. All animals should be free, not chained or caged."

She understood. Caroline had visited a menagerie once, and she was certain that each animal contained within was either miserable, bored, or both.

"Nobody should be chained, caged, or claimed or owned by another," he said more quietly before he looked back out and over the horizon.

Such a statement should not have surprised her. His family did not own slaves and abhorred the very idea. Wyndham, and his father, had both argued for the end of slavery, not just the abolishment of the slave trade, which occurred in 1807.

There was honor in Wyndham and that was something she admired.

She also found him likeable, which she certainly had not expected when she had first met him or when she had been filled with lust at the sight of his naked chest.

Goodness, just the reminder of him standing in the office, his banyan open, hair tousled from having just risen from the bed…

It certainly was a warm day and Caroline used her straw bonnet to fan her face, yet it gave no relief from the desire that had been sparked in her body from a once dead flame.

Chapter Twenty-One

"How much do you know of your father's duties?" Sterling asked Caroline after they had traveled a good distance in silence, with nothing but the crunch of the wheels along the ground, birds above, or the whispered conversation between Malik and Kaya.

He had often wondered what it would be like to experience the sensation of being in love but accepted that it would never happen. Such was for younger men like Malik, who likely wasn't above twenty years of age.

"What was your question?" Caroline asked.

Sterling returned his attention to Caroline, who had grown rather tense. It had been a straightforward enough question, not a rebuke of Hallaway. He was simply curious since women usually had little to do with estate management.

"Is there something specific you wish to ask?"

"I wondered if he discussed matters involving the estate with you, or do you only copy his reports and accounting?"

"We have had many discussions," she answered. "After my return, it was just the two of us at dinner, along with Livia of course, before William returned from England. He had gone there for his formal education and to attend university and remained another year to enjoy London and a Season," she explained. "When it was just Father and me, he would tell me about his days, his duties, his concerns, and plans."

"Had he done that before you traveled to England?"

Caroline chuckled. "I used to follow my father, pestering him with questions about the grapes, wine, and all areas of the estate because I was fascinated, especially that first year after having lived in England. Unfortunately, my mother forced me to return to the house and learn all the necessary tasks that a woman should put her mind to, which did not include stables, barns, or fields."

The lessons had not taken because he could still recall how she rode past the window with a good portion of her leg on display. Perhaps she had always been a hoyden if her interests had been more in what her father was doing than her mother and had been forced to become a proper miss suitable to attend a Season.

"What lessons did your mother attempt to impart?" he asked with a chuckle. He had a very good idea because of the women he had met in Society, but being raised with only brothers, there might be duties he was unaware of.

"Embroidery, watercolors, etiquette, the proper running of a household, and how to play the pianoforte," she answered. "I am certain that more was taught to me but I no longer recall and found that very little of it has been of use, though I can mend clothing as a result of the embroidery."

"As well as run a household," he reminded her. "You are, after all, the temporary housekeeper."

"Yes, there is that, I suppose," she answered with what he believed was a forced smile. If she did not like performing these duties then she should resign, especially since neither his mother, nor Caroline's father, had been paying her for being in that position.

"Mother would be pleased that I took something from those lessons," she murmured before she turned her eyes on the horizon, an end to their discussion.

They stopped briefly so that they could relieve some discomfort, then stroll to stretch their legs, being mindful of the dangers that might be on the ground and waiting to strike, even though they walked in the tracks already made by the wagons because the sound would have already disturbed any poisonous reptiles and sent them scurrying, it was wise to remain cautious.

The four of them then settled in the back of the wagon where they opened the basket of food and enjoyed a midday meal.

"How much further do we need to travel?" Sterling asked.

"We are halfway to our destination," Malik answered. "This is where we always break for meals and to give the cattle a longer rest."

They had stopped occasionally for that reason since the left and Sterling was beginning to remember how long, and tedious, this trip could be. He had only remembered the visits, not the length of time it took to get to Stellenbosch and then return home.

He'd also been in the back of the wagon with four younger brothers and they would play games until they grew tired, and then often bicker, before they grew bored enough to sleep while his father drove the carriage and his mother sat beside him. Servants had never accompanied them on their trips to Stellenbosch. It had only been family.

"Shall we continue?" Malik asked as he returned with Kaya by his side.

"Yes," Caroline answered brightly and put the remains of the small repast back in the hamper as Malik climbed onto the seat of the wagon and assist Kaya.

Sterling also adjusted the blankets beneath his bum, as well as the pillows for his back so that he could continue his conversation with Caroline. How much knowledge did she possess about Wyndview Farm and her father's duties? He also wanted to discover more about Caroline Sutcliffe.

Instead, he watched as she adjusted her seat to face forward and prop her head in her hand, elbow on the edge of the wagon. While some of her face was shaded, other parts were not and revealed the delicate bone structure of her jaw and long neck. A few of her dark curls had escaped from her hat and bounced behind her shoulders. There was a blissful smile on her lips…lips that he would not mind tasting.

Nearly four years she had been a widow and he could not help but wonder if she missed the intimacies she would have shared with her husband.

Nor could he deny his desire. It had begun the first time he had seen her face when she had come looking for her daughter and increased when he found her in the office late at night and glimpsed the swell of her breasts above the bodice. Then there was the ball where she was the most beautiful woman present and then they had waltzed and no woman had ever been so perfect in his arms. But when his desire really became undeniable for her was when they were outside and talked for over an hour.

He wanted Caroline. Yet she was not a widow who would seek a lover, but one who was respectable, thoughtful, and kind, or she would not put up with so much from his mother.

Therefore, no matter how much he wanted her, it would not be right to seduce her. No doubt, she would reject him. He would rather converse with her than risk her avoiding him for the rest of his visit.

As THE WAGON crested the hill, Caroline glanced down and into the valley where Stellenbosch sat and could not help but smile. It was a picturesque town surrounded by mountains and fields planted with grapes and corn.

"I had forgotten how excited I became as a boy when we arrived in this very spot and knew that I would soon see my grandparents and second cousins," Wyndham murmured.

"Do many still live here?" Caroline asked.

"My grandparents are gone. I am not certain of the others. It has been so long…"

Caroline turned away as Sterling trailed off, likely lost in memories.

As the wagon arrived in town, residents that she recognized came forward to greet them. When Kaya's mother saw her daughter, she rushed forward for an embrace.

"Go," Caroline insisted. "Enjoy time with your family. Both of you."

"When would you like to leave, Mrs. Sutcliffe?"

The sun would set soon, which meant that Kaya and Malik would not have much time with their family, nor would Wyndham who needed to reunite with family. "The day after tomorrow, at sunrise," she finally answered.

"I will see to the horses and wagon," Malik offered as Wyndham helped her from the wagon and retrieved their valises.

"Caroline," Mrs. Cloate called and came forward. "It has been too long and we are so happy you have come to visit. Malik and Kaya's parents have been eagerly awaiting your arrival."

How could Mrs. Cloate know that she would be here when she hadn't even known until yesterday afternoon, unless…Had Lady Wyndham planned this all along and sent word ahead?

"The cottage you usually occupy has been dusted and swept, and the bedding was changed."

Caroline had no words and was certain she looked confused as she stood there, her mouth hanging open.

Mrs. Cloate then smiled at Sterling. Caroline realized that the woman did not know who he was.

"The Earl of Wyndham," Caroline somehow managed to make the introductions.

"Sterling!" she exclaimed and held out her hands to him.

"Aunt Fenna," Sterling returned with a smile.

"My, how you have grown," she said, taking his hands. "You were just a boy when you were last here."

"It has been a long time," he chuckled.

"The two of you will dine with me tonight. Tomorrow, I will invite your relatives together for a feast," she announced.

"I would like to freshen first, if you please," Caroline told her.

"Yes, of course." She led Caroline to the small, whitewashed cottage in which she had always slept. They stepped inside and Mrs. Cloate lit a lamp illuminating the room that held a table, stove, cupboard, and two small beds against opposite walls.

Caroline walked forward and placed her valise at the foot of the bed she always slept in. "Where will Lord Wyndham be staying?"

Mrs. Cloate's face began to pinken as she bit her lip and glanced around. "I am afraid that we have no place for my great-nephew."

If Mrs. Cloate had anticipated Caroline's arrival, why had she not been expecting Wyndham? That was assuming his mother had written, though Caroline still could not understand how she could have known… She pinched the bridge of her nose. If she gave it too much thought, she would end up with a headache. She would simply make do while they were here and ask questions when they returned to Wyndview Farm.

"I can sleep in the back of the wagon," Wyndham offered much to her surprise.

"You most certainly will not," Mrs. Cloate argued. "You are an earl."

"Mrs. Sutcliffe cannot do so."

"Of course not, it is much too dangerous."

"What of the floor in the home of a relation."

"That is not done either."

"I will not allow anyone to give up a bed for me since I was not expected."

"I have the perfect solution," Mrs. Cloate announced.

"What would that be?" Caroline asked.

"If we hang a curtain down the center of the room, then it is just the same as having two separate rooms."

Except, it wasn't. They would still be sharing a small cottage with no chaperone.

"I am certain that my nephew is a gentleman and there should be no worries," Mrs. Cloate continued.

It did not matter if he stayed on his side of the curtain or not, others would know that they had shared the cottage, alone, together, all night.

"Now, come along. Dinner will be ready soon."

She glanced across the room as Sterling placed his valise on the floor beside the other bed, accepting their situation without argument.

In that instant, Caroline realized that she would get no rest that night. Not while temptation slept on the other side of a curtain pretending to be a wall.

CHAPTER TWENTY-TWO

NOT ONLY WAS the meal filling, but Sterling enjoyed the conversation in his great-aunt's home. There were a few relatives from his mother's family present—men he had played with when they had all been boys. They laughed and teased and made him long for the days when his family had still lived at Wyndview Farm. Further, he wasn't the Earl of Wyndham here. He was Sterling.

Memories that he had forgotten reemerged and a sense of nostalgia filled his being.

If only his father's older brothers had not died without heirs, Sterling might have spent his life here. Except, he would not have met Caroline. There would have been no need for an estate manager because that had been his father's position and would have been Sterling's.

His life would have been extraordinarily different.

Except, it wasn't and it did no good to wonder who he would have been if his father hadn't inherited the earldom.

The cousins he used to play with when they were children had married and now had children of their own who played the same games.

An ache of longing for the same—a wife to love and children—grew in his chest as the night grew long. He wanted what his cousins had but as it had not found him yet, it might never.

He glanced over at Caroline. She had managed to find love

and had a daughter, but she had also lost him and was now a widow. Had she wanted to marry again or was she content with her life at Wyndview Farm?

Sterling was happy for those who found love and shared a joyful family. For him, it would likely be an amicable marriage to produce an heir and a spare.

Except, he did have four younger brothers. His father had been the third son and unexpectedly inherited, so his brothers or one of their sons, when they managed to marry and have them, could replace Sterling one day.

Should he force himself to fulfill his duty and stay unhappy?

More importantly, why hadn't the option ever occurred to him before?

No, he was not going to settle. If he were not as lucky as his cousins, then he would simply not wed but the name would continue.

This holiday was turning out to be enlightening with discovering perspective to his situation and returning memories once lost.

And he was also able to spend this visit with Caroline, who seemed to enjoy his family and was certainly familiar with them. All in all, he was very glad his mother had forced him to come to Stellenbosch, not that he would ever tell her because she would meddle even more until he sailed away.

However, he faced one difficulty—sharing a cottage with the woman he had desired since he arrived at Wyndview Farm, with only a blanket to separate them.

With temptation so close, it was unlikely he would get any sleep at all.

CAROLINE SLOWLY STROLLED back to the cottage following dinner and visiting with Wyndham's family. She still couldn't believe that they would be sharing the same cottage. A one room cottage. Certainly, there had to be one relative with space for him, shouldn't there be?

Except, the extended family she met tonight had large families so likely every bed in their houses was taken.

This still wasn't right. She was overcome with a nervousness that she had not experienced since the first time she spent the evening with her husband and that had been the night after they wed.

Of course, her nerves were for different reasons as she had known that she would become a wife in truth and was not certain what to expect. Tonight, she would just sleep in her own bed while a man she desired to fulfill her growing needs was on the other side of the room. Thank goodness there were two beds because she wasn't certain what she would have done had there been only one.

She nearly shivered at the possibility then reminded herself that she was a respectable widow and that Wyndham was her father's employer. She was a companion to his mother, among other things at Wyndham Farm. Despite how cordial and friendly some of their conversations had been, there would be nothing more between her and Wyndham.

Wyndham pushed open the door of the cottage then lit a lamp. Caroline was grateful to find that someone had already been there and a rope had been tied down the center of the room from which blankets hung. It would save them from having to figure out how to do it themselves.

She then realized that the bed she usually chose was the one closest to the door. If Wyndham needed to leave for any purpose, he would have to cross over to her side, which she did not like.

"Do you mind if we switch sides?" she asked.

He arched a blond brow, humor in his blue eyes. "Not at all, Mrs. Sutcliffe."

"Thank you." She picked up her valise then slipped between the slight gap where two blankets met.

Lord Wyndham followed her, and Caroline was startled when he joined her.

"I am only retrieving my bag."

"Oh, yes, of course," she nearly stammered.

Why was she being such a ninny?

Despite what anyone would believe, she would stay on her side of the room and Wyndham on his, well, as soon as he returned to it and they would not see each other again until morning after they were once again fully dressed.

"Good night, Mrs. Sutcliffe," Wyndham said as he crossed back to his side of the cottage.

It was then that she opened her valise and drew out her nightrail. Caroline glanced back at the blanket shielding her from him.

Did she dare slip out of her dress and into her nightrail? To do so would leave her exposed. Or did she sleep in her shift?

What if the blanket fell away?

She could not take such a risk and put the nightrail away. She would sleep in her dress. It would not be so uncomfortable. Then tomorrow, after he had left the cottage, she would change into a fresh dress.

Yes, that is what she would do.

"How often do you visit Stellenbosch?" his voice came from the other side of the blankets.

"Once a year. Sometimes twice," she answered. "Your mother enjoys visiting her family."

"And this is where you stay each time?"

"Yes."

"What of my mother. Where does she sleep?"

He likely assumed that his mother had better accommodations. "We share this cottage," she answered as she removed her boots.

"What of her maid and whatnot?"

"Your mother can survive without a maid, and she had me." Caroline rolled down her stockings and draped them across the end of the bed.

"Yes, I suppose," he murmured.

She then pulled the coverlet back on the bed and glanced at the blankets one more time to make certain they were secure then climbed under the covers and turned on her side, pillow bunched beneath her head and stared at the blanket that separated her from the Earl of Wyndham.

She had heard rustling on the other side and wondered if he had not been concerned that she was present and had disrobed to put on a nightshirt.

Her husband had never worn one but surely Wyndham did, especially in a situation such as this.

Except, he had not known the sleeping arrangements until they arrived.

What if he had nothing to wear and nothing was covering his chest any longer?

Heat swept up her body and Caroline silently lectured herself not to think of Wyndham's chest or any other part of his anatomy.

"May I ask something of you?"

"Yes," she answered slowly.

Just because she was having impure thoughts about Wyndham did not mean he thought of her as anything more than his mother's companion to be forgotten once he was gone.

"Please call me Sterling."

Her face heated with the very idea. It was too personal. "I could not."

"I am rarely called by my name, tonight being an exception, and we are sharing a cottage, sleeping in the same room, so I believe formality is no longer necessary."

But it was. Being on a first name basis was too personal...intimate. Yet, she couldn't make herself voice the objections.

"I shall call you Caroline and you will call me Sterling."

She was certain she heard a smile in his tone.

"It would be nice to hear my name for change instead of my

title such as when we were at dinner tonight."

"Your mother addresses you by your given name," she reminded him.

"That is different. She is my mother, and as you and I seem to be becoming friends, in addition to these sleeping arrangements, you should call me Sterling and I shall call you Caroline."

Caroline was not at all comfortable doing so but … "If you insist…Sterling."

"I do, Caroline."

Warmth swept through her and Caroline realized that she was in trouble. Not only did she want Wyndham, but she was beginning to like him more than she should. There was no future and thus, she must limit her emotions to a temporary friendship, if that, because she was still far beneath him.

Oh, she should not have thought about being beneath him because it conjured other images. This was going to be a very long night.

CHAPTER TWENTY-THREE

STERLING BARELY SLEPT. Caroline did not snore, but he could hear her soft breathing. And every time she moved, the bed creaked and he wondered if she would sleep better if she did not have to do so alone.

The temptation to slip through the blankets and seduce her was nearly impossible to ignore, but he did not leave his bed.

Who could blame him for wanting her? She was beautiful, put together perfectly, kind, intelligent, and mature. And, she was not innocent, but had been married and birthed a daughter, so it would not be as if he were ruining her.

He feared that she would reject him, which would make for a very awkward day in Stellenbosch, and an even more uncomfortable day as they traveled back to Wyndview Farm.

His thoughts of Caroline and how he would like to be in her bed, after he had lifted the hem of her nightrail and tossed it on the ground, had him aching with need.

In fact, even when he finally was able to sleep, his dreams were filled with her. If matters continued to progress in his manner, he may need to find privacy to release some of the tension that had developed before he…well…that would be rather embarrassing.

With those thoughts and his continuous need, Sterling rose for the day, dressed, then left the cottage in search of a very private place, which he found behind the mews with nothing around him except the back of the stable, vineyards to either side and mountains ahead. Secure that he was alone, and that it was early enough for a good portion of Stellenbosch to still slumber, he unfastened the placket on his trousers and took himself in hand. If anyone came upon him, he would simply make the excuse that he was relieving himself, just not in the manner another would assume.

WHILE SHE COULD have slept better, at least Caroline got some when she had feared that she would get none.

However, she did wake with the sun, which was her habit. For the longest time, she laid there debating if she should get up and dress quickly before Sterling awoke or if she should lie there and wait until she was certain that he was gone. But as she was trying to decide, she heard movement on the other side of the blanket. If she had not been mistaken, Sterling was getting dressed and then moments later the door to the cottage opened and closed.

As soon as he was gone, Caroline scrambled from her bed and quickly withdrew a clean dress and shook it out. She then slipped out of the wrinkled one that she slept in and pulled the other one over her head and fastened the buttons. She then rolled on her stockings and put on her boots and waited.

She had not expected him to awaken so early. Then again, she did not know the habits of the Earl of Wyndham, or Sterling, as he wanted her to call him. It was still too intimate and she likely would not do so in front of others or they would assume something more had happened in the cottage last night than it did.

Her face heated at the very idea of anyone in Stellenbosch assuming that she and Sterling had been intimate.

The moments ticked by and he had not returned.

She had assumed that he might have gone outside to relieve himself, and she had a similar need and had noted the chamber pot in the corner but had thought it more important to change before he returned.

Except, she was also becoming uncomfortable and hoped that Sterling did not return before she finished making use of it.

He did not, and she waited a little longer before she finally gave up and left the cottage to step outside.

Where could he have gone?

Chapter Twenty-Four

AFTER STERLING HAD taken care of matters uninterrupted, he returned to the cottage only to find Caroline outside. Few residents were out yet.

"Do you always wake this early?" he asked once her reached her side.

"Yes," she answered brightly. "Do you?"

"No," he grumbled.

"Did you not sleep well?" she asked with concern.

"I had difficulty getting comfortable." Let Caroline think it was the bed and not thoughts of her.

"What do you suppose we do now?" she asked.

"We could walk," he suggested. "I would like to see how much Stellenbosch has changed since I was last here."

Eventually they would return to the home of his great-aunt because she had promised to provide meals, but he wasn't ready to go there yet. It was likely too early to knock on their door. He also wanted to be alone with Caroline.

They walked in silence along oak-lined streets protecting whitewashed cottages then past the farmhouses with the Dutch gables and finally came to the fields of grapevines where workers were just beginning their day. The town was nearly twice the size it had been when he had visited as a child.

A peacefulness had settled around Sterling that he had not experienced in a very long time. It was the quiet. It was not having to make any decisions. It was not having to worry about Trade Wynd or the earldom. And it was because Caroline was by his side, with no need to fill the silence, but just be.

Maybe his mother was right in that he truly needed a holiday. But tomorrow they would return to Wyndview Farm where he hoped to take part in the harvest, learn the answers to his questions, and then he would sail for Madeira.

Sterling glanced down at Caroline, who stared out over the valley. His only regret in leaving so soon was that he would not have a chance to come to know her better.

He returned his gaze to the horizon. Besides grapes, there were also rows of corn further out, which did remind him of one question. "We grow wheat, barley, rye, and oats. Have we grown corn?"

"A letter has gone to Lord Avery to ask his opinion and the benefits and value of such a crop."

"Why not me?" he asked.

Her face started to pinken. "I suppose the letter should have gone to you. It is just that…"

Sterling chuckled. "I would have asked Avery if your father would have asked me. Avery has managed and adjusted the crops on our estate until they were to his specification, so he should do the same here."

If he weren't mistaken, she sighed with relief.

Why was everyone afraid of him? Caroline, especially, should know by now that he was not disagreeable. Except, she had witnessed some conversations he'd had with his mother, and those had not been very pleasant, so maybe she did fear his displeasure. If that were the case, he needed to somehow prove to her that he was not a difficult person, and that he was no threat to the life she shared with her father, brother, and daughter at Wyndview Farm.

"SHALL WE RETURN?" Caroline asked.

"I suppose we should." He let out a sigh as they started to return to town.

When Sterling asked why they had not written to him, she had not wanted to tell him that it never occurred to them to write the owner when it had been Lord Avery who first began writing and asking about the vineyard and then other crops, plants, trees…everything that grew on the estate.

Also, she had not been careful in her response, but fortunately he assumed that the letter had come from her father, even if it may have been written in her hand.

At least Sterling wasn't angry, but she really did need to remember to write to him first on any matter that concerned Wyndview Farm.

No, her *father* needed to write him first.

"I joined your father in the vineyard a few days ago."

Caroline tried to remain relaxed as if he had not said anything alarming. "I hope you found him informative and that he was able to answer some of your questions."

"He did not have much to say, even though I attempted to have a conversation, but he only cared about the grapes." Sterling chuckled. "I thought we could discuss some of the questions from my review of the reports but I might as well have been invisible, though he was very clear when he told me that the grapes would be ready when they were."

Caroline winced. That was not how one treated their employer. "At this time of year, Father is preoccupied with the harvest because he knows it is a source of income for not only Trade Wynd but Wyndview Farm as well. If the wine crops fail, so does the vineyard," she explained. "He thinks of little else."

No matter the time of year, her father thought of nothing else, which was why she had taken over his other duties.

"I gathered as much, but as you already explained that he does speak with you and you know what is in the reports, perhaps you can tell me why he decided to plant tobacco and then stopped?"

"Your brother, Lord Avery," she answered knowing that he already possessed such information.

"Your brother said the same, but no further explanation was provided."

"Should they have not taken instruction from your younger brother?" Was that what bothered him? It was the second time he had mentioned it but admitted that he would have asked Lord Avery himself. Maybe that is how it should be—all correspondence regarding anything grown at Wyndview Farm should be directed to Sterling even if he was going to then ask his brother.

"That is not my concern," he assured her. "Avery is a botanist and studies other sciences. If he thought tobacco would bring additional income to Wyndview Farm, then he was welcome to instruct your father to see that it was done."

"Which he did." Caroline was still not certain what Sterling's question was.

"Why did he cease growing tobacco after only two years, or do you know?"

"Oh, that is a simple explanation," she answered. "Which was explained to your brother."

Wyndham arched a blond eyebrow. "I, too, would appreciate an explanation."

"Tobacco is a lengthy process," she began. "Seeds are sown in August and September, the plants then need to be thinned in October, then in November, transplanted to the field. In January, it is primed and topped."

"Is it because the process is too involved?" he asked.

"Partially," she answered. "The first difficulty came when the tobacco needed to be cut near the same time as grapes. While tobacco is hung for curing, the grapes needed to be crushed. Twice the number of servants were needed for the month that it took to accomplish both tasks."

He nodded, his blue eyes gleaming with engagement.

"After the wine was barreled, the tobacco then needed to be

pressed and shipped and it became difficult to manage both."

"I can see where it would, except the cost of extra workers did not offset the income from tobacco. It was still a profitable venture."

"It would be if you owned enough land," she corrected.

"I own several hectares," he reminded her.

"Yes, you do, much of it taken up with grapes, wheat, barley, rye, and oats, besides the kitchen gardens and fruit trees."

"I still do not understand. There was enough land to plant tobacco for two years."

"Tobacco grows best in previously uncultivated ground so land needs to be cleared before each planting. You would soon be out of land, though after a few years, you could likely replant in the first field, and rotate, as many crops are, but you would need more land to rotate, or so it is assumed. The difficulty was addressed to Lord Avery, but a response has not yet been received. Which was difficult when it took three months for a letter to be delivered and another three months for the reply to be received, and why many decisions were made without consulting the owner."

"You are very well-informed and knowledgeable about the growing of tobacco," Sterling remarked when she was finished.

Had she provided too much detail? Except that was what had been included in the letter to Lord Avery. She could explain that it was only because she had copied her father's letters, but the lie was become more uncomfortable and she really hoped that he asked no further questions.

"It was discussed," she finally said, which was the truth, because it had been, at length, just not with her father.

Wyndham tilted his head and slowly nodded. "Yet, your father seemed surprised that tobacco had been grown at all the one time that I was able to sit down and meet with him."

✦ ✦

CHAPTER TWENTY-FIVE

Caroline chuckled. Yet she sounded nervous, which piqued his curiosity.

"As I told you earlier, my father is only thinking about grapes and wine this time of year."

It was an assurance that he appreciated but an estate manager shouldn't be focused only on one task while the rest of the estate was ignored, and something he would give further attention to, and observe once they returned to Wyndview Farm.

As they neared the home of his great-aunt, Malik approached, his chin high, shoulders back and spine straight.

"Lord Wyndham, may I please have a moment of your time."

Sterling straightened, grew stern, and tried not to smile. Malik would not have approached had Kaya's father not granted permission to marry his daughter. Yet Malik's hands were shaking. Was he afraid that Sterling would deny his request? In any other circumstance, he might question the man further, but Malik may view it as torture if he did, so Sterling decided to make the matter easy for his employee.

"If it is to ask my permission to marry another servant in my household, then I grant it."

Malik's eyes widened as his jaw seemed to drop. He had probably been working up the bravado to approach and likely rehearsed a speech in his head and was full of nerves while doing so.

"Congratulations, Malik," he offered.

"Thank you, Lord Wyndham. Thank you very much." Then in a blink he turned and ran off, likely to tell his future bride.

"That was good of you," Caroline said.

"Good of me to do what?"

"To save him from having to ask you when he was terrified of doing so."

"He was nervous, not terrified."

"Then you did not see how much his hands trembled." She chuckled. "You are a good employer, Lord Wyndview."

"Sterling," he corrected.

"Sterling."

"If I am, why do the servants appear to be afraid of me? They are certainly nervous in my presence and never speak."

"You gave no warning that you were going to arrive and none of them know your character and likely fear what you may do or the changes you may make."

"There is no cause for concern."

Caroline stopped and turned to face him, suddenly serious. "Please do not make light of their circumstances. They cannot know if you mean to sack them or increase their wages. The life of a servant is precarious and often decided on the whim of an employer. *Everyone* on your estate is loyal and their priority is seeing that Wyndview Farm not only produces the best wine, but that every other aspect is successful as well. They have a mind to increase the earnings and eliminate waste, not only for you, but because it is also their home and they take pride in their duties. As you have never had to worry where your next meal may come from or where you might live, you cannot understand their concerns when the absentee owner of an estate suddenly makes an appearance seven years after he inherited that estate."

Sterling sobered. Not only had Caroline's impassioned speech taken him aback, as if she had a personal stake in what happened, but she had also humbled him. Perhaps she was more sensitive to their plight because she was forced to return to her father because she had no means to support a child.

He really should be more considerate and sensitive and would begin doing so now.

Then maybe everyone at the estate would not fear him so much.

CAROLINE SURPRISED HERSELF with the emotional speech to Sterling, but he needed to understand what he so easily disregarded.

"You are correct," he said after a moment. "I should have realized…"

"Lords usually do not give much consideration to those in their household so long as there is no upset," she explained and knew it to be the truth. Or at least that was what she had observed when she was in London and how her own grandfather treated those who worked for him.

"Do you think it would make a difference if I said anything?"

Was he truly so concerned that his servants may fear him? "I do not think that is necessary."

"They do not leave the room the moment you walk in, or keep their eyes down, and not speak in your presence. It is all rather disconcerting if you must know the truth."

She supposed there could be several reasons. One being they didn't want to be asked questions that Caroline would not want them to answer. "They likely only need time to become used to you," she finally suggested.

"I may be gone by then."

"At least they will then know you are not a horrid employer." She shrugged.

"I suppose," he said quietly.

She would have never guessed that when he arrived that Sterling cared about being liked.

Maybe it wasn't so much liked as he didn't want to be feared.

"Mrs. Sutcliffe, Lord Wyndham."

They both turned to find Kaya hurrying toward them. Caroline hoped that Malik had told her the news and that she wasn't here to beg for Sterling's permission.

"Thank you, Lord Wyndham," she gushed after she quickly curtseyed and then turned to Caroline. "The wedding is to be today."

"So soon?" she asked in surprise.

"We need to return to Wyndview Farm tomorrow. Who knows when we will return and Malik and I want to be wed now, and in front of our family."

"Then I am happy for you," Caroline replied. What more could she say?

"Promise you will be there." She turned to Sterling. "And you too, of course, Lord Wyndham, that is, if you would like to, but I understand it…that is…it is presumptuous of me."

"I will be happy to attend your wedding," he finally said, much to Caroline's relief because she feared Kaya was about to dissolve into a puddle for even speaking to Sterling, but she had been so excited that the words were likely out before she realized that an earl usually does not attend the wedding of a servant.

$$\ast\!\!\ast\!\!\ast$$

CHAPTER TWENTY-SIX

THE WEDDING AND following celebration, which was not a wedding breakfast, was unlike anything Sterling had ever witnessed.

The bride and groom had said their vows on the steps of *Moederkerk,* the Dutch Reform Church, surrounded by family and friends. They were then escorted to a field where chairs and tables had been placed, the latter loaded with food. After everyone had eaten, the musicians set up and began to play with everyone dancing as it grew dark. Then torches were lit and more food and drink were loaded on the tables.

There was freedom and happiness. Distant relations approached not only to greet Sterling but to reminisce about their childhood, sharing stories. Memories came flooding back and he ached for what had been and wished he could be nothing more than the keeper of Wyndview Farm, not the Earl of Wyndham.

He was told that the feast had been planned for him as soon as he arrived so that he could visit with family, a celebration of his return, even if it was only a visit. It had become a wedding celebration instead but he did not mind because it would have been odd to have a celebration just because he had visited Stellenbosch.

He also danced, more than he ever had at any ball, including two with Caroline, one being a waltz.

"Do you think they are even married?" he questioned. "There

was no special license, nor were the banns read."

"I overheard her mother say that they were married in the eyes of the lord and by a minister and that was good enough."

"Perhaps for them, but by law?" he asked.

Caroline chuckled. "I am not certain the same rules apply to the Dutch as they do the English, but I do not think anyone will claim that the marriage is not real especially since the bride and groom have already left, which could leave Kaya ruined if anyone objected."

Sterling was rather envious of Malik. He would like nothing better than to spend the whole of the night in a bed with Caroline exploring her as she explored him.

Sterling pulled her closer than was proper when they turned, but he did not care, nor did he think any of the others in attendance noticed. Many were already deep in their cups, and not only the men either.

His mood was light and if they were alone, he might risk kissing her. Instead, Sterling enjoyed having her in his arms, her steps matching his without hesitation or misstep. They moved as one, breaths mingled, eyes only on each other. His heart pounded as desire filled his body, yet he managed to keep everything in check so as to not embarrass himself, but they would be sharing a cottage again tonight.

Did he dare seduce her?

Was it even right to do so?

Or would he rise early again tomorrow and hide behind the mews a second time?

Bloody hell!

He had never wanted a woman as much as he wanted Caroline.

FOR A GENTLEMAN that she had feared when he first arrived,

Sterling now warmed her heart. If he hadn't proved it before today, he showed himself to be far from pompous, strict, or unyielding. He had laughed, danced, spent time with his family, and teased his cousins. Now he was dancing with her. His hand resting on her back warmed her skin. Her blood pounded in her veins and when their eyes met, longing filled her being. Her breasts tightened and her nether regions ached.

It had been so long since she experienced the need to be out of her clothing and be touched, to experience release, then be filled and soar again.

Caroline took in a deep shaky breath.

If only… But she couldn't. It was too risky. He would be gone and she would remain here.

Yet, she was likely worried for nothing and Sterling had no desire or intention to seduce her, but she wanted to be seduced.

She was also afraid and as a widow, there were simply risks that she could not take no matter how much she ached for him.

As the song came to an end, they parted. Her face was heated and likely flushed because of her wicked thoughts.

"The party is coming to an end," he observed and she looked around to note that the musicians were putting away their instruments and women were taking food into their homes. Some groupings lingered and talked, but several people were slowly making their way home.

"We do leave early tomorrow," she reminded him.

"Then we should also turn in."

It was unlikely that she would get any sleep tonight with her bodily state, but she had little choice because some risks were not worth taking, otherwise, she would likely attempt to seduce him.

Sterling opened the door when they reached their cottage and she stepped in, followed by Sterling who lit a lamp. As she crossed the room, he reached out and grabbed her hand.

Caroline turned to look up into his blue eyes.

"I mean no insult to your respectability, but I must tell you that all I have been able to think about all day and evening was kissing you."

Her heart pounded heavily as he tugged her closer.

"You must know that it's not just a kiss, and I will understand if you reject me and I will never speak of it again, nor will it change anything between us. But I want you, Caroline."

Did she dare?

Oh, she wanted to.

Caroline gazed into his dark and intense blue eyes. Her need and desire doubled.

CHAPTER TWENTY-SEVEN

"I CANNOT," SHE whispered.

Sterling let go of her hand. He was disappointed but understood. It was a risk he had to take, even if he expected rejection. "I understand."

"I do not think you do," she returned. "I have wanted, needed, since…" She shook her head. "I would take you as a lover, but it is because of what I fear happening why I do not."

He turned back to her. "What is your fear? I would never harm you."

"I know. It is not that," she answered. "I cannot risk finding that I am with child after you have sailed back to England."

She was not rejecting him, and he well understood her fear, but it was not something that concerned him. "Dear Caroline, there are ways to prevent such from happening."

She frowned, confusion in her brown eyes, which shouldn't surprise him. She had been a wife, and likely never had another lover, so her husband would not have taken such precautions.

"Do you trust me?"

She stared up into his eyes. "Yes."

"Will you have me?"

"Oh, yes,"

Sterling did not give her a chance to change her mind but swept Caroline up in his arms and carried her to his bed. It was narrow, meant for a single person, but that did not matter. He needed her.

Coming over her, Sterling kissed her deeply. Caroline returned his passion, tangling her tongue with his until they were both nearly out of breath before he moved his lips to her jaw then neck, and down her chest until he reached her bodice. Sitting up and straddling her, he carefully undid each button until the dress loosened then slid his hand inside to caress her perfect breasts then roll a nipple between his finger and thumb.

Caroline moaned, arching her back. He wanted…needed more and pulled the dress and shift down, then freed her arms from the sleeves. He then bent forward to take one perfect peak in his mouth.

Each moan pushed him further to the edge, but he needed to bring her pleasure. He couldn't just take his own and with those thoughts, he stood and pulled her shift and dress over her hips then down her legs and tossed it on the floor, leaving her naked before him. She was perfection! Full breasts, tapered waist, and wider hips. No, she was not a thin miss with bones protruding at her ribs or hips, but curved, rounded, and soft, wearing nothing but her stockings and boots, the dark curls at the apex of her thighs beckoning.

He should pause to remove her boots and his own, as well as his clothing, but he was too eager and once again took a nipple between his teeth as his fingers caressed and slipped through the curls in her nether regions. Caroline's thighs parted and she arched, meeting each caress, pushing into his hand and then she cried out as she was overtaken by her release.

He quickly undid the placket of his trousers and freed his member before positioning himself between her thighs. He glanced up at Caroline. Her eyes met his and then she nodded. Sterling pressed forward as she gasped and soon her legs were about his hips as he filled her and withdrew then filled her again. When she cried out a second time, he withdrew and spilled his seed on her stomach before he collapsed at her side.

He had imagined a slow seduction of teasing to heighten

sensation, but their joining had been none of that, and even though rushed, it had been perfect.

CAROLINE WAS CERTAIN that her heartbeat would not return to normal anytime soon.

Until he touched her, Caroline had no idea how much she had truly needed him, the intimacy. She just prayed that matters were not awkward between them after this. Or worse, that he was a rake, and now that he had made a conquest, he would be done with her, and treat her as someone easily discarded, forgotten then ignored as if she no longer existed. She had seen it happen often enough in London and hoped that Sterling was not so callous.

It would also be best not to let this happen again, but she hoped that it would.

He would be leaving after the harvest so why shouldn't she take him as a lover until he was gone? Widows in London did it all the time.

Unless he decided that he was no longer interested, which would be quite disappointing and possibly humiliating.

Slowly she sat up and noticed the substance on her abdomen. "I never knew what it looked like before."

Sterling chuckled and rolled away from her then walked to the pitcher and bowl on a small table and returned with a towel that he used to wipe her stomach before he returned it. When he started back toward the bed, her body was finally beginning to cool and she suddenly became very aware that she was naked and he was not, though his member was on display.

He paused at the end of the bed, then removed each boot and set them aside before he rolled down each stocking. As the back of his fingers brushed her inner thighs, Caroline's body quickened again. Was it because it had been so long that her body craved more before it had to go without again?

He must have noticed because Sterling then took a finger and caressed up the inside of her thigh stopping just before her curls. Caroline could not have held back the moan if she wanted to.

He straightened then and before her very eyes first removed his boots then his clothing. His perfect chest and abdomen were the first to be revealed and it was so much better than she remembered, and then he pushed his trousers over his hips then tossed them aside.

Goodness! She was not the only one who was ready for intimacy a second time, and he was magnificent.

Sterling leaned forward and kissed her deeply, caressed her once again, knowing exactly where to touch and how, and almost before she could prepare, her release came over her with such power that she cried out again. This time he didn't wait but filled her completely and Caroline met him thrust for thrust, over and over until she reached her climax again, but he continued, over and over. Then he was gone, and once again spilling his seed onto her belly.

Goodness!

CHAPTER TWENTY-EIGHT

STERLING AWAKENED MORE content than he had been in a very long time. Beside him, on her side was Caroline, as naked as she had been when she fell asleep. He was curled around her, a hand on her breast, his body coming alive again.

The passion that had come over him last night was unlike any he had ever experienced. He could hardly keep control enough to bring her pleasure and his came on him quickly.

Caroline snuggled back against him and if she kept doing so he would be waking her in the most pleasant of ways. Perhaps he should wake her now so that they could enjoy each other once more before they were forced to return to Wyndview Farm.

It would be difficult to be lovers there. She lived with her father and he lived with his mother, and servants were often around, so it would be complicated to get away without someone knowing. He supposed that they could sneak out to meet, but in doing so it tarnished what they had shared as if they were doing something wrong.

Perhaps they were, but he didn't care. He wanted to share as much with Caroline and enjoy her company and share a bed until he had to board a ship.

Given that his time was short, Sterling kissed Caroline's neck as he trailed his fingers over her abdomen with every intention of waking her with pleasure when someone began pounding on the door.

"Mrs. Sutcliffe. Lord Wyndham. We have the wagon ready."

What the blazes was Kaya doing up so early? She had been married yesterday. If anybody should be snuggling and naked in bed right now, it was her and Malik.

Caroline pushed him away and jumped from the bed. "We will be out in a moment," she called.

Sterling was slower to get out of bed but he watched as Caroline rushed to roll on her stockings and her boots then pulled her shift and then dress down over her head before she disappeared behind the blanket. A moment later she stepped back through the blankets, her hair brushed and valise in hand.

He hoped she had no regrets because he certainly had none.

CAROLINE'S HANDS HAD been shaking as she straightened her gown and tried to repair her hair.

She had been intimate with Sterling last night—twice—then slept naked with him. She had not even done that when she was married. Had she turned completely wanton?

Did she care?

No and she had no regrets. She may never have this opportunity again and she was going to take something for herself.

Caroline finished shoving her items into the valise and stepped between the blankets to find Sterling already dressed and putting his belongings in a bag.

"Are you ready to return to Wyndham Farm?" he asked.

"I suppose I am."

"Last night…"

Her heart nearly stopped because she feared he was going to say it was a mistake and would not happen again and that it would never be discussed. She tried to prepare herself.

"…was more than my apparent meager imagination."

Her face heated.

"Would you like to be lovers until I leave, or was last night all?"

Carolyn looked into his blue eyes and read the warmth and sincerity there. "I would like that, so long as I am a lover and not reduced to a mistress." A lover bespoke of an agreement, equals. A mistress was a kept woman, which she would never allow herself to become.

"Lovers until you decide no longer." He then leaned in and pressed his lips against hers. "Until we are alone again."

Which would be Wyndview Farm.

Caroline was also more relaxed than she had been when they set out for Stellenbosch. Maybe it was because she had come to know Sterling a little better, or maybe it was because of what they shared last night, which also left her exhausted and Caroline found herself taking naps, as did Sterling, likely making up for the sleep they had missed.

But when she had finally rested and thought over everything that had transpired since Sterling had arrived at Wyndview Farm, she grew curious and given they were alone in the back of a wagon with no place to do, Caroline decided to ask.

"I have a question. You do not need to answer me, but it is a curiosity."

"What would that be?"

"You seem distant from your mother, sometimes angry. Bitter."

"That is because I am. Or I was when I had first arrived. My irritation now is because she is trying to manipulate my time here."

"Many mothers are the same when they want a son to marry." She chuckled. "I believe she attempted to do her best to introduce you to each marriageable girl at the ball."

Sterling groaned. "Yes, well, I do not need her assistance as it relates to any part of my life. She forfeited that privilege long ago."

"Oh." Caroline had not expected such an answer. "Why?" She

then threw up her hands. "Never mind, you do not need to answer that question."

Sterling stared at her for a moment as if he were trying to decide if he was going to tell her. "She abandoned me."

CHAPTER TWENTY-NINE

STERLING PUSHED HIS fingers through his hair. He did not want to talk about his mother.

"I do not understand."

How could she? Sterling was certain that his mother would have been too proud to let anyone know that her husband had left her behind.

It was a private family matter…except, Sterling wanted to tell Caroline. Maybe then she would understand.

"She left us."

"What do you mean she abandoned you?"

Sterling then went on to explain how when his parents sailed to the Cape Colony with Caroline's family that his father had returned to England without his mother.

"She stayed here and your father went home. Therefore, she abandoned you?"

"Yes!" Maybe now she would understand.

"I was fourteen at the time. How old were you?"

"Ten and eight."

"Your brothers, were they much younger?"

"Damian was six and ten, Elliot four and ten, Jules three and ten and Avery was only eleven."

"Did you all live at home?"

"No. They were at Eton and Cambridge. I had already finished my studies."

"You were an adult who claims to have been abandoned by his mother."

When Caroline worded it so slowly and deliberately, it sounded ridiculous.

"My brothers were also affected, especially Avery, who was only eleven," he reminded her. "A boy. That is who she abandoned." Maybe now she would understand.

"There had to a reason. A woman simply does not up and leave her children never to return."

"She did."

Caroline narrowed her eyes. "Tell me the whole of it. You are leaving something out. Unless it is too private of a matter."

Sterling withdrew what remained of the wine after they had shared their midday meal from the basket and took a drink before he passed the bottle to Caroline, who declined.

"I am reluctant to tell you because it does not show my father in a very good light."

"Then maybe you are casting too much of the blame on your mother."

"I was, or I did, but not any longer." He then began at the beginning, piecing together the story as he knew it from his father and his mother and presented it in the order of how the separation occurred. He even told her how they were not allowed to talk about her and that she wrote to them regularly.

"You have held onto the bitterness of her not returning when you are the one who cut her from your life."

He pulled back at her scolding.

"By your own admission, you stopped opening her correspondence. At least she reached out to you."

He didn't like that Caroline pointed out his fault in the matter, nor did he want to admit it to himself. "Avery had the most difficult time of it. He was always reading scientific journals and studying plants, but even more so when we realized she would not return. He became sadder, quieter."

"I am sorry for that. Did she write him?"

"Yes, and I know Avery returned her letters, though he snuck them into the post."

"I think you need to forgive yourself, Sterling."

"I did nothing wrong," he objected.

"When your mother abandoned you, as you say, you turned your back on her. Did it ever occur to you to write and ask why she never came back?"

He hadn't because he had accepted his father's explanation, even though he knew there was more. He knew because his father would mumble about his mother when deep in his cups, which he denied the next day after he was sober.

CAROLINE DID NOT question Sterling any further but left him alone with his thoughts for the remainder of their journey. She hated the pain that he must have suffered when his mother did not return, but she also thought that Lady Wyndham had been treated unfairly. Except, had she been separated from Livia, she would not have asked permission but would have gone to her anyway.

She also had not known the family then, at least not as she did now, and it wasn't her place to judge Lady Wyndham, her family, or Sterling.

When they finally arrived back at Wyndview Farm and entered the lavender sitting room Lady Wyndham loved, Livia spotted her and ran into her arms.

This may have been the longest she had been away from her daughter and Caroline suffered a wave of guilt for not thinking about her daughter more often, but she realized that the travel to Stellenbosch had turned out to be something just for her.

However, now that she was back, her responsibilities settled on her shoulders.

But first she needed a private audience with Lady Wyndham.

Chapter Thirty

THE CLOSER THEY came to Wyndview Farm, the more Sterling was reminded of his duties. He had been gone from England for nearly a year, but he was also confident that his brother had Trade Wynd well in hand. He had been trained to supervise all operations along the docks, ships, and cargo while Sterling had seen to those duties required by an earl, so therefore, there should be no concerns.

Was he even really needed in England?

When he had arrived here eight days ago, he had been determined to meet with his estate manager, have only limited contact with his mother, and then be gone. That was also before he had truly met Caroline, listened to his mother's explanation of what had happened, and decided that he wanted to take part in the grape harvest.

He'd been assailed by memories from this youth, when his brothers had played here, and when he had visited his cousins and Sterling realized that he had been his happiest at Wyndview Farm and he might just be happy again.

He couldn't help but compare the difference of how his life had been before his father inherited the title and after. His life would have been much different if it had never happened and maybe there would have been more days like yesterday instead of what he faced upon his return.

He also couldn't help but compare who his father had been

and what he had become. Sterling did not like that he'd also become more like the man who had been forced to return to England.

He did not want to be so unyielding, unforgiving, and strict. It was unfair to him and those around him and there was no reason why he could not return to England a better man than when he had left and a happier man.

It would be difficult to leave Wyndview Farm, especially Caroline, but he could not remain here for good. He had responsibilities that could not be ignored. He just wished that he could take Caroline with him.

The thought gave him pause. Was she becoming more to him than simply a friend and temporary lover?

Sterling followed Caroline into his mother's sitting room, somewhat unsettled at his recent revelation but not displeased either. However, it was certainly something that he would need to give deep consideration to before he made any decision as to his future and hers.

"We saw penguins, Mama!" Livia chirped.

"Penguins?" Caroline asked before she sent a searching glance to his mother.

"Yes, dear. Yesterday was quite lovely and when Livia told me that she had not yet seen them, well, of course we needed to picnic at Boulder Beach."

"Did you enjoy yourself, darling?" Caroline smoothed her daughter's dark hair then squatted down to look her in the eyes. "I missed you."

"They were funny." Livia giggled, ignoring the last part of what Caroline had said. "They walk like this." Livia put the heels of her feet together and hands down at her side and mimicked the small steps and waddle of a penguin.

"That is a very good impression," Caroline praised her daughter.

Sterling's heart warmed watching Caroline. It did make him long for children but only under the right circumstances. One of those being that he would not wed unless he found love. He would not have an empty marriage of simple compatibility and titles or rank for the purpose of uniting families and begetting heirs. He would not settle and bring children into a marriage that might turn bitter.

He assumed that Livia had been born of love, which ignited some jealousy that someone had won Caroline's heart. Yet, it should not matter. They were forming a friendship and they were lovers.

Excellent lovers together. Never had he experienced such passion with a woman. No lover in his past had ever been so responsive to his touch. Nor had they been so free to enjoy their own pleasure, which only heightened his. There had been no hesitation, nor practiced skills of a mistress. Instead, theirs had been a joining of all-consuming passion and pleasure, which he hoped to experience again.

He needed to be with her again, which was why he would put his mind to opportunities for him to be alone with Caroline.

"Did you enjoy your holiday?" his mother asked.

Sterling blinked and hoped that he had not missed any other questions or comments while his mind had been lost in what he planned to do with Caroline.

"Yes, I did."

"Were you able to spend time with your distant relatives?"

"Yes. We even attended the nuptials for Kaya and Malik."

It had been his mother's intention to see that Malik received permission from Kaya's father so she might as well know that the two had also wed.

"Already?" she complained. "I wish I would not have missed it."

He was rather glad she had because had his mother been with them, then she would have shared the cottage with Caroline. Not him.

"Is there any word on when the grapes will be ready to be harvested?" Sterling asked.

"It will be at least a few days," his mother answered. "Halla-way said it will not be today or tomorrow. Beyond that he does not know."

Sterling gave a nod of acceptance. He may just go ask the man himself or he may follow along as he tested grapes again to see how much more he could learn.

"As you will not be able to meet with him today or tomorrow, why don't you visit the penguins?"

He frowned at his mother. "Why would I want to visit the penguins?"

"You delighted in them when you were a child, and the seals, if I recall correctly. I also know that it has been some time since Caroline has been to Boulder Beach. You should also take a picnic and enjoy the day."

Sterling frowned. Why did she want him gone when he had just returned after being away for three days? Was she hiding something from him or would she rather not have him around even though she claimed that she hoped he would remain longer?

"I have already been gone for three days, Lady Wyndham," Caroline said. "I cannot take another day from my duties. I need to be available if my father needs my assistance as I need to be available to you as your companion."

"Or housekeeper," Sterling added. "I do not believe your father needs a secretary at the moment."

He really needed to see that she began receiving wages for at least one of the duties she performed.

"Nonsense, Caroline," his mother dismissed. "We have eve-rything well in hand. Those menus have been planned as you required. The maids see to the upkeep of the house, and the laundress has not shirked her duty in seeing that linens and clothing were cleaned. Your father does not need you and Livia spends all day at her lessons. Go! Take a picnic and enjoy. Soon enough the harvest will be upon us and there will be no time for rest."

If it were just him and Caroline, Sterling would not mind

going to Boulder Beach. Except the penguins were not what interested him. But with his mother more concerned with having him out from underfoot, he was reluctant to leave.

His eyes shifted to Caroline. Maybe it had nothing to do with him at all other than he served a purpose. Maybe she wanted her companion to enjoy more leisure and the privileges usually afforded the granddaughter of a baron.

Was his mother reminding Caroline that she was not a mere servant? She had tried to play matchmaker at the ball and no doubt as soon as the harvest was complete and Sterling had sailed for Madeira; his mother would begin having teas and inviting eligible bachelors to spend time with Caroline.

His mother wanted her to marry!

This was all designed so that Caroline could remember what it was like to be free of responsibility as she had been before she married and became a mother and his mother was using him for that purpose. No doubt his mother anticipated that Caroline would begin to long for the life she once had and would be more willing to enjoy tea with bachelors and possibly consider a different future.

She should have someone who loved and cared about her, especially after he was gone. But that did not mean he needed to be happy about it.

"Well, if you will excuse me, I think I will go find Hallaway in the fields to see what I can learn."

"What about Boulder Beach?" his mother asked.

Sterling turned to Caroline. "Would you be available to go to the beach to picnic and view penguins tomorrow?"

Caroline glanced at his mother with suspicion in her eyes. Was she also wondering what his mother was up to?

"Oh, you must go, Mama. You will have so much fun," Livia insisted.

Caroline laughed and patted her head again. "Very well, darling, I will visit the penguins while you are at your studies."

"Until tomorrow, Mrs. Sutcliffe." He then turned on his heel and marched out of the parlor. His mother may think they were going to picnic and watch the penguins and seals, which they likely would, but Sterling had no intention of letting a chance to be alone with Caroline to enjoy some of what they did in Stellenbosch slip away.

NOW THAT STERLING was gone, Caroline intended to have a necessary discussion with his mother.

"Go along, Livia. Remind Cook that Lord Wyndham has returned and will be dining with his mother this evening. Remain there until I come for you."

"Yes, Mama," her daughter answered before skipping from the sitting room.

"How did you enjoy Stellenbosch, Caroline. And please, tell me, that my son relaxed some of his uncompromising demeanor and enjoyed himself."

"Did you send word ahead to expect us? Mrs. Cloate did not seem at all surprised when we arrived."

Lady Wyndham busied her hands by smoothing her gown. "I may have written that Kaya and Malik wished to visit on the matter of their courtship and that I would facilitate their wishes."

It was not an answer. At least, not fully. "Did Mrs. Cloate know when we were going to arrive?"

Lady Wyndham's cheeks turned pink. "Yes. I wrote to her ahead of time and mentioned that I hoped that you would accompany the couple."

She had been manipulated. She could not understand why, when all Lady Wyndham had to do was ask and allow her a little time to prepare for the trip.

"When?" Caroline demanded.

"The day of the ball."

She had not even been aware that a servant had been gone

long enough to deliver a message and return.

"Did you also inform her that your son would be accompanying us?"

Her cheeks grew darker, but she did not answer.

Except…Oh, this was confusing. "Why would you say that he would go to Stellenbosch when you insisted that the two of you visit Cape Agulhas?"

"Oh, I knew the captain of the ship would not consent to sailing there," Lady Wyndham dismissed with a wave of her hand. "I had already asked. He promised not to tell my son, though."

When had she done that? Lady Wyndham rarely left the house.

Caroline frowned. Except there were times when she was not about but Caroline had always assumed she was resting. Now she questioned how often Lady Wyndham did leave and wondered where she went.

"As I knew that my son would never agree to travel there by wagon or horse and be gone for a fortnight, I provided an option that was more reasonable after he had denied my first two requests, I assumed that he would be more inclined to accept the third."

"Why were you so certain that I would go as well? I could have insisted on remaining here since a chaperone was not truly needed for a lord and his two servants, as you know?"

"I really did not insist, if you recall. I knew that you would never allow Sterling to go on his own because of what he might learn."

And the reason why she had tried to remain back at Wyndview Farm and keep Wyndham here too. There were those in Stellenbosch who had met her father and mother, when she had been alive, and were aware of the difficulties of late. "You wrote and asked them to keep our secrets?"

"That is true, but I could not allow you to know they had warning, or Sterling for that matter."

"Why?" she asked with exacerbation.

"Because then he would have never gone."

"You could have told me."

"Then you would not have gone."

"Why did either one of us have to leave?" she nearly yelled.

Lady Wyndham had been acting strangely and treated Caroline differently ever since her son had arrived and she could not figure out why. She would ask Lady Wyndham, but she was fairly certain that she would not provide a completely honest answer.

"You need to leave the estate more often and my son needed to be reminded of his heritage and what Wyndview Farm represents to our family. It is not simply another business owned by Wynd Trade. My ancestors are from here and this land came to the family through the Dutch who lived here long before the English. This land came to us through marriage and it is in his blood."

Caroline understood such motivation. She was not happy but understood. However, she had one more question.

"If you had explained your purpose then why wasn't Lord Wyndham provided with a separate accommodation?"

"I have no idea to what you refer," she murmured and smoothed her skirts again.

Yes, she did!

Caroline pulled back in horror, embarrassment, and humiliation. Had she wanted her…well, as a widow she could not be ruined. Did she believe that if her son enjoyed some bed sport that he might be more agreeable? Had she made certain that Caroline accompanied him, shared a cottage so that Wyndham might…

She had no idea that Lady Wyndham would think that she would easily succumb to lust and seduction. Was it because her father was only an estate manager and since they were nearly beneath notice that it was acceptable without repercussions?

"Calm yourself, Caroline!" Lady Wyndham ordered.

"It is not so easy to do, Lady Wyndham."

"I know what you have just assumed and conjured all kinds of ideas in your mind as to why I would put you in such a position. That was not my intention."

"Then what was?" she demanded.

"Nothing that would have brought harm to you, of that you have my assurance."

Yet it had. She was reminded of what it was like not to sleep alone and how comforting it was to have a warm chest at her back and a heavy arm on her waist, and gentle breath on her neck. It had made her ache with longing for what she would never have again.

And it angered her that Lady Wyndham would put her in such a position. Even if she had remained in her own bed and Sterling in his, her reputation was still at risk, which proved how little she meant to the Wynd family.

"If that is the case, next time you believe your son might need something, please do not include me in your plans." With that rebuke, Caroline turned and marched from the room before her tears were noted by Lady Wyndham. She rushed to her home and locked herself inside her chamber where she cried for what she would never have again or wouldn't once Sterling was gone.

CHAPTER THIRTY-ONE

STERLING WOKE WITH two purposes for the day. First, he was going to apologize to his mother The second, he was going to make certain there were horses available. He did not want to take a wagon to Boulder Beach. He did not want servants to drive them in a wagon because then he and Caroline would not be alone and it was very important that they did not have anyone else about.

When he reached the dining room, he found his mother sipping tea and approached.

"I would like to apologize."

Her eyes widened in surprise. "There is no need, Sterling."

"There is." He understood so much more, including his responsibility, after talking with Caroline. "I should have written you back after I read your first couple of letters. I should have written and asked why you had not returned or asked you to come home. I am sorry that I accepted what Father told me and did not inquire further. You tried to reach out to me and you were ignored."

"I understand, Sterling."

"You should not. I should not have ignored you when I came home on holiday. I should have noticed that you were unhappy."

"You were not supposed to see it. I hid it from you intentionally. A son is not supposed to worry about a mother. It is the mother who worries about her children."

"I still should have realized."

"It does not matter, Sterling."

"A part of me may always be upset that you did not come home, but Father carried most of that responsibility. He made you to be the villain and I did not question it."

Her smile was gentle and there were tears in her eyes. "I accept your apology, Sterling."

He smiled. "I am glad I came to Wyndview Farm, and not so that I could evaluate it from the only perspective of a part of Trade Wyne"

"I am as well, Sterling." His mother smiled, a mist in her eyes, which did make him uncomfortable.

"Well, I should be going since Caroline and I are off to see penguins." He laughed as he left the dining room and waited for her to join him on the terrace.

"I assume you can ride, since I did see you do so the first day of my arrival," he said as soon as he joined her. It was also a sight he would never forget.

"A horse?" she questioned.

"Yes."

She held out her arms and looked down. "I am not dressed for riding a horse. Please excuse me."

It had not seemed to bother her previously. Then again, she had only rushed to warn her father that his employer had suddenly arrived. This time they would be riding away from the estate.

When she returned, Sterling had anticipated that she would be wearing the type of riding habit often seen in England, but Caroline had only changed into a different dress.

"Did you change your mind about going?"

"Not at all." Caroline grasped her skirt and spread her arms to demonstrate the fullness. "I refuse to put on the stuffy riding habit that I wore during my first Season. It did well enough for that mild climate, but it would be sweltering before we ever neared the beach."

He supposed she was correct and then considered his own clothing that was no different from what he wore back home. He too would be overly warm, and likely miserable.

"Please excuse me."

He hurried back into the house and up to his chamber where he removed his cravat and suitcoat, leaving only his linen shirt, trousers and waistcoat and boots. He had seen other local men in Cape Town and the surrounding dressed similarly or even less properly than he was now and decided that he did not care what anyone thought. After he retrieved the worn leather hat that he had procured in Greece after his face had burned during the crossing of the Mediterranean from Italy, he once again joined Caroline on the terrace.

Caroline was just tying the ribbon of her straw hat beneath her chin when he arrived.

At his appearance, she arched a brow. "Goodness, such impropriety for an earl is unheard of."

"Yes, well, upon reconsideration, I would also rather be comfortable." He gestured to the door. "Shall we?"

She gave a nod then walked past him, through the house until she exited onto the front drive, Sterling following. Waiting was a stable hand who held the reins of two saddled horses, as requested. A footman held a basket of foodstuffs and a maid held a blanket.

After giving Caroline a leg up, she got herself situated, making certain that her legs were covered and then she took the reins and then blanket, which she draped over the horse while Sterling tied the basket to the back of his saddle then mounted his horse and took the reins from the stable hand.

"Are you ready?" he asked.

"I look forward to our outing, Lord Wyndham."

"I believe my mother is attempting to organize my life," Sterling said once they were on the main road.

"Why do you think so?"

"She claims that she does not want me to leave Wyndview

Farm until it is necessary, yet she does not appear to want me around either."

"Perhaps she does not want you to grow bored while you wait to meet with my father," Caroline suggested.

"No, I think it is more. I get the distinct feeling that she does not want me spending too much of my free time at Wyndview Farm." He glanced over and waited to see if Caroline would have a response. She was looking straight ahead, pearly teeth biting her bottom lip.

Strange.

"Would you know why my mother keeps sending me away?"

Caroline winced at his question.

"What are you keeping from me?"

"It is not for me to say."

"If it is about me, you most certainly are at liberty to say."

"Your mother's concerns are inconsequential given the reason for your visit. They are truly harmless."

"What the hell is that supposed to mean?"

Caroline straightened. Likely because of his sharp tone.

"I am sorry but if you must know, my mother is the most maddening and frustrating woman alive."

Sterling had not expected Caroline to agree with him but was surprised at her giggle.

"Please tell me what my mother is about?"

She glanced at him, indecision in her brown eyes. "Do you promise not to say anything to her?"

"That would depend on what you tell me."

"Then I will not tell you anything unless you promise me."

"I cannot make such a promise when I do not know what my mother is up to or what you might tell me."

"Then I suppose we are at an impasse, Lord Wyndham."

"What happened to calling me Sterling?"

"I will not do so if you are going to take such a tone."

For just a moment, he was shocked by her reproach, but soon he was overcome with laughter. Nobody had ever spoken to him that way other than a parent.

"I am sorry, Caroline. Forget my demands and let us enjoy the day." He didn't want to spend it arguing. Besides he could ask his mother when he returned now that he knew she definitely was up to something.

CAROLINE WAS ALREADY keeping her own secret and did not want to keep Lady Wyndham's as well. She was not going to lie to Sterling but she also wasn't going to pretend that she wasn't aware that Lady Wyndham had plans for her son. However, if he wished to know what those were, Sterling could ask his mother directly.

It was going to be difficult enough if he ever learned of her deception, and she prayed that he never did.

At first, she feared what would happen if he learned, now she worried about his reaction because she had come to care for him.

Where had that thought come from?

She could not *care* for him.

They could share friendship, desire, and intimacy, but under no circumstances could she develop any deeper emotions.

They were lovers and nothing more and, in few months, he would be gone. She would carry on as she did before and he would do the same. If they were lucky, they would have fond memories and then she would return to doing what she needed to for her family.

"Are you upset with me?"

Sterling's question intruded on her thoughts.

"No, why would you ask?"

"You not only grew very quiet, but there is also an expression of serious concerns on your face."

Yes, well, she was worried. "I was thinking about the duties that I have avoided for the fourth day in a row." It wasn't necessarily a lie because her duties were exactly what she feared he would learn about.

"Ah, we have arrived."

Sterling led the horses down a small slope before he dismounted and tied them to a spindly bush then lifted Caroline effortlessly from her mount and lowered her until her feet were once again on the ground.

There was barely any space between them and as she had in the past, Caroline became acutely aware of Sterling. Except now, she had so much more to remember than a bare chest.

He lifted his hand and tucked a wayward curl behind her ear before he leaned forward and pressed his lips to hers then pulled away.

"Shall we picnic on the beach or on this rise?" he asked as he untied the basket.

Caroline walked a little further, before some of the small boulders that the beach was named for and the sand began. From here they could see the ocean, and the penguins—the reason they were here.

The waves were gentle and the breezes were light, but still enough to cool their skin in the heat. Dozens of penguins frolicked in the water and walked along the beach while seals sunned themselves on the boulders.

"Here!" she said before she returned to her horse and retrieved the blanket then shook it out and spread it on the ground.

Sterling joined her and set the basket in a corner then took a seat next to her.

"I had forgotten how much I enjoyed watching the penguins when I was a boy."

At least his mother's plan was working.

"I am also glad that your mother insisted that we do this."

"And though I do not appreciate how she has been attempting to manage us, I do not mind in this moment."

Neither did she. They were in a perfect setting, it was a beautiful day, and nobody else was around.

Sterling leaned forward and opened the basket and took out roasted chicken, fresh bread, plums, which had been recently picked from the orchard, and strawberries from their fruit garden, wine, glasses, plates and utensils—everything that they needed to enjoy a repast, including napkins.

Caroline added a few choices to her plate while Sterling opened the wine and poured two glasses.

"Cook apologized that the wine comes from another local vineyard, but since we do not bottle ours at the vineyard, it was impossible to enjoy something we have grown."

Caroline laughed. "Do not tell the owner of Wyndview Farm, but I do enjoy drinking Groot Constantia on occasion."

"As does a good portion of the world," Sterling grumbled. "They sell more than we do. Even Napoleon in exile receives cases of Constantia."

She had not meant to introduce what appeared to be a bitter topic. "Your wine does sell well does it not?" she asked when she truly did not know. Yes, they produced it, but once it was shipped, Caroline did not know where it was bottled, or what type of profit Trade Wynd earned.

"It does well, and I should not complain."

Yet, she sensed that he wanted to. "Are you going to brood for the rest of the afternoon because I enjoy your competitor's wine as does a former emperor who waged war that killed thousands over your wine?"

She meant to tease him into realizing how ridiculous his complaints were but Sterling grew serious.

"I am sorry. I should not complain. Hundreds of men died because of Napoleon, your husband included, which makes my complaint rather selfish."

Caroline had not even been thinking about Peter when she mentioned the deaths. "Do not concern yourself. It has been three and a half years and I have not forgotten."

"I suppose you wouldn't."

She did not want to think about Peter and changed the subject.

"You said that you send the wine to England, America, and the Caribbean. What do you bring back?"

"Sugar, molasses, tobacco, and cotton," he answered and then started telling her how many ships Trade Wynd owned. Where they sailed. What they imported, what they exported. It was all fascinating that a cargo ship filled with wine would return filled with sugar—coveted items on both sides of the Atlantic.

"Have you ever wanted to visit America or the Caribbean?" He had already visited several countries on the Continent, but the one that most fascinated her was Greece.

"I would, but I have been gone for almost a year and cannot take more time to sail across the Atlantic."

"Maybe you can in a few years," she suggested.

Caroline understood that he had duties in England but if she had access to a ship to take her anywhere that she wanted, she would travel the world.

It was a silly thought, especially when she may not even be given the opportunity to return to England.

"Where do you suppose your mother will send you tomorrow?" she asked.

Sterling snorted. "There are not many places left to visit. At least few that are close because I am not going to ride in a wagon for a full day again.

Caroling chuckled and leaned into him. "Was your bottom sore?"

"I expect that it is also bruised," he grumbled before he began to smile. "Maybe I should ask you to take a look to see if it is. I would be happy to check you for bruises as well."

"I am certain you would." Caroline laughed as her blood heated.

"But when and how?" he straightened and glanced around.

"Certainly not here!" she objected. They were out in the open and anyone could decide to visit the beach and watch the penguins.

Sterling leaned in and took her hand then kissed the back of it. "I do want to…be alone with you again in a setting where no one will find us."

"I would be agreeable to such an arrangement."

"Then we are back to my original question. When and how?"

Never had Caroline been so happy that she had insisted on the back parlor as her chamber. "Simply cross the terrace."

"Your house?"

"Do not use the front door, but the one a little further down."

"To the parlor?" he asked with a frown.

"It is where I sleep and have since I gave my brother back his room when he returned from school."

"What of Livia?"

"She is above-stairs in my old chamber. I am the only one on the ground floor."

"I cannot believe your family allows you to sleep in the parlor."

"I have made it into my bedchambers and it is treated as such by my family so I am never disturbed." Except for the one time she had slept too late, right after Sterling had arrived, and woke up to Livia standing by her bed afraid that she was ill.

He started to grin. "What time should I call?"

"Not until everyone is asleep. I do not want to have to explain to my family or your mother and I certainly do not want servants gossiping."

"Does that mean you will make me leave before the sun rises?"

"As much as I may not want you to, I am afraid that I must insist."

Chapter Thirty-Two

AFTER HE HAD dined with his mother, Sterling had gone to the office to review the quarterly reports once again. He then tried to read the local newssheets, and then a book, but nothing held his attention. And every time he looked at the clock, he would swear that the hands had not moved.

However, when it finally started to grow dark, he knew the time was near and waited in the office for his mother to retire and for the servants to find their beds. Only then did he go up to his chamber where he could look out the window to the house Caroline shared with her family.

A few lights remained burning in the upper level, as there were in the parlor. Those were the ones he did not mind, but he waited for the upper level to go dark, then waited another half hour to make certain that everyone was asleep before he quietly left the house, crossed the terrace and tapped on the door that led to Caroline's chamber.

She opened immediately then pulled him inside.

"Did anyone see you?"

"No."

"Are you certain?"

"I promise."

Only then did she blow out a breath.

"I promise that nobody will ever know," he assured her.

"I hope you speak the truth."

"I do." Then he kissed her, first in a chaste manner, but then they grew more heated as Caroline's arms came around his shoulders. As he devoured her mouth, he walked her back to the bed on the far wall then leaned over until she sat then came over her.

He had wanted her since the picnic, especially when she had opened the upper buttons of her gown to cool her skin and he had glimpsed her creamy breasts. Had they not been out in the open, he would have pleasured her then and taken great delight in doing so.

Caroline pushed his coat off his shoulders. Sterling stood only long enough to remove it and then toss it on the floor. Then Caroline set to work unbuttoning his waistcoat, which soon joined the suitcoat, and as she pulled his shirt from his trousers and slipped her delicate fingers and palms up his chest, he pushed her skirts higher and higher, caressing her inner thighs until his fingers met her curls.

Caroline sucked in a breath and then he touched her just as he lowered his mouth to hers once again.

As before, she was the most responsive woman to his caress, which only further heated his blood, while he tried to bring her close then back away, prolonging her pleasure instead of sending her over the edge too quickly, she was not patient and each time he shifted, she followed until her body convulsed with her release.

Only then did he break the kiss, stand, and undo the placket on his trousers.

Caroline sat up, reached out, and wrapped her hand around his length. Sterling groaned as his knees nearly buckled. He needed to make her stop or this would end before he joined her and with that, Sterling lifted her hips and thrust forward. Caroline fell back on the bed with a moan then clutched the coverlet as he remained standing, filling her over and over until she put a fist in her mouth to keep from crying out as her climax racked her body again. Only then did he allow himself to follow and pulled away at the last minute.

As Caroline lay there panting, he fell to the side of her while also trying to catch his breath.

"I think I like having a lover," she said quietly.

Sterling leaned over and kissed her. "I know that I do."

CAROLINE AWOKE WITH a smile. After she and Sterling had been intimate, they shared brandy and talked on several topics from the Season in London to Trade Wynd and he spoke of their other vineyard in Madeira, which he had never visited but his younger brother managed. They discussed politics in England and in the Cape Colony, and books, and his brothers until they both tired. Afraid that he would fall asleep, Caroline made him get dressed and go home. Only then had she crawled into bed and fallen asleep instantly. Now she was awake with the sun, happy and content.

She did like Sterling. She liked him very much, but they were lovers and becoming friends. That was all they would ever be. Nothing more. It was far more than friendship, but she was reluctant to call it love. Except, she feared that it was too late.

Maybe she just didn't want to admit it to herself yet, and likely never would. There was no place for love between them when their relationship was of a short duration. Besides, gentlemen like Sterling did not fall in love with their lovers and that was all they would ever be.

With those thoughts, she pulled herself from the bed and prepared for the day then joined her daughter and Beatrix for breakfast before she went over to see if Lady Wyndham needed anything today. When she entered the sitting room, Caroline was surprised to find Sterling there as well.

For a moment, she wondered if Sterling had confronted Lady Wyndham about why she kept sending him away even though she wanted him to remain in the Cape Colony. She suspected that would anger him, but the two appeared to be amicable, without the tension that usually emanated in the room when the two were together.

"Ah, Caroline, you are just the person I was hoping to see this morning."

"You did not greet me in such a manner," Sterling complained. Caroline would have thought him angry if she hadn't seen the quirk at the corner of his lip.

"Good morning, Mrs. Sutcliffe."

"Lord Wyndham," she nodded before she returned her attention to his mother. "How may I be of service, Lady Wyndham."

"I am to understand that the grapes may be ready as early as tomorrow."

Sterling straightened and looked to Caroline for clarification, but she was as surprised as him. "My father did not mention it to me."

"He and I spoke of it yesterday while the two of you were at Boulder Beach."

Why hadn't her father told her? She needed to make certain that all was prepared. Were there enough baskets? Had the vats been thoroughly cleaned? Had the remaining barrels been delivered?

She had been gone for four days because Lady Wyndham brought her into her plans to see that her son remembered where he came from and she had neglected her duties.

"I will go speak with my father directly to see how I may be of service." Caroline smiled and tried not to rush from the room, but she could not help the panic that stirred. If everything wasn't prepared, then they could suffer a setback. It was imperative that everything be done in a specific and timely order.

"Shall I go with you?" Sterling suggested.

"That is not necessary, Lord Wyndham. I will report back any news that my father has that he has not shared with your mother."

❧❧

CHAPTER THIRTY-THREE

STERLING POURED ANOTHER cup of coffee and looked over at his mother. "Was Mrs. Sutcliffe acting strangely or was it my imagination?"

"She always gets anxious before the harvest," his mother dismissed with a wave of her hand. "No doubt she will return after she has spoken with her father."

"Why would she be anxious?" He asked out of curiosity. "It is her father who is the estate manager and oversees the harvest and I assume he's training his son William to take over when he is ready to enter retirement."

"That is correct."

"Then why did Mrs. Sutcliffe feel the need to hurry to her father, almost alarmed?"

"There are two reasons," she answered. "The first is that everyone knows how important the grapes and wine are to the estate and if something were to go wrong or the wine did not turn out as it should, it could jeopardize their positions, Hallaway included, which would affect Caroline and her daughter."

Sterling nodded because it was something that he could understand. A bad crop of grapes could lead to a financial loss and the need to let employees go.

"What is the second?"

"Caroline gets overly concerned for her father," his mother explained. "She is a doting daughter who sees her father as an aging man who should not work so hard or spend as many hours in the sun as he does. His walking the fields and tasting the grapes are not so much a concern, but his participation in the harvest does give her concern. No doubt she is going to lecture him that he will supervise the cutting of the grapes then stop him from taking part."

"Is Hallaway infirm?" Perhaps he needed to interview William soon to see if he would be up to the task of taking over his father's position.

"He is not; I can assure you."

"If that is not the case…"

"She is an overly protective daughter. Hallaway may be getting on in years, but he can still supervise the harvest. That man knows more about grapes and the making of wine than your father ever did."

Such a statement took him aback because Sterling had always believed his father knew everything and that nobody could know more than he did. But he had also been a boy when he had made those assumptions.

"Perhaps I should join her. I would like to know more about how Hallaway can tell that the grapes are now ready when they were not yesterday or that they will be tomorrow. Is it because of color? Is it because of taste?"

His mother sat forward and this time it was her who was alarmed. "Oh, that is not necessary. You will only be in the way."

In the way? Why did his mother and Caroline want to keep him from the vineyard? He had every right to be there—he bloody owned the estate.

Sterling placed his cup in the saucer that rested on the table. Then stood. "I think will visit anyway. And I promise to stay out of the way."

Caroline and his mother were behaving oddly. All was well until his mother informed Caroline that they would begin to harvest the grapes tomorrow. It was then that her entire demeanor changed. The smile was gone and there was concern in her brown eyes and then she could not wait to be away from them. What truly had her concerned?

Yes, Hallaway was older but from what Sterling had seen he was quite capable to continue in his duties.

Something was very odd and he wanted to find out exactly what.

"I have an excellent idea, Sterling," his mother called after him.

Sterling stopped and turned to face her. If she was going to offer a suggestion that would keep him here instead of going to the vineyard then he would know that the two were hiding something from him, though Sterling could not imagine what that would be.

"What is it, Mother?" he asked with barely veiled impatience.

"Go fetch Caroline and bring her back."

That was not what he expected. "Why?"

"She will fret when there is no reason. I do not think you realize how much she fusses and she needs a distraction."

He had yet to see Caroline *fret* or *fuss*. Though he had only once been present when the father and daughter were together so he really could not judge their relationship.

"Visit Table Mountain," she offered brightly. "You have not climbed it since you were a boy when you were accompanied your father."

"But never you," he reminded her.

"I do not do well with heights and climbing in a skirt is difficult."

"Then will not Mrs. Sutcliffe have the same difficulty?"

"Oh, Caroline does not wear a skirt when she ventures up to Table Mountain. At least, she hadn't when she visited last year when William returned from England."

If she didn't wear a skirt… "I will fetch her and return shortly," he announced. "Please make the arrangements for a wagon, horses, servants, a picnic…whatever we will need." He tried to sound authoritative, just solving a difficulty, and hoped that his mother had no idea the thoughts that flashed through his mind. If she wasn't wearing skirts, then that could only mean that Caroline would be in trousers, which was something he wanted to very much see.

CAROLINE STOOD BEFORE her father; hands fisted on her hips. "Why did you not tell me that you plan on harvesting tomorrow?"

"You have been busy."

"I am never too busy for something this important."

"All is ready. I can assure you. Would I let the harvest happen too soon or too late?"

"What of the vats? Are they all sufficiently cleaned and ready?"

"Yes, they are."

"Have all the baskets been loaded into the wagon?"

"Yes."

"Has every servant been informed of their duties?"

"You behave as if I have never overseen the harvest before, Caroline."

"We have never harvested grapes while the Earl of Wyndham has been here."

"I know grapes. I know harvesting. I know making wine. I would not shirk any duty that could affect the quality we will produce."

Caroline stared at her father. He was correct. When it came to his estate manager duties, the grapes and making of wine had never been a concern. It was everything else.

"Check for yourself. You will see that the vats are ready, that the barrels have arrived, and the wagons are loaded with baskets to bring into the field."

"I will!" she announced and marched away to the barn.

Four days she had been absent. Four days she had allowed Lady Wyndham to dictate where she went and with whom when the woman knew that Caroline was needed here, especially at this time of year.

Just because her father always had the harvest in hand, and that it was the only thing he cared about, did not mean he couldn't forget something important. William would not know if anything was neglected because he had not been part of the harvest before. He arrived last year just as they were about to load the last of the barrels on a ship.

She should have been here so that he was taught everything that was necessary.

What if Father had only rambled on, as he tended to do, without imparting any true knowledge?

Except, the servants knew what to do…

Still, she needed to make certain for herself.

When she stepped inside the barn, Caroline paused and took in the activity then inspected the vats, wagons, baskets, then the cellar where empty barrels waited to be filled.

There was nothing that she needed to do. Everything was well in hand.

While she was relieved, there was discontent.

They did not need her.

Once William was trained, she would not be needed any-where.

❧ ❧

CHAPTER THIRTY-FOUR

"IT IS AN art," Hallaway had explained after Sterling had found him and asked how he knew the grapes would be ready.

Hallaway picked a grape and handed it to Sterling. "Taste."

He did, but it tasted no different than any other grape. There had to be a difference and he wanted to ask questions because this was what Sterling had wanted to learn since he was a boy, which left him torn. Did he stay and take in everything that Hallaway might teach him, or find Caroline?

She had been alarmed and upset when she fled his mother's sitting room.

Except, he had been under the impression that she would be by her father and watching so that he did not overexert himself but she was not to be found.

"Where might your daughter be?"

Hallaway shook his head. "Caro worries too much. About me. About the grapes. About the harvest."

Just as his mother had claimed.

"She is fretting in the barn and once she sees that all is as it should be, she will be back to stay at my side so that I do not overdo."

"Is there a reason she should be concerned."

Hallaway laughed. "As I said, she worries too much." He then walked on, stopping and examining grapes. Sterling followed, torn with whether he should stay and learn or find Caroline.

When Hallaway reached the end of the row and turned to Sterling. "Is it your turn to hover? Did Caro send you in her stead?"

"No, of course not," Sterling insisted. Except, he had every right to be there. He owned the property.

"What if I am simply here to observe and learn," he returned.

"To what purpose?" he countered. "You will be gone soon and it might be another seven years or more before you are back." Hallaway walked to the next row and continued examining grapes.

Had his estate manager insulted him for being an absentee owner? It wasn't as if he could abandon England, the estate there, and Trade Wynd to grow grapes in the Cape Colony.

Except, he wanted to. If he could, he would leave England behind and remain here, on Wyndview Farm and with Caroline and live a simpler life.

No wonder his mother hadn't rushed to return to England.

Unfortunately, he had responsibilities that he couldn't shirk and he had already been away too long.

"Your father trusted me," Hallaway reminded him. "Unless you have complaints."

Sterling took a step back. He was being dismissed by his estate manager. Such would be unheard of in England.

"Do you have complaints?" he asked pointedly.

"No. None."

Hallaway nodded. "Then do not concern yourself with learning what I know. Find my daughter before she is overset."

Overset? Sterling could not imagine Caroline being overset any more than fretting or being fussy, and it was rather laughable. Then again, he had not known her long, nor had he been present during a harvest.

"If you do not take her away, and back to your mother, she will be back by my side, a nuisance and distraction that I do not need."

He spoke as if Caroline was a child, which she most certainly was not. No, she was a fully grown passionate woman who would be dressed in trousers if he took her to Table Mountain.

"I will do as you ask, but tomorrow, I will want to learn."

Hallaway nodded then shooed him away without looking up from his grapes.

It was very disrespectful, but the man did know what he was doing better than anyone else so Sterling did not take offense or discipline him. Instead, he went off to find Caroline who was standing at the entrance of the barn when he came across her.

She did not appear worried or concerned, but sad.

"Is all well, Caroline?" he asked, using her given name since no one was near enough to hear them.

She turned and frowned. "It is. All is well. In fact, it is perfect!"

Then why was she upset?

"I suppose I should return to the house and see what other matters need my attention."

She then turned and walked away from him.

"Nothing," he said as he caught up to her.

"How would you know?"

"Because my mother said so. In fact, she suggested that the two of us visit Table Mountain and have a picnic."

Caroline stopped and faced him, hands on her hips. "That will be yet another day away from Wyndview Farm. Do you know how long it takes to climb to the top?"

He did not know. It had been years since he had done so.

"Hours!"

It had seemed to take a while when he was a child, but all things seemed to take too long when there was anticipation.

"Then we will climb, picnic, and come back down."

"And likely not return until after dinnertime," she argued.

"Why does that matter?" Did she not want to be with him or was she afraid of being away from the estate? There was nothing that needed her attention. She wasn't even a true servant. She lived here with her daughter, father, and brother because she had needed a home. She was only a companion to his mother and acted the housekeeper because there was a need, not that she applied for the position.

"I have been gone too often and for too long."

"What would you do today if you remained?"

Caroline blinked and looked up at him. A frown on her lips and eyebrows drawn together. "I suppose nothing," she answered after the longest time, her tone quiet and defeated.

He did not understand why she was bothered, but there was often much he did not understand about women and chose not to press for answers. "Then you are free to accompany me."

Caroline sighed. "I suppose I am."

If she had any less enthusiasm, she would be asleep, but Sterling did not let her lack of desire to affect his mood.

WHEN STERLING HAD asked what she would to today if she remained, several areas that needed her attention came to mind. Except, she could mention none of them because if she did, he would then ask questions that Caroline was not prepared to answer. So, instead, she would be hiking to the top of Table Mountain.

Caroline stared at her appearance in the mirror and reconsidered for the tenth time if she should dress in this manner. Except, she really had no choice because climbing the mountain in a skirt was perilous. One wrong step on the hem of her dress could not only cause her to trip but send her falling. It was better that she wore a pair of her brother's cast-off trousers, which had to be belted at her middle with a rope. Her light woven cotton shirt that she had purchased in town had been made by one of the local women. Lastly, she slipped on the boots she usually wore when working in the gardens. Finally, she had tied her hair back and away from her face. Caroline also added a hat to shield her from the sun, not that it would do any good to save her from the heat.

Though few would remark upon her appearance at Wyndview Farm, or even in town, Sterling may have quite a different opinion. He was used to the ladies in England. Ladies who wore pretty dresses, not trousers. However, she would not know until she faced him and with those thoughts, she kissed Livia goodbye then made her way to the main house.

At her appearance, his left eyebrow rose, as his blue eyes widened, no doubt in shock and disapproval.

"I feared you would find an excuse not to go at all." Lady Wyndham chuckled.

"I may not yet," Caroline answered.

"Why would that be?"

"I fear that your son might be scandalized by my appearance." Caroline offered in grave seriousness.

"Surprised, yes. Hardly scandalized," he answered as the corner of his mouth tipped.

"I will see if the servants to accompany you are ready," Lady Wyndham started for the entry.

"Are you certain that they want to go?" Caroline asked.

"Oh, yes," Lady Wyndham assured her. "I asked for volunteers and Malik and Kaya were quick to respond. They enjoy such activities."

They had also only been married for a few days and likely wanted to spend more time together. Such was young love.

"Your clothing is casual. Perhaps I should change," Wyndham said.

"The climb can be difficult at times, but worth the effort. However, if you do not want what you are wearing to be potentially damaged, I would suggest changing into something that you would not mind becoming dirty or possibly torn. The path can be steep and rugged in places."

"Cook has readied a picnic to carry in shoulder bags so that your hands are free," his mother said.

"Why would we need our hands free?" Sterling asked cautiously.

"Well, for one, it helps with balance. The second reason is that you will have a walking stick so that your presence warns away any snakes that may be further up the trail."

Caroline did not like snakes, but with warning of a stick hitting the ground, they slithered away. It was when snakes were surprised and cornered that unpleasant consequences occurred.

"Mother, what is this?" Sterling lifted an old worn leather satchel with a long strap that could be worn over a shoulder.

"Yours, dear."

A faint smile formed as his blue eyes warmed.

"It was discovered when your chamber was being prepared upon your arrival. I thought you might like to take it with you."

"I thought it had been lost when we moved," he murmured and opened the flap.

"There are stunning views from the top. Perhaps you might want to sketch them," his mother said right before she left them.

He withdrew a sketchbook and pencils and Caroline came forward as he flipped to the first page.

"There is nothing in it."

"No, there would not be," he answered then closed it. "I had not used all the pages in my other book and was saving this one for the voyage but could not find it once we sailed. I thought it had been packed way in the trunks that were stored below but when we unpacked after arriving in England, it was not there either."

"You never told me that you drew." How many layers were there to Sterling? Every time she learned something new, Caroline realized how much she had misjudged him when he had first arrived.

"I no longer draw," he answered and placed the items back in the leather satchel.

"Why?" Caroline asked with concern.

"Because with adulthood comes responsibilities that do not allow for such frivolity of sitting around sketching or drawing whenever a person feels like doing so."

That was rather harsh and Caroline found herself stepping back.

"That is truly a shame!" his mother criticized on her return. "You were quite talented."

"I accept that there is bias in your opinion."

"It was also something you enjoyed, Sterling. You were rarely without your sketchbook when you lived here."

"I was also a boy."

Caroline now knew why Lady Wyndham had left the satchel out. His mother wanted to remind him of what was important because she feared that he would never be happy. It was the same reason she had sent him to Stellenbosch, then to Boulder Beach, and now Table Mountain.

As much of an inconvenience as it was to be gone, Caroline also realized that Sterling would not go to these places on his own. Besides, she certainly wasn't needed in the vineyard, so why shouldn't she enjoy her time with Sterling before he was gone?

❧ ❧

CHAPTER THIRTY-FIVE

STERLING'S MOUTH HAD gone dry when Caroline stepped into the sitting room wearing old, worn trousers and a loose cotton shirt. No wonder women wore skirts. If they went about dressed in this manner, it would be impossible for men to accomplish anything because they would be too busy lusting after them.

He should probably not follow her on the trail because he would spend too much time watching her perfect bum and would be in an uncomfortable state by the time they reached the top.

His mother picked up the leather satchel. "Perhaps Livia would like to draw if you are not going to."

It was almost as if his fingers tingled with the very idea of grasping a pencil again. He had enjoyed it in his youth, but duty had forced him to set it aside. However, there was no reason why he could not take pleasure in it while he was here, and when he sailed home. Once he was back in England, he could set it aside again.

"No, I will keep it."

He lifted the satchel and flung the strap over his shoulder so that it crossed his body instead of dragging down his arm. It had always been too big for him when he was younger. Now it was perfect.

They set out, the four of them in the back of the wagon, each person carried a satchel that held what they would need when they arrived at the top such as a loaf of bread, wine, cups, dried meats, cheeses, and fruits. He had added heavier items to his and Malik's satchels while Caroline's and Kaya's satchels held the lighter picnic necessities.

The driver would remain at the base of the mountain with the wagon and horses while they hiked up.

He knew that his mother had once again found an excuse to send him from the house, but he no longer minded since he was able to spend the day with Caroline, the surprising delight he discovered at Wyndview Farm who was right in front of him, walking stick in hand, satchel at her side, hiking up the mountain with her perfectly rounded bum pulling at the fabric of her trousers.

Maybe that was what he should sketch once they arrived at the top, though it was a sight that Sterling doubted he would ever forget.

CAROLINE HAD FORGOTTEN how difficult the climb could be but once she gazed out and across Table Bay and down the Cape Peninsula, she was awed and quickly forgot that she had been out of breath and perspiring by the time they reached the top.

Sterling came to stand beside her.

"It is beautiful, is it not?"

"Spectacular," he agreed, then took a deep breath.

"Are you thirsty, Lord Wyndview?" Kaya called.

Caroline turned to see that the servants were setting out the picnic for them to enjoy.

The climb had been just as difficult for those two, but given Sterling was an earl, he might not invite them to sit.

"As I am certain you are," he responded as he walked to where the blanket had been spread out.

"Join me, Mrs. Sutcliffe," he called.

Caroline wandered over and settled on the blanket. It was good to rest her legs.

"Malik, Kaya." He gestured to areas of the blanket not yet occupied. "We could all use with a rest and I am certain you are as famished as I am."

The newlywed couple shared a look of uncertainty before they slowly walked forward and dropped to their knees.

The food they had brought was arranged in the middle and while Caroline first poured water for everyone, Sterling opened the bottle of wine.

"When I told the other stable hands where we were going, they insisted that the climb was impossible and that we would turn around and return to Wyndview Farm," Malik told them.

"Difficult, yes. Impossible, no."

Caroline had heard the same before she, her father, and William had made the climb not long after they had first arrived. He had also hired a guide to bring them to the top.

After they had finished eating, Kaya and Malik wandered off and Sterling took the sketchbook out of his satchel and settled upon a boulder and began drawing.

Caroline was the one who gathered the food and returned the remains to the various satchels and then settled on the blanket and looked out to enjoy the fabulous view and waited for Sterling to be done sketching and for Malik and Kaya to…whatever they were doing since they had wandered a little further away. She hoped that they were careful and did not get too close to the edge.

When she grew tired of the view, Caroline watched Sterling. He hardly looked up but concentrated on the book held in one hand and balanced on his knee while he sketched quickly. Then he would sit back and study what he had drawn before he returned to sketching. By the intensity on his face and complete concentration on what he was doing, Caroline determined that Sterling may have forgotten that anyone else was with him. Not that she minded since she enjoyed watching him and admired his profile, form, and the character that she had discovered beneath his cool and stern exterior.

However, curiosity did get the best of her and Caroline pulled herself to her feet and wandered over to where he sat. When her shadow fell over him, Sterling quickly closed the sketchbook, hiding what he had drawn.

"You are not going to show me?"

"I would prefer that you were not aware of my lack of talent."

"You will not show me one?" she begged him.

He tilted his head back and studied her. "Just one?" he asked.

"Just one."

He grinned and opened the book to the first page and held it up for her to see.

At first, she wasn't certain what the sketch was but then slowly realized. "Is that…"

"Yes. It is your bum. I had ample time to study it as we climbed, and I enjoyed it very much."

Her face started to burn. "I cannot believe that you…that…" She could not even find the words but sputtered and gestured. He had sketched every detail, including the patch she'd sewn on one side to cover the rip from when her brother had owned them, and the wear of the rope about her waist.

Sterling only laughed, closing the sketchbook.

"What are you going to do with it?"

"I thought to frame it and hang in my office at home, back in England, to always remember you by."

Panic seized her. "You would not dare."

"Why would I not?"

"What if someone asked?"

Sterling chuckled. "I would never reveal a name," he promised. "I will simply explain that it was an inspirational view from my time spent in the Cape Colony."

Caroline did not know what to say and she truly hoped that he was teasing and that nobody else ever saw the drawing.

"We need to go so that we are back before it gets dark." She then stomped away and hoped that she could find a way to get that drawing away from him and then she had another disturbing thought. "What else did you sketch?"

"Various things." He gestured to the scenery.

Oh, she wanted to believe him but there was too much humor in his eyes. She needed to see what was in that sketchbook. If he drew her bottom from memory, what else had he *remembered*?

Just the very idea caused her face to burn and she quickly turned away and started folding the thin blanket to shove in her satchel.

CHAPTER THIRTY-SIX

S TERLING FOUND HIMSELF chuckling at various times as they climbed down the mountain only to have Caroline look back at him over her shoulder and glare.

Oh, if only she knew the sketches he had made, she would be furious. They were certainly different than what a boy of fourteen sketched, and far more scintillating, and they were his.

Nobody would ever see what was within those pages because they were his memories of a remarkable woman. There was no doubt that in the years to come, when he was back in England, he would likely look through the pages often, simply to remember her.

His heart ached at the very idea of leaving Caroline...of leaving Wyndview Farm.

Was it because of her that he wanted to stay, or did he also want this life? The one he had been denied.

When she glanced back again, her dark eyes narrowing, he knew in that moment that it was mostly because of Caroline.

Despite his earlier insistence that it would be impossible to know someone well enough to determine if he wanted to spend the rest of his life with her, it had happened. He had fallen in love with Caroline and he wanted to be with her whether it was here or in England, or both as often as they managed to sail between the two.

Once they were again headed back to Wyndview Farm, they

spoke little. In fact, they were all exhausted from the climb. Kaya and Malik had fallen asleep, as well as Caroline, who had drifted off, her arm cradling her head on the side of the wagon while Sterling was coming to accept that he had fallen in love when he thought it was something that he would be denied.

He also wasn't certain what to do with such information.

Did he tell her?

What if she rejected him? What if she only saw him as a temporary lover, and that was all she wanted? Then what would he do?

It was likely best to just wait before he told her. The harvest would begin tomorrow and instead of confessing his heart, he would do his best to make her fall in love with him too.

He still wondered why his mother kept sending him away, and he had a new question. Why did she always insist that Caroline accompany him?

He had been under the impression that his mother was going to try and arrange a match for her with a local gentleman or military man? Did she now want to play matchmaker for him and Caroline?

Was it her plan that Sterling decide to never leave and forget about the earldom and leave Damian to manage Trade Wynd in his absence? Or did she expect him to take Caroline with him, which included her daughter Livia?

Or maybe her sending him off was for reasons he did not understand, which meant that he needed to ask her directly because Sterling knew she was up to something, he just didn't know what. Therefore, as soon as they arrived back at Wyndview Farm, he jumped out of the wagon and strode into the house, leaving everyone behind and went in search of his mother who he knew would be in the lavender sitting room.

"What are you about, Mother?"

"Whatever do you mean?" she asked innocently.

"Almost from the moment I arrived, you have been sending me places. First, I had to accompany you and Mrs. Sutcliffe to a ball. Then you sent me to Stellenbosch, also with Mrs. Sutcliffe."

"It was for Kaya and Malik," she insisted.

He would wager that they had been used as an excuse.

"When we returned, you suggested that Mrs. Sutcliffe and I visit Boulder Beach and then today, you sent us to Table Mountain. My question is, where do you plan to send me tomorrow and will you insist that Mrs. Sutcliffe accompany me?"

"Her presence is a convenience because she knows the area better than you and if I am to be honest, I worry about Caroline."

Some of his irritation slipped away. "Why?"

"She has taken on more responsibility than you could possibly know. Wyndview Farm is her home and nothing is more important to her, except for her daughter."

"Wyndview Farm is her father's responsibility," Sterling reminded his mother. Caroline's father was the estate manager, not her.

"I think she fears that she might be asked to leave if she has not created a position where she is needed. I also think she needs a purpose. She was rather lost when she arrived."

"If she is so devoted to Wyndview Farm, how did you convince her to leave so often?"

His mother's cheeks started to turn pink.

"When I questioned Mrs. Sutcliffe, she gave me the impression that she knew what you were about."

His mother gasped. "Caroline would not dare betray my confidence."

"Aha! You do have an ulterior motive."

"What did Caroline tell you, dear?" she asked calmly as she folded her hands onto her lap.

"Nothing. What are you about, Mother?"

His mother drew in a deep sigh. "I worry about you as well, Sterling."

"Why? I am perfectly content."

"Content is not happy."

Bloody hell!

"It is preferable to miserable, which I am not, so there is no cause for you to worry."

"Of course there is," she argued. "I want to see you happy."

He crossed his arms over his chest and studied her. "Why do you think that I am not?" he asked out of curiosity.

"Because when you arrived, you were just like your father *after* he lived in England."

He would like to argue, but his mother was correct. It was no different from when he conducted business with those he had not met personally. It was important to establish that there was no time for triviality in business dealings and that he expected all matters to be completed as expeditiously as possible. After all, not only was he an earl, but he was respected because of the power of Trade Wynd, a lucrative import and export business rivaled only by the East India Company. Trade Wynd was influential politically but had no part of the military, which was preferrable as it allowed them more freedom to trade.

So, yes, he had been arrogant and expected Hallaway to report to him almost immediately. And that was when his intentions and expectations started to change.

"Such behavior is not a benefit to you or anyone around you. Do you really want to turn into the same strict taskmaster as your father with schedules to be kept, which meant that being early was on time and demanded exactness from everyone?"

No, he did. He just hadn't truly realized just how rigid and unforgiving he had become. But he also knew that he had changed since that first day. Whether it was from being here or remembering a time when his family had been happy, being without responsibilities or Caroline, or everything combined, he did not know, but he was happy. Happy with his life, fortunate that he had come to Wyndview Farm, elated to have met Caroline and glad that he had forgiven his mother.

Sterling nearly sucked in a breath.

He had forgiven her and all the anger and animosity that he had carried for so many years was gone.

"The reason I have been sending you places is because I wanted you to remember how he was then. How we were. How you could be."

"Mrs. Sutcliffe knew your plans, did she not?" he asked.

"Yes. She was reluctant to help because she believed she was needed here, but in the end she agreed."

"So, you have been manipulating both of us." Caroline thought she was assisting his mother, and him apparently, while his mother hoped he would find happiness and because she worried about Caroline.

"Yes, I have," she admitted without guilt.

Sterling pinched the bridge of his nose and blew out a breath. He wanted to be angry with his mother for directing their lives but could not find it in himself. But, if he thanked her, it would only encourage her to keep on interfering and he wanted his relationship to continue on its own terms to see where it would end.

Besides, the harvest began tomorrow and neither one of them could be gone.

"Very well," he finally said and turned to leave, not certain what else he could say to her, only to find Caroline standing in the doorway, concern in her brown eyes, and hand on her chest.

Sterling nodded to her and left the sitting room. They would talk later, when they were alone, though he was not yet certain that he was ready to reveal that he had fallen in love with her.

CAROLINE FEARED THAT Sterling would be angry when he learned. After he had asked her yesterday what his mother was up to and she confirmed that it was something, but would not tell him, she knew that he would demand answers but didn't think that he would wait a day.

Except, he didn't appear to be angry. Maybe frustrated but

not upset as she would have expected after he had first arrived.

Caroline had no idea how he had been as a child, so she had no comparison. But he had become more approachable and less arrogant since his arrival. Further, he was an excellent lover.

She was also falling in love with him, which scared her. Would her heart mend after he was gone? It had taken time before she could think of Peter without hurting. How long would it take for her heart to recover from the loss of Sterling?

She closed her eyes and pushed her thoughts away. It would do no good to worry about a future when she had no intention of changing her present, knowing just how much she was risking her heart every time they were together.

Lady Wyndham smiled, quite pleased with herself, or maybe it was relief that she and her son had a conversation without anger. "I am certain that you want to retire early tonight since the harvest begins tomorrow."

"I do," she admitted, knowing that it was unlikely to happen if Sterling came to her room again tonight.

Lady Wyndham stood and let out a sigh of content.

"I will bring Livia to you in the morning."

Lady Wyndham nodded as she walked to the window over-looking the gardens. Then she suddenly tensed and sucked in a breath.

"Lady Wyndham, what is it?"

"Caroline, dear, I need you to remain calm," she said slowly. "You cannot rush out there, do you understand?"

She had no idea what Lady Wyndham meant and slowly crossed the room to see what had Lady Wyndham worried.

"Sterling is there," she said quietly.

"I do not under…"

Her blood ran cold and she turned to run from the parlor but Lady Wyndham grasped her wrist.

"Calm, Caroline. If you rush out there…"

Oh God, how could she remain calm?

CHAPTER THIRTY-SEVEN

STERLING STEPPED OUT onto the Terrace and took a deep breath and intent on finding Hallaway for instructions for tomorrow when he noted Caroline's daughter, Livia, standing near the gardens.

As she was the most important person in Caroline's life, and Caroline was important to him, it would be remiss of him to not come to know Livia better, but as he took a step forward Sterling realized that she was not simply standing there, but she was as still as a statute, which was very odd for a five-year-old. And it was only then that he noted what she was facing and his blood ran cold—a cobra, risen from the garden, its hood spread and ready to strike.

Sterling did not dare approach or he may be seen as an aggressor. Instead, he held his place and hoped that he did not startle Livia when he spoke, though she likely heard him exit the house and hoped that whoever was behind her would come to her rescue.

"You are doing well, Livia," he said only loud enough for her to hear and kept his tone gentle and calm. "Now I want you to do as I say. Do not answer me. Do not nod your head. Just do exactly what I tell you."

He took a deep breath and hoped that the lessons from his childhood and what he had been told to do in this situation held true.

"With your left foot slowly step back."

Olivia did exactly what he said.

"Now very slowly step back with your right foot."

Again, she did as he said.

"Very good. Now your left foot again."

She followed his instructions slowly and carefully each time he told her to move. Sterling's heart pounded against his chest as fear rose that the cobra would strike before she was far enough away.

He repeated his instructions, but her steps were smaller than his and it took twice as long as it would have taken him. Anxiety and fear filled his being. Livia would not survive if she was bitten, and Caroline would not survive losing her daughter.

The door opened behind him and he feared that it was Caroline and when she realized what her daughter faced that she'd panic. She hoped she would remember to remain calm until Livia was safe.

"You are doing very well, Livia. Now, slowly step back again."

He kept calling instructions for her to step because she did not do so on her own. Whenever he paused, she remained still.

She trusted him and Sterling could not fail her.

"Another step, Livia."

And, just as she did, the cobra disappeared into the foliage, likely putting as much distance as possible between it and the humans.

"You are safe now. It is gone." At his words, the child turned and ran to him, tears streaming down her face. Sterling bent down to catch her as tiny arms wrapped around his neck as she sobbed on his shoulder.

A warmth that he had never experienced swept through him, replacing the terror that had risen when he saw the cobra.

Sterling had never comforted a child before and acted on instinct by holding her close and patting her back. Only then did he notice Caroline beside him, frightfully pale, tears in her eyes.

"Thank you," she whispered. "Thank you for saving my daughter."

It was not necessary to thank him because anyone would have done exactly what he had if they had come across Livia. He just happened to be the first person who saw her.

It took some time but Livia finally fell asleep. Caroline could only hope that she did not have nightmares and that because she was a child, might forget this incident.

Caroline had praised her over and over for being brave and remembering the lessons she had been told and even though her daughter calmed, Caroline's hands still shook.

It had taken everything in her being not to run to her daughter or call out. Instincts to save Livia were in opposition to what needed to be done in that situation. Instead, she stood helpless while Sterling gently called out instructions and Livia slowly obeyed. Caroline was certain that she did not breathe until Livia was in Sterling's arms.

Thank goodness it had been Sterling who came across Livia because Caroline was not so certain she wouldn't have panicked and thus put her daughter in worse danger, just as Lady Wyndham had feared when she kept telling Caroline to be calm.

She wanted to thank him again, but the later it grew, and when he didn't come, Caroline assumed that he would not. Therefore, she started to prepare for bed when there was a quiet tap on her door. When she opened, she found a concerned Sterling on her doorstep but he was looking behind her as if he anticipated to find someone else there.

"How is Livia?" he finally asked.

"She is finally asleep." Caroline stepped back and opened the door further so that he could enter.

"I hope that she does not suffer nightmares."

"I fear that may be me," she responded honestly. "Thank you. I do not know what…"

"It did not," he cut her off.

"We have told her what to do since she was a…" Caroline offered a dry chuckle. "I was going to say child, which she still is, but one never knows if a child truly listens or even remembers."

"She listened," he reminded her. "She also followed instructions."

This had been the most terrifying day of her life.

Sterling reached out and took her hands in his. "You are trembling."

She had been since she'd stepped out on the terrace and saw her five-year-old daughter slowly backing away from a cobra and had been unable to help her.

"Do you have brandy? If not, I can return to the house and bring some back."

"We do," she murmured, pulling away and going to the sideboard in the dining room to retrieve a bottle and two glasses. When she returned, Sterling took them from her and poured.

"Thank you," she offered when he handed her a glass.

She took a sip and closed her eyes and welcomed the burn down the back of her throat then warmth in her stomach before she looked at Sterling.

"I wish you would have told me what my mother was about."

Caroline sank down onto the bed, thankful to have something else to think about. "To tell you the truth, I did not know what to do. When she asked me to assist, I did not know you, but I knew your mother and she asked it of me."

He stared at her not saying anything and she waited to see if he was angry with her even though he had not been upset with his mother.

"I understand," he finally said. "At least you did not lie to me when I asked."

"I did not tell you anything," she reminded him. There was

much that she wasn't telling him.

"No. You held my mother's confidence, which I respect, but you let me know that my suspicions were correct when you could have lied to me."

Her stomach tightened. Did he believe an omission was the same as a lie?

"It has been a difficult position," she answered honestly. "Except, I think that after Stellenbosch, I went along not so much because she asked, but because I wanted to share those adventures with you." She gazed into his blue eyes so that he would know she was sincere.

"That is good to know," he chuckled. "There is still something that my mother said that concerns me."

Her stomach tightened, because Caroline was certain that she already knew or maybe it was because of her guilty conscious.

"When my mother said that you took on more responsibility than I can possibly know, what did she mean?"

Caroline stood and strolled to the window. "It is her opinion, that is all. I simply do my part in being of assistance where I can be."

"Companion, sometimes gardener, secretary, and house-keeper?"

Caroline shrugged, not really answering because she could not look him in the eye and lie.

"Has the brandy helped relax you?" he asked.

"Yes," she answered quietly. "Though, I do believe that it will take time before the terror is truly gone."

He came up from behind and placed his arms around her and kissed her cheek. "Would you like for me to stay with you tonight?"

She did, if only for the comfort of his arms, but feared that her daughter might suffer a nightmare and come to her bed and Caroline did not want Livia to discover Sterling there. First, she did not want to have to explain and second, she couldn't have her daughter telling anyone.

"It is probably best if you leave," she finally said. "There will be an early start tomorrow and I may go above and watch over Livia."

"I understand." Sterling kissed her cheek again and then walked to the door "Sleep well, Caroline, I will see you tomorrow." Then he was gone.

Caroline watched as Sterling crossed the terrace then returned the brandy to her office and washed the glasses so that her father did not ask questions.

There was so much more to Sterling than being an arrogant earl, unyielding owner of vineyards, and an incredible lover. He was strong, yet vulnerable, and a man who had saved her daughter.

He was also her friend and she would miss him terribly when he was gone.

But, most of all, she was in love with him, even more so after he had remained calm to save her daughter.

CHAPTER THIRTY-EIGHT

STERLING WOKE WITH anticipation of the grape harvest. He wanted to be present and work alongside everyone as his father had done.

After pulling himself from the bed, he dressed in a pair of worn trousers and pulled on an older linen shirt then slipped on his boots. It was going to be hot and grueling work. Sterling grabbed his old leather hat and hurried down to the dining room only to be brought up short to find his mother breaking her fast with Livia. That was very odd but he was certain there was a reason.

"Where is everyone else?"

"Cutting the grapes," his mother answered. He glanced at the clock. It was eight in the morning. "Already?"

"They start before the sun is up," Livia said.

"Before the sun?" He looked at his mother.

"Yes, dear. It is hot laborious work so they begin work at four-thirty or five. Torches are placed along the vines and lit so that the workers can see. When it is bright enough out, they are extinguished. When it becomes too hot to work outside, everyone retreats to the shade or in the barn."

If they started so early, then everyone had been at work for almost four hours. He had wanted to start work with them.

"Thank you, Mother, I will see you later. Enjoy your day, Livia." He grabbed a piece of bread then headed out of the house and made his way to the slope that led to the rows of grapes and paused to look down. At the far edge of the field, workers were bent over, cutting the bunches and dropping them into the baskets beside them. When he saw Caroline, he hurried to join her.

WHEN A SHADOW fell over Caroline, she looked up to see who it was and her heart swelled to see Sterling happy and relaxed. "Good morning, Lord Wyndham."

"Good morning." He then looked around. "I had not realized that there were so many that worked outside the house."

"Every servant in your household, with the exception of Cook, the butler, and those too old, are cutting grapes. You will likely not see a maid or a footman or a stable hand until the harvest is complete. We need everyone to get it done in a timely manner."

"Then who sees to the rest of the estate?" he asked with a frown.

"There are a few who will tend the animals and the rest of the crops and vegetable and herb gardens, but only so much as to make certain all is well and then they join us. Periodically servants will go to the stables, see that the chickens are still in their coop, check on the livestock, and then return here. Not everything is completely abandoned, they just do not receive as much attention."

"Do you have one of those that I could use?" he gestured to her vine knife.

Caroline arched an eyebrow. "You want to cut clusters of grapes."

"It is my vineyard. Should I not also participate?"

"That is why owners have servants," she reminded him. She had expected him only to supervise.

"Do you have another or do I need to ask someone else?"

She pulled her spare knife from her apron pocket and handed it to him.

He studied the curved blade then squatted beside Caroline. "Show me."

"Very well, Lord Wyndham." She then lifted a bunch of grapes, cut the stem, then gently dropped the bunch into the basket beside her. It was already half full. "It is that simple."

"It appears so, but I am certain it is more difficult than it appears."

She chuckled and returned to cutting the grapes, certain that by the time they reached the end of the row his back would ache and possibly the hand that gripped the knife would be cramping. In fact, she was certain of it because she had experienced it herself every year since her return and she had begun helping with the harvest.

"Thank you," he said a moment later, after he cut another bunch and dropped it into the basket.

"For what?" she asked.

"For making me realize where my anger came from and that I was being an arse." He chuckled. "I even apologized to my mother. You are good for me, Caroline."

Her heart stilled for a moment, but his words did not mean that he thought of her other than as a friend and lover.

"Nobody calls me to task as you do. Nobody argues with me, except maybe my brothers. Everyone else accepts my decisions, and behavior, without argument."

"Few people would quarrel with an earl," she said. "I tend to forget that you are one." He had become Sterling, a gentleman that she enjoyed being with.

"Maybe if the title was stripped away, I would find out what people actually thought of me."

"Or simply, what they thought, much like your relations treated you while we were in Stellenbosch," she said. "They would feel freer to offer an opinion."

"No doubt I would be greatly humbled." He chuckled.

"A little humbling is not a bad thing, Lord Wyndham."

When he lifted a bunch to cut, she noticed that the grapes were not as ripe as the others. "Not that one." Then explained why they would be left for now.

"I should not have assumed that all grapes would be fully ripe at the same time." He chuckled. "Afterall, not all apples fall from a tree on the same day."

She appreciated that he listened and when uncertain, asked. He wanted to learn and he allowed her to teach.

She would not have imagined the arrogant earl who had first arrived would have listened to anyone, not with the way he had demanded to see her father.

He had changed.

But so had she. The worry and tension that often accompanied her had lessened. Maybe it was because she had taken time away and enjoyed his company. But she also knew that once the harvest was done, she would have to return her attention to the other needs at Wyndview Farm, and she would likely welcome the work as it would serve as a distraction from what she would lose when Sterling sailed away.

CHAPTER THIRTY-NINE

WHEN ALL THE ripened bunches had been removed from those first vines, he lifted the basket and they moved past other servants cutting grapes to the vines that still had bunches and continued to cut. When the basket was full, he took it to the wagons and returned with an empty one. This continued until grapes had been cut from the entire row.

It was backbreaking work and the hand that clutched the knife began to ache. He was hot and his shirt was soaked with sweat and every time he bent over, it dripped off his nose. He was not alone because everyone was in a disheveled state. Even Caroline, who had her hat in place, had sweat dripping down her neck and her dress was damp.

Sterling stood and looked around. They were only halfway through the third row with dozens or more to go.

As much as he wanted to quit and rest, nobody else did, nor did they complain of the discomfort, so he got right back to work. Only when a horn blasted just as they reached the end of yet another row did everyone stop. There were some groans from the workers as they stood. Some placed palms against their lower backs, others stretched then wiped their brows with handkerchiefs.

Mr. Hallaway was standing on the back of the wagon. "No more cutting today." He yelled out. "Eat a meal, drink water, rest, and arrive in the barn in an hour." He then jumped down and two workers led the horses away, one following the other and both carried baskets filled with grapes.

"Cook will have fruits, bread, cheese, and cold meats waiting," Caroline said as she started to walk back toward the house, the other workers accompanying them.

He had assumed it would be food for them, but she meant everyone and he was surprised by the tables now on the terrace loaded with food and jugs of water as well as pitchers of lemonade.

The workers formed a line, filled plates then found a place in the shade.

Sterling went directly to the jug of water, filled a glass and drank deeply. Many of the workers had canteens with them that they drank from while they worked. If he had one, he would do the same. Caroline had shared hers, but he had been careful not to drink too much.

He then filled a plate, surprised that he was not as hungry as he thought he would be and selected more of the lighter fruits than the heavier cheeses. He then found a place to sit and relax near others, but not so close as to be intrusive since many looked at him with curiosity.

Caroline had disappeared into her home and he assumed she had decided to find a cooler place to rest, but she wasn't gone long before she returned and handed him an empty canteen with a smile.

"Thank you."

She then filled a plate and joined him. They ate in silence, which he did not mind. Those around them talked quietly and he could only assume that it was because they were more tired than he was since they had already been working hours before he arrived.

When the horn was blown again, everyone got up, returned their plates, cups and eating utensils to the tables, refilled their canteens, then started walking toward the barn.

THE FAMILIAR SIGHT of long tables, baskets of grapes, and empty buckets in the middle welcomed them and her father assigned jobs to each person as they entered. She was sent to the table to inspect the grapes for freshness before they were tossed in the large vat, but Caroline waited to find out where Sterling would be assigned, which turned out to be destemming. She then took a place at the opposite end of the table and across from him. She told herself that it was simply to observe and help if he needed assistance.

Except, he didn't need any guidance. Once the man next to Sterling explained that all he needed to do was pull the grapes from the stem and put them in the bucket, he set to work and only occasionally looked up, and at her.

She smiled in return and started inspecting the grapes to make certain they were ripe enough to use for wine, discarding those that were too old or too damaged.

He would smile at her too. No, it was a grin, as if he were fully enjoying himself.

Then again, it was the first day and by the time they were finished, he would likely collapse in his bed, too exhausted to visit hers.

Caroline sighed and returned to inspecting the grapes. She would miss him very much when he was gone.

There was less banter around the table than normally accompanied the harvest, but she assumed that it was because Sterling stood among them. If she did not know him as well as she did, she too would have been intimidated.

Maybe they would become more relaxed tomorrow. That was, assuming Sterling returned the second day of the harvest.

She glanced at him again and smiled. He would be back and return each day until all the grapes had been cut, destemmed, and crushed. Of that she was certain.

They worked quickly through the afternoon because the workers were experienced. After a few hours, everything that had been cut that day was now in the large, slightly angled vats for what came next.

Chapter Forty

Sterling straightened his fingers then made a fist, then straightened his fingers all over again. He needed to loosen his hands from the stiffness of holding the knife then gently pinching grapes while he removed them from the stems.

It was not a complaint and he looked forward to doing it again. But now that the grapes were in the vat, he waited to see who would be crushing them, and if he were to be honest with himself, he hoped that he could participate.

"Come along." Caroline tugged on his shirtsleeve and led him to an area where others had gathered and were removing their stockings and shoes and rolling up their trousers.

"Do I get to crush the grapes?" He hoped he did not sound too excited.

"Yes. Do what they do and I will return shortly."

He, like the others, sat on a bench and rolled up his trousers, removed his boots then stockings before he walked to a large basin where their feet and legs were washed. Caroline and a few other women came out from behind a screen. The bottom of her skirt was pulled up and tied at her waist, revealing the lower portion of her legs starting just below her knees.

His pulse increased, but he seemed to be the only man who noticed that the women were showing their legs.

He supposed that they were likely used to seeing such and in truth, he had barely glanced at the other women but he could not ignore Caroline's shapely caves and delicate ankles and feet.

It was odd to sink into the grapes and feel them crush between his toes. It was also harder than he had anticipated, almost like stepping into thick mud, denser than he thought it would be instead of rolling away and parting.

Caroline joined Sterling and pulled him into a line that faced another and everyone locked arms.

"What now?" he asked.

"We all stomp at the same time, and keeping our arms locked."

"Why?"

"Because it is easy to lose balance and we cannot have anyone falling into the grapes. Bare feet and legs only."

He nodded and understood. No doubt the more grapes that were crushed, the slipperier it would become.

"Just move with me. First right and then left as we move to one side of the vat until we reach the end and come back, opposite of those across from us."

He nodded and followed her lead stomping and crushing. The level of grapes they started with slowly decreased and by the time they were finished, all the juice had run into barrels, the skins and seeds left behind, and his thighs burned. Sterling was seriously concerned that he might not be able to step out of the vat and then down the ladder without his legs giving out.

"That is all for today," Hallaway called as the last sealed barrel was rolled down the ramp and into the cellar.

"It will be easier tomorrow," Caroline whispered as she stepped out ahead of him.

"I am not so certain," he laughed.

"Work will be divided by Father. Most will cut, but some will be sent to the barn to begin the work of destemming and crushing as buckets are filled. It is only the first day that everyone cuts."

"Where will we be?" he asked.

"That will be determined tomorrow, when my father decides

who will do what after he observed everyone today. Though, he may as your preference since you are the owner."

"That would be wherever you are," he whispered so that nobody could hear, but he did wonder if he would even be able to move tomorrow since almost every part of his body ached. Yet he also had never felt better.

CAROLINE DID NOT expect Sterling to come to her chamber that night. She was certain that he would collapse from exhaustion soon after he dined with his mother, which was why she took time with her bath.

It was one thing for her five-year-old daughter to bathe in the kitchen near the stove, but Caroline did not want to do so in a room that her father or brother could walk in. They may have no objection to bathing in the lake with the other men, but she preferred far more privacy.

After she pulled the hipbath into her chamber and filled it with hot water, Caroline sank down as far as possible. She was sore, which was not unusual following the first day of harvest. She knew that her legs and arms would be stiff when she woke tomorrow morning, but they all needed to endure for the days to come in order to make wine.

She was trying to decide if she should also wash her hair or just go to bed when there was a quiet knock on her door.

Her eyes flew open as she looked across the room.

Her heartbeat increased and Caroline pulled herself from the bath then wrapped a towel around her body before walking to the door and cracking it open just a little to see who was there.

"Are you going to let me come in?" he asked.

"Why are you not asleep?"

"Because I wanted to see you."

"Give me a moment." She then shut the door in his face and

rushed to her bed and pulled on her dressing gown and secured it at her waist before opening the door again.

"Have I disturbed you?" he asked with a frown as he entered.

He, too, had bathed because his hair was still damp.

"I was bathing." She gestured to the tub.

"Do not let me stop you from doing so." Sterling grinned. "I can even be of assistance in helping scrub the places that you might not be able to reach."

Her body warmed at the very idea of him assisting her, but that would be too intimate. Which was a strange thought since they had already seen each other completely unclothed.

"I thought for certain that you would be asleep by now," she said again.

"Because I am a pampered earl who is not used to hard work?" he countered.

"Because you are a gentleman who has never taken part in harvesting grapes before. It is hard work and no doubt several people who were beside us today are already asleep."

"Not you," he reminded her.

"Because I had duties when I returned home. Only after Livia was asleep was I able to take a bath."

He nodded and stalked toward her. "What were you wearing when you answered the door? You hid yourself."

"A towel," she answered.

"Is there anything on beneath your robe now?"

"That is a rather personal question, Lord Wyndham."

He grabbed the tie at her waist and pulled her forward until she was pressed against his body as his mouth devoured hers. Heat swept through her entire being.

His nimble fingers untied her dressing gown and pulled it open then brought his hands to her breasts before one hand caressed down her stomach until he reached her curls and then he touched her.

Caroline's knees nearly gave way and she had to clutch his shoulders to keep from collapsing. She thought they would move to the bed but he turned her away from him and brought her back against his chest. As he kissed her neck, he caressed a breast and teased a nipple while his other fingers brought waves and waves of pleasure until a release so powerful that swept from her womb and through her entire body. Only then did he sweep her up and place her on the bed.

She lay there with no strength to move and tried to catch her breath as Sterling stripped every piece of clothing from his body and came over to her. Caroline parted for him and gasped when he filled her with one thrust.

For a moment, he didn't move. She stared up and into his blue eyes and then Sterling kissed her. So gentle, sweet, and caring that her soul ached from the beauty of it and her heart swelled further with love. Then he moved, but slowly, deliberately, and watched her face and eyes until she once again reached the heights of passion that sent her soaring again, her body splintering right before he groaned and withdrew.

Only then did he fall away from her, breathing deeply.

Once she recovered, Caroline turned her head to look at him.

"I did just bathe."

He chuckled then swept her up in his arms before crossing to the tub and lowering her back into the water.

"Then I suppose it is my responsibility to bathe you all over again."

CHAPTER FORTY-ONE

THE NEXT MORNING, Sterling was awake before the sun. He was not going to be late again. In fact, he arrived before Caroline.

"Did you oversleep?" he asked quietly.

"No. I needed to take my daughter to your mother and break my fast," she returned. "I am surprised you are here so early."

"Why? Because I was late yesterday, or because I didn't retire until later than I should?"

He chuckled when she quickly looked around. He knew that nobody was close enough to hear his comments. Work hadn't even begun yet.

As the torches were lit, the workers took empty buckets and walked to the end of the next row of grapes and started cutting bunches as they had done the day before and he could not help but smile, even as his muscles protested from the overexertion of yesterday.

"You are the first person I have seen who was almost gleeful to be cutting grapes."

"That is because this is something that I always wanted to do."

"Then why did you not?" she asked.

"I did not live here," he reminded her.

"That is your fault. You have been an earl for almost seven years. You could have participated at any time."

"I wish I would have," he admitted almost to himself. "Honestly, I did not think about it. It was something I had wanted to do as a child and followed my father around, but I was always too young to participate."

"Is it everything that you had hoped it would be?" she asked with a laugh.

"It is more," he answered honestly. "Grapes and wine are in my blood, and that goes back generations. I should know every process from the planting of a root to loading the last barrel of wine in the cellar. It is so much more than reports and income."

Sterling surprised himself at the passion behind his words.

Trade Wynd and the earldom existed before the vineyard became the property of the Wynd family. The part of him that was English, the earl, understood his place in Society, the importance of their import-export business. The Dutch side of him, and only since he arrived at Wyndview Farm, felt the tradition and history of the vineyard deep in his soul.

Before he came here, his life was one of duty and Sterling knew what was expected of him. He took his seat in Parliament, gave careful thought before voting on issues, and built their business beyond what his father established, like those before him, which would leave them wealthier. He was content and had not given thought to whether he was happy or unhappy because that wasn't what was important. At least it wasn't supposed to be to the Earl of Wyndham.

His father had taught him what was important and that was the earldom and Trade Wynd and that was all that mattered. At Wyndview Farm, he had discovered so much more and his mother had been right to make certain that he remembered who he had been and who the family had been before. He would likely be sailing away a changed man and uncertain when he would return.

Sterling glanced at Caroline who was bent over and cutting the stem of a bunch of grapes. He wanted to take her with him but was uncertain if she would go.

Once enough buckets had been filled for the vats, Hallaway selected workers who had been cutting grapes and instructed them to go to the barn, leaving the rest to toil in the sun. As Caroline remained to cut, so did he since Hallaway hadn't given him instructions on what he should do.

The rest of the day was spent much like the first, sharing conversations with Caroline and some of the others around him. However, when it came time to crush the grapes, and after they had shared the midday meal, he had been sent to the barn to help with the barrels. First, positioning them at the lowest point of the vats to collect the juice that flowed from an opening, surprised by how much a vat of grapes produced. He was then shown how to seal the barrel, then rolled it to the cellar and with the help of others, lifted it to a shelf so that it could rest on its side as the wine fermented while waiting to be shipped.

A CHILL SWEPT over Caroline's body after Sterling had left her bed and returned to the house.

For nearly two months, they had spent the days harvesting grapes, side by side, teasing and talking, and at night, he came to her after everyone had retired.

They were not always intimate. Sometimes she simply lay in his arms as they talked of their past, what his life was like in England. He talked about his brothers and his education. He described some of the debates in Parliament and the issues he cared most about.

Caroline did not have anything of interest to share with him. She was the daughter of an estate manager who had gone to London for a Season because her grandfather was a baron.

He insisted that her life was not so simple, she claimed that it was and it pained her not to tell him the full truth about what she had become.

Some of their passion has lessened, but tenderness grew. They weren't as hurried but took their time in caresses and learning each other's body in a way that only heightened her pleasure, a slow build to release that left her satiated in ways she had never imagined.

These past two months, the days and the nights, she would cherish for the rest of her life. She had loved again, and she would not regret one moment after he was gone no matter how much missing Sterling hurt.

What saddened her, and likely the reason for the chill, was tonight may have been the last that they shared with the other. Sterling did not say so, but the harvest was complete, the barrels of wine were stored and there was nothing left to do except to clean the baskets and the vats and store everything that was not needed until next year.

They were not needed for that, which meant that Sterling would want to meet with her father.

That frightened her more than anything.

So much could go wrong. Her chill might as well be foreboding and Caroline might not breathe again until he was safely away. She might suffer from an aching heart from the loss but at least her family's position would be secure.

She was also ill from guilt, as well as heartache.

She was so deeply in love with him, but she kept secrets. Maybe she would have confessed the truth to him or even shared her emotions. The closest that he had come to admitting any emotion for her was when he proclaimed that she had made him a better man and that he would miss her, and that he had come to Wyndview Farm because of Trade Wynd but had discovered someone he deeply cared about, a friend that he hadn't known he needed.

Not a love, but a friend and lover.

There had been so many opportunities to tell Sterling the truth, but the fear of what his reaction would be was too frightening to contemplate. She had argued with herself these past weeks that he was more understanding now than he had been when he arrived and maybe if she explained the difficulties she had faced, and her father, that he would accept that she had needed to take over the duties of the estate manager, but the risk of losing everything kept her from confessing.

Now, it was likely too late.

Exhaustion eventually took over, but that did not stop her from dreaming—nightmares mostly of her fears visited and her world crumbled and by the time she finally rose from her bed, she was more exhausted than when she had fallen asleep.

So much had been neglected since Sterling arrived and during the harvest that she could not put those concerns off for another day, so she dressed and made her way to her father's small office and made a list of everything she needed to accomplish. But, as she was writing, she remembered that a list had already been prepared and she had tucked it away in the office that Sterling used when he had returned and she had been afraid of being caught.

Had he found it? If he had, did he assume that she had only written from her father's instructions?

Caroline's stomach tightened.

She did not want him to leave hating her. Had he remained the unpleasant Earl of Wyndham whom she would not have associated with, Caroline's conscience likely would not have suffered because of her duplicity, but that had not been the case, and she feared that she would be left with second-guessing her decisions in the days to come.

CHAPTER FORTY-TWO

THE DAYS HAD been enjoyable, even when his body ached while he cut and stomped grapes and when he lost sleep so that he could be alone with Caroline.

Today, he woke up with a heavy heart. His time at Wyndview Farm would soon come to an end. There were only two things left to do. The first, and his reason for coming here in the first place, was the long-awaited meeting with Hallaway. The second, he needed to tell Caroline that he had fallen in love with her and that he did not want to live without her in his life then ask her to marry him.

What if she declined his request?

What if she did not love him as he loved her?

She had been clear that they would be lovers and that she would not be a mistress, but certainly, her emotions had grown just as his.

But, what if they hadn't?

That was his biggest fear and why he had said nothing these past few months because he did not want what was left of his time at Wyndview Farm to be ruined with heartache and rejection.

He had been a coward, and still was, and willingly admitted to that fact, but now was the time, whether she accepted him or not.

Sterling had never been afraid of anything in his life until now.

He had also never been in love.

"You seem troubled this morning, Sterling," his mother greeted him when he joined her to break their fast. "I thought your mood would be excellent now that the harvest is done and you can put your mind to the reason you came here to begin with."

Did he confide in her?

He had come to understand his mother more. They talked each evening over dinner and he *listened*, for a change. Except he had never really confided in anyone something so personal and was not comfortable even telling his mother.

"I do have an appointment to meet with Hallaway," he answered.

"Is that what disturbs you?" she asked with a frown.

"No," he answered. "I am certain that now that his mind is off grapes and wine, he will be able to answer the other questions."

He filled his cup with tea and looked over the various breakfast dishes that had been prepared, not truly hungry. There was too much on his mind. It wasn't the estate. It was Caroline and the fear of rejection.

"What is on your mind, dear?" his mother asked softly.

"I am thinking about what needs to be done. What I need to do next."

"Do any of those decisions involve Caroline?"

He glanced over at his mother and narrowed his eyes. "Why would you ask?"

She chuckled and set her teacup aside. "It is obvious that you have formed a tendre for her."

How could she possibly know?

"It has been whispered about by the servants of how the two of you worked side-by-side every day of the harvest, that the two of you spoke quietly and there were times that Caroline blushed, and you would laugh. Such teasing usually only occurs when there is attraction." She arched a brow. "Or even love."

He did not want to have this discussion with his mother.

"She would make a fine wife, Sterling."

He already knew that and did not need his mother to convince him.

"Follow your heart, Sterling. If you think with your head, you might talk yourself out of love or let fear control your decision."

"I promise to make decisions with my heart *and* my head," he said.

"Just your heart," she reiterated.

"I do not even know if Caroline loves me."

"I do know that you love Caroline." It wasn't a question but a statement.

Except, she never claimed that Caroline loved him, which was his main concern.

Sterling finished his tea, took a last bit of his breakfast and stood. "I will see you later, Mother."

He then made his way to the office for his appointment with Hallaway only to find his son, William, waiting instead.

"Where is your father?"

"He…well…he…there were matters…um…"

"What matters?" Sterling asked.

"He is recovering," William blurted out.

"Recovering? From what?"

"The, erm, harvest takes more out of him…he is not as young…"

That had been a concern. Not that Hallaway was frail, but he was getting on in years, a bit eccentric, and only worried about the grapes.

"How long have you been back at Wyndview Farm?"

"Approximately nine months."

Sterling nodded. "I assume you attended university."

"Yes. My father wanted that for me and my grandfather arranged it."

"Why did you return when you could have done almost anything you wanted in England?"

"I did remain there for over a year after. I attended a Season. I went to house parties. But I was not wealthy nor titled and when my grandfather passes, my cousin will become the next baron, so friends soon fell away as I pursued areas of trade."

"What would those be?"

"I began to apprentice for a vintner. I know wine. Or I know wine from the Cape Colony. Father had been teaching me about planting, harvest, how to care for the vines before I left for university so I assumed I would do well in that trade."

"Did you?" Though, he presumed that he did not since William had returned to Wyndview Farm.

"I would have, except I did not like being a merchant of wine and discovered what I really wanted was to make wine like my father so I came home."

Sterling leaned back in his chair and studied William. "Have you learned anything more since you returned, such as the duties of the estate manager or were you only interested in grapes?"

William's face colored with embarrassment and he grew uncomfortable.

"To be honest, Lord Wyndham, I had hoped to learn all that I could so that when my father retired that I might be able to take his place as your estate manager."

William was still young for such a duty, but since he was already learning, and Sterling did not anticipate that Hallaway would retire all that soon, he saw no reason not to consider him. "I will keep that in mind when the time comes."

"Thank you, Lord Wyndham."

With that out of the way, Sterling leaned forward. "Since you have been assisting your father, maybe you can answer some questions that I have."

His eyes grew wide. "Yes, of course."

An hour later, William walked from his office having answered all of Sterling's questions. He could easily forgo the meeting with Hallaway, but he did want to have one appointment with Hallaway and that was to instruct him to train William and when the time came, he would evaluate the son as a possible replacement.

The more he thought about it, the more irritated Sterling became. Hallaway was his estate manager, therefore he should have been present for their scheduled meeting. Yes, William had offered a reason for his father's absence, but Sterling knew when a man was making up an excuse, therefore, Sterling decided to search for Hallway himself, but not on foot. The estate was too large and it would take too much time, so he made his way to the stables.

CAROLINE NEEDED TO check that oranges were being harvested along with the lemons, as well as what remained of the peaches this late in the year. The pomegranates were ready to be sold, now that they had taken what they needed from the estate, but arrangements had to be made to take the excess fruit to be sold to the ships that stopped to replenish their supplies. They had good luck the past two years and even though there wasn't much increase in the coffers, it was better than letting it rot because there was too much to be eaten by those who lived on the estate.

Though she supposed that the fruit should be crated and then taken to the Trade Wynd ship that would take Sterling back to England.

Yes, that was where the fruit would go and she would give instructions to one of the groundskeepers.

She would then need to meet with another to make certain that the fields would soon be plowed so that the wheat and oats could be planted and then the barley.

All of this included taking a tour with the groundskeeper who oversaw these areas and who had once reported to her father.

She also needed to meet with the maids who took care of the kitchen gardens, the vegetable gardens and the herb gardens. The days had been hot and without much rain and she needed to make certain everything was receiving enough water.

The stables were another matter, as well as checking on the chickens, ducks…there was much but Caroline could not make herself leave the house.

Her nerves were on edge because her father and William were meeting with Sterling.

All she could pray was that Sterling accepted her father's eccentricities of being focused on grapes and that William's answers to the questions were enough to satisfy Sterling and leave no concerns.

However, if he insisted on his father answering since he was the estate manager, they could all be in trouble and that was what worried her.

Even as early as this morning she begged him to review the reports but he waved away her concern with, "You worry too much, Caro."

Maybe she did, but she had to worry for both of them since he wasn't concerned.

She was going to be ill.

In retrospect, she should have just sat down with Sterling and explained and made an argument for her brother to take over her father's position, beg forgiveness for her deception, and hope that he understood, but it was too late for that now.

Unable to remain in her house, but not willing to stray too far until after the meeting was complete, Caroline made her way to the kitchen where she met with Cook for more meal planning. However, it wasn't completed because they did not know when Sterling would leave. They would not need as much food, nor as many courses once Sterling was gone so it was difficult to plan.

Caroline next met with the maids to make certain the dusting, sweeping, polishing, and laundry that had been neglected during the grape harvest would soon be completed so that everything was back to a normal schedule.

When she stepped out onto the terrace, she walked toward the gardens that she had intended to weed right after Sterling had arrived but Lady Wyndham had kept her from doing so. But, as she neared it, noting that the weeds were now twice as bad, she remembered the cobra that had stared at her daughter from within. She stopped walking and slowly backed up, then returned home and wrote a note so that she remembered to warn the groundskeeper before he assigned someone to remove the weeds.

When she heard their door open and close, she rushed out to meet her father and William to find out how the meeting had gone but the only person there was William.

"How did the meeting with Lord Wyndham go?" she asked and then nearly held her breath.

"Well, considering."

Her chest tightened. "Considering what?"

"Father was not present."

"Where was he?" Caroline cried.

William shrugged. "He wasn't with the grapes, in the barn, the cellar, and not even with his experimental grapes. I would have kept looking for him but I did not want to arrive late for our appointment."

"Have you seen Father at all today?"

"When we broke our fast. I assumed he was going where he always did when he left."

This was not something they needed right now. "What was Wyndham's reaction to father's absence? What did you even tell him?"

She listened patiently to everything William told her and only breathed a sigh of relief that Sterling may have been mildly irritated but received William well. Still, she wasn't so foolish as to think that he would not still want to meet with her father and if he were missing, she was afraid of where he might be.

"He is probably with Mother. It is what he does at the end of the harvest. Go find him and bring him back. I want to know why he did not meet Wyndham as promised." Except, she was afraid she already did have the answer.

CHAPTER FORTY-THREE

STERLING STEPPED INTO the shade of the stables to ask for a horse when a lad of no more than ten ran up to him.

He was one of the younger stable boys but that didn't mean he could not do the job.

"How can I help you, Lord Wyndham?"

"I need a horse saddled."

"Right away. I will bring you the horse, but someone bigger than me will have to saddle it," he answered seriously as if Sterling would not have already known that. The saddle probably weighed more than the boy.

"What you need that for?"

That was a rather impertinent question. Nobody ever asked him why he wanted a horse in England. They just got one. Still, Sterling answered, "I need to find Hallaway and thought it would be quicker if I rode."

"I know where he is."

This took him by surprise. "Where is he?"

"He is with the grapes," the boy answered cheerfully.

"The harvest is over," her reminded the lad.

"Mr. Hallaway is always with the grapes, every day all year."

That made no sense. Hallaway was his estate manager and had many other duties besides the grapes and wine.

Sterling frowned and stepped from the stable, confused by what he had been told.

Maybe that was why William knew so much. Maybe he had already been acting as the estate manager. With that thought, Sterling returned back inside and approached the boy.

"If Hallaway is always with the grapes, who is managing the estate?" he asked and waited for the boy to name William.

"That would be Mrs. Sutcliffe."

"You mean William, her brother," Sterling corrected.

"No. William follows her a lot but it is Mrs. Sutcliffe who—"

"—Johnny, who are you talking to and what are you telling him?"

Sterling looked up to find an older stable hand approaching with concern. He had worked next to the man when they were cutting grapes—Lyle was his name if Sterling remembered correctly.

"I was just telling Lord Wyndham about Mrs. Sutcliffe."

"You are mistaken." There was more warning than correction in Lyle's tone.

Did everyone know that Caroline was doing the duties of the estate manager?

Wasn't her being her father's secretary, mother's companion, temporary housekeeper, and sometimes gardener enough? Maybe that was why they were confused—because she did so much because everyone knew that women were not estate managers.

"Thank you," he said. "I will not be needing a horse now."

Sterling stepped back outside and wondered what to do next.

The boy had to be wrong. If Caroline was the estate manager, he would know. She would have told him.

Once again Sterling returned inside.

"If Mr. Hallaway is not with the grapes, where might he be?"

"Oh, that's easy," Johnny answered with a grin. "The cemetery just down the road by the old church."

Bloody hell! What was going on at Wyndview Farm?

"I believe I will need that horse after all."

IT TOOK ALL afternoon of walking the estate with the groundskeeper and taking notes before Caroline knew everything that needed to be accomplished. She then discussed those with the groundskeeper and in the order in which they should be done, her concerns, and solutions. With her notebook in hand, she returned to her house to write more detailed notes that would be needed when she prepared her next quarterly report to send to Sterling. She also needed to update the records on how many barrels of wine they had produced this harvest and the anticipation for next year. Those amounts were all fresh in her mind since the last barrel had been stored yesterday. She had just failed to make note of it because she had been tired and then Sterling had come to her room.

By the time she had finished, neither William nor her father had returned and it worried her. So much so that she had to search for them herself, only to find her father walking back with William, a bottle in his hand.

Caroline groaned and rushed forward.

"Caroline," her father greeted happily. "It was an excellent harvest. I was just telling your mother all about it. She would be happy, and proud of you."

"Come along, Father. Let us get you inside."

She and her brother ushered her father around the main house and then onto the terrace so that they could enter their own home.

"I will brew some tea. Very strong tea," Caroline said and rushed to the kitchen. When she returned, she took the bottle from him and handed him the tea.

At least he wasn't too deep in his cups, just enough that it put him in a pleasant mood. She supposed it could be worse.

"Father, you need to listen to me," she began.

"I listen, Caro. I always listen, but you do not hear me."

"Oh, Father, but I do. You just refuse to understand."

"What would you have me understand?"

"It is imperative that you meet with Wyndham tomorrow. You must also be able to answer any question he has about the estate."

"William met with him," her father dismissed.

"William is not the estate manager, you are," she reminded her father. "If you do not meet with him, there is a very good chance that you will be sacked. If that happens, you will never be able to work with the grapes again. You will not be able to tend the vines that Mother cultivated. They will belong to another. We might even be forced to return to England and you will not be able to visit mother any longer. Do you understand me?"

He drew in a heavy breath before he blew it out. "I understand, Caro. I will do as you ask, but only for you and your mother's vines."

"Why wait until tomorrow when we can discuss the estate now?"

Caroline whipped around to find Sterling standing at the entry to the sitting room. His blue eyes were hard and jaw tight, looking very much the gentleman from that first day he had arrived at Wyndview Farm.

Behind him stood William, helplessly holding his arms out.

Her heart sank to her stomach.

"Good evening, Lord Wyndham," Caroline greeted him.

"Are you drunk, Hallaway?" Sterling demanded.

"Tipsy, perhaps."

Why couldn't he claim to be drunk? Then maybe Sterling would put off this interview.

"Then there is no reason why you and Mrs. Sutcliffe cannot return with me to the house. I have a few questions regarding the estate."

"I thought William answered them all," her father returned.

Oh, she did not need her father to be difficult. He had just promised her that he would be prepared...*tomorrow*.

"He is not the estate manager. You are the one who currently holds that title."

Her father was going to be sacked and they would all be forced to leave. It was exactly as she feared.

"Come along." He looked at Caroline, his blue eyes boring into hers. "You as well."

Oh God. He knew.

CHAPTER FORTY-FOUR

BETRAYAL ATE AT his soul.

How could he have been so wrong about Caroline?

She had lied to him from the moment they had met. While he could understand her duplicity at first, he thought they had become close enough that she could tell him anything and he would understand, even the truth about her father.

Instead, she'd said nothing and pretended that she was simply a daughter who assisted her father.

He harrumphed and took a deep drink of brandy while he stood at the window and kept an eye on the terrace below, awaiting the return of his *lover*.

She'd made a fool of him while he had fallen in love with her.

Her duplicity hurt deeper than if someone would have plunged a knife into his heart and Sterling was not certain what he should do or how he should even react. However, when he finally saw Caroline and William return to their home with Hallaway, he decided not to put off his plans until tomorrow and followed. He had not even bothered to knock but entered. He did own the home. When William saw him and started to object, he motioned for him to be silent then walked to the sitting room and listened as Caroline begged her father to prepare for the meeting.

She was scared.

When he returned to his house and office, Sterling assumed they followed. When he stepped behind his desk, he noted that they both hovered near the door.

"Please take a seat."

Caroline drew in a deep breath then did as he asked.

Her father, not nearly as concerned, followed.

He then picked up the list that he had found in his top desk drawer, written in Caroline's neat penmanship, outlining the schedule of what needed to be taken care of after the grapes were harvested and the juice sealed in the barrels.

He handed it to Hallaway. "Did you instruct your daughter to prepare this schedule and tell her what must be done in which order?"

Hallaway frowned, then looked at Caroline, his blue eyes full of confusion.

Sterling set it aside.

He then pulled out the parchment with the list of questions he had asked William.

"How much wheat was harvested last year and why do you believe we should plant more?"

Hallaway stared at him blankly and Sterling knew instantly that his estate manager could not answer so he asked the next question, and the next, and the next, without any response from the man he paid to manage his estate.

"Mr. Hallaway, I find that I must relieve you of your position as my estate manager. You have failed in your duties; therefore, you will no longer work for me."

"No," Hallaway argued. "I must tend to your grapes and make the wine."

Sterling frowned. Did Hallway not grasp the precarious position he had put himself in? Yes, the grapes were important but so was the entire estate.

His mind was failing and he was forgetful of nearly everything except winemaking. That was what one of the men who took care of the vines finally confided in him.

"A senility," another had said.

Something that both daughter and son had hidden from him.

He glanced at Caroline who understood the full weight of his words because she had lost all color, but he would discuss her transgressions with her later.

"You may go, Mr. Hallaway."

He stood, as did Caroline.

"Not you, Mrs. Sutcliffe. We still have matters to discuss."

For the first time since he came across the two, Hallaway appeared concerned.

"Go on, Father," she said quietly.

"It has been a most interesting day," Sterling said once they were alone.

He did not think Caroline could get any paler but she did.

If he were the same person who had arrived at Wyndview Farm, this matter would be dealt with in a cold, efficient manner, but he had changed, though a part of him wished that he would not have so that this would be easier.

"I toured the estate today, on my own. It is something that I should have done before now, but there was no need. Or, I did not believe that there was one since Wyndview Farm had been prospering under your father's guidance."

Sterling got up from his desk and walked to the sideboard and poured a glass of brandy. And offered her one.

"No thank you."

"Are you certain?"

Caroline gulped and nodded.

He took a drink, his back to her.

He still loved her and hated that he did. How could he still care when he knew that she had lied to him for weeks.

Did he even truly know her?

Perhaps that was what angered him the most. While he was falling in love with her, Caroline was dishonest about who she was. Had their friendship been real or was she just doing what she thought necessary, including becoming his love, so he would never learn the truth?

Sterling returned to the desk and settled back in his seat and took a sip of his brandy. "I now know what my mother meant when she said that you have more responsibility than I knew and that you deserved a holiday. I assumed she meant being a mother along with everything else. That wasn't it, was it, Caroline?"

She did not answer but glanced down at her hands.

"And now, after today, I have come to realize that not only are you the companion, housekeeper, and sometimes gardener, but you are also the estate manager for Wyndview Farm, is that correct?

"Yes," she finally answered.

"In fact, you might as well be the Mistress of Wyndview because you manage not only the estate, but the house, everything inside and out." His voice rose. "Is that what you truly want? Is that what you were hoping to gain?"

Caroline looked up, her brown eyes hard and her once pale cheeks flamed red.

"I have never aspired to be the Mistress of Wyndview. I assisted where I was needed. Whether you approve or not is not my concern. Your mother was happy with my position here."

"She does not own the estate, Caroline, I do."

"Oh, I am aware, Lord Wyndham."

"What was your game? What were your intentions? Did you have an ulterior motive for becoming my friend? My lover?"

"You think so little of me?"

Sterling truly did not know what to think and was still coming to terms with the revelations of today. But, instead of answering her, he shrugged, which was not well done of him.

She straightened and glared, right before she slapped him soundly across the cheek.

"I had no ulterior motive for anything that I did, Lord Wyndham. Did you?"

"What does that mean?"

"If you think so little of me, then maybe it was because I meant so little to you. A dalliance to keep you entertained before you sailed away." She turned and stalked to the door. "I hope that it made your stay at Wyndview Farm enjoyable." Then she was gone.

Sterling hurried after her. "I am not done with our discussion, Mrs. Sutcliffe."

She whipped around and glared at him. "I very much am, and I will be going. It is my daughter's bedtime and I must see to her." With that she turned and stomped to the door leading to the terrace before she turned. "If you would have but asked, I would have explained, but I will not tolerate being demeaned in such a manner, especially after...it shows that I was mistaken about you."

"As I was about you, Mrs. Sutcliffe."

Sterling stood there for a moment then turned around and strolled back to his office, settled behind his desk and lifted the glass of brandy. He may be angry and hurt over her deception, but there was no woman that he admired more.

He took a sip of the brandy and closed his eyes as it burned down his throat. He also still loved her. It was a shame that he could never trust her and maybe that was why he had conde-scended to her to coolly—so that she would hate him and then he would never know if she could have loved him or if she would have rejected his offer of marriage had it been made.

CAROLINE STORMED INTO her house and then her chamber and slammed the door and started to pace. How dare he accuse her of wanting to be the Mistress of Wyndview? How dare he accuse her of having an ulterior motive for becoming his lover?

Caroline may not have wanted brandy when she was with Sterling but she certainly wanted one now and marched out of her chamber and went to her office where she grabbed the decanter and a glass before returning to her room and shutting the door again.

She poured then took a deep drink and gasped at the burn before taking a more moderate sip.

She knew why he was angry. He had every right to be because she had not been honest with him. However, that did not give him the right to treat her with such cold disdain. It was almost as if he hated her, which made her question whether he had ever cared at all.

Had their forming a friendship come about because he had nothing better to do while he was waiting for the harvest? As for being his lover, was that for the same reason? She knew that men enjoyed bedsport. She had heard rumors before she was married and understood it fully once she was a bride. Was that all she had been to him?

To think she had fallen in love with him!

"Was it all worth it to you?"

Caroline whipped around to find Sterling standing in the doorway that led to the terrace. He had not knocked again and walked in as if he owned the place. It didn't matter that he did, he should have had more respect.

"Was what worth it? And I would appreciate you knocking next time."

"At least, tell me why."

"Why what?" She wasn't certain what he was asking.

"Why you took over for your father."

"I assumed that you already had that information." It had been only a matter of time before someone said something and she was lucky that it hadn't occurred before now.

"I would like to hear the reasons from you." His tone was calmer and she dare not assume he understood.

"Because he could not any longer." It was the truth and she was tired of deceptions. Enough damage had already been done and matters certainly could not get worse.

"Then why did he not just resign?"

"It is not that simple, Lord Wyndham." It was impossible to call him Sterling any longer. That relationship was over and it pained her greatly.

"Explain it to me, Caroline."

She turned away at hearing her name on his lips and fought the tears of everything that had been lost today. "What does it matter? You have made up your mind and sacked my father. If it did, you would have asked when I was back at the house. Instead, you treated me as if...as if you had no heart, much like you behaved when you first arrived."

He sucked in a breath at the insult, but she did not care.

"I am sorry for that," he offered. "I truly would like to know."

There was sincerity in his eyes and in his tone, but did she trust that it was true?

Did it matter?

"When my parents first came here, they saw it as an adventure. A new experience. And, like your parents, mine were very happy here. It was my mother who took the most interest in the grapes. To father, it was another crop to manage along with the others. He understood the importance and that the wine needed to be superior or Wyndview Farm would fail, which he could not allow."

"May I have one of those?" He pointed to her glass of brandy.

"I will return in a moment."

Caroline left to retrieve a glass and tried to find more composure before she returned and handed it to him.

When she didn't pour the brandy, he did.

"The vineyard was my mother's favorite place. They enjoyed spending time there together and she was the one who started experimenting with grafting roots. She would spend hours while Father saw to the other duties required of his position."

She paused and sipped before she continued. It wasn't so much that it was difficult to talk to Wyndham, because she was used to having conversations with him. It was the fact that he was watching and waiting to disapprove that put her on edge. Still, she pushed through so that he would know her reasons, even if he never understood.

"As you already know, my mother died while I was sailing back to the Cape Colony. What I also found when I arrived was my father in deep mourning."

Those were difficult days, for her and for him.

"Your mother was concerned, obviously, but she also had patience. She knew that it was a difficult time and that he would return to his duties fully or so she had hoped."

"Yet he did not," Sterling reminded her, his tone cold.

"No, he did not," she admitted. "He would have resigned except he was anchored here because Mother loved it so and she is buried down the road."

"Are you saying that your father fell into a melancholy state?"

"He was in mourning as any husband or wife would be after losing their spouse. It was no more than that, or so I thought at the time. I assumed that he had just decided that there was no point in working as hard. He only had himself to provide for. That is, until I returned. I encouraged him to resume all his duties and that if he did not, your mother would write to you and that you would likely be sacked. I did not know at the time that you never read letters from her."

She took a deep breath then sipped the brandy before she could continue.

"As it was also January, I reminded him of how much mother would be disappointed if he allowed the grapes to die on the vine without being harvested for wine. That is what motivated him the most and I hoped that by the time the harvest was complete that he would have had a change of heart and resume all his duties. Your mother thought the same."

"He did not?" Sterling asked.

Oh, she wanted to believe that Sterling did care and was trying to understand, but after the way he had spoken to her at the house, she feared what he might say when she was done. Yet, she continued.

"No, he did not. I tried everything that I could but he only cared about the grapes and wine. I had told him that if he did not return to his other duties that he was likely to lose his position.

He asked me what other duties, as if he had forgotten, and I came to realize that he had. A senility had set in and he only cared about the grapes or anything my mother had touched, and the rest well, was not his responsibility, as if it had never been. Therefore, I was left with no choice but to step in and assume his responsibilities while I tried to remind him of everything he had managed before. My biggest fear was that you would learn but your mother assured me that you would never visit and never know. I trusted in that."

He nodded, sadness in his blue eyes and maybe he was understanding.

"Your mother also did not feel it was necessary to tell you because the estate was being managed just as well as it had been under my father's supervision." She took a deep breath, straightened her shoulders and lifted her chin. "That is how I became your estate manager."

He just stood there and stared at her and it became very hard to hold onto her false confidence.

"So when I arrived, you decided just to lie to me."

"I did not see it so much as a lie as an omission," she reluctantly admitted. "We assumed that you would tour the estate, review the reports and accounting and leave. You did not."

"Had your father met with me when I asked him to and provided me with the answers I needed, I may have left fully ignorant of what was occurring on my own estate."

Caroline drew in a shaky breath. He was still angry. He had only appeared calmer.

"My intention had only been to remain a sennight, or fortnight at the most."

"I am aware."

"It was my mother who kept me here, and your father by avoiding me, that led to my discovery of what you were doing."

Oh, if only her father had just reviewed the reports, been able to remember, and care what was written within, had his meeting with Wyndham and answered all the questions correctly, he would have been gone before...before everything.

❧ ❧

CHAPTER FORTY-FIVE

HE UNDERSTOOD HER reasons and her actions but he couldn't forgive her deceptions.

"You could have told me at any time while we traveled, visited Boulder Beach, hiked to Table Mountain. Then there were the days we worked side-by-side during the harvest, or maybe when we lay in your bed!"

She drew back as if struck.

"Yes, I can see where you did not have ample opportunity."

He pushed long fingers through his hair and sipped the brandy.

"Did it ever occur to you to explain? What did you fear would happen?"

"Happen?" she repeated. "When you first arrived you were so unapproachable, rigid, cold that I feared…I feared that my father would be sacked and Livia and I would lose our home. We had nowhere else to go. If we returned to England, a home with my grandfather would only be temporary. He had made that clear after my husband died. He was willing to allow me and Livia to live with him while Peter was off at war, but when he was killed, I became my father's responsibility and no longer his. That is the reason I returned here, and I wanted to be with my parents. If he allowed us, my father, William, Livia, and myself to return to his home, it would again be temporary. Then what would we do? At my father's age, he was likely not to find another position.

William had little experience, and my skills are for a position that is only allowed for the employment of men."

He pulled back at her impassioned speech. He had not expected her to so vehemently defend her reasons.

"Remember when I told you that the reasons your servants avoided you was because they did not know what to expect? I reminded you that you had never needed to worry where your next meal may come from or where you might live so you couldn't understand their concerns or fear of being sacked. I was not only speaking about them but myself as well. Not just for myself, but Livia."

He remembered. He had been taken aback at her rebuke of his privilege.

Her eyes watered and Caroline turned away from him and wiped the tears away.

"Perhaps that is true when we first met, and I can understand your reluctance to confide in me, but we grew closer and you still said nothing."

"By then I feared you would be even angrier at not having been told right away and I was correct."

"You should have told me," he ground out.

"Yes, I should have and in retrospect, wish I would have, but the longer I avoided telling you, the more difficult it became. I was afraid of what you would do or say and now I know and it is worse than my original fears." Tears filled her eyes and she did not try to hide them any longer. "I was desperate to protect my father, our place at Wyndview Farm. If he lost the position or if you did not accept William, we would be destitute. I needed to protect my daughter." She practically yelled.

He turned away and strolled to the window looking out as he sipped his brandy.

He did understand, but had she ever truly cared about him, or had she done what she felt necessary to protect her family. Was that why she became his lover?

While he was falling in love with her, she may have only

been trying to keep him happy until he was gone.

Sterling's heart clenched, the pain nearly agonizing, and perhaps now he understood why some of his colleagues swore off love.

CAROLINE WAS NOT certain what to expect from him next and as much as she wanted to ask him to leave, she couldn't. Not when what became of her family was still held in the balance.

"Was it all pretend?" he asked quietly then turned to face her. "Was any of it real or were you just afraid of being caught?"

"It was all real and I cherished the time that we spent together."

"Yet you continued to lie even after we became close."

"I did not lie. I simply did not tell you."

"A deception all the same." He shook his head. "I had fallen in love with you, did you know that?"

Caroline gasped and stepped back. Her heart started pounding.

She never dreamed that he would care so deeply for her. She had simply assumed she had been the only one to fall in love.

"I was going to ask you to marry me and take you back to England. You and Livia."

Oh God, what had she done? If only…She closed her eyes. It was too late for second-guessing decisions already made that had altered her future.

"Except, I am not certain if I fell in love with you are just the image you presented of yourself."

"It was one secret," she whispered "One."

"Yet, it is my trust that has been lost and I am not certain it can be regained." He drained the brandy from his glass.

No matter what she said he would not believe her. Her deception had destroyed everything, but she had to be honest, even if she had not been until today.

"I did fall in love with you, Sterling. I was never going to tell you because I never dreamed you would feel the same. I accepted that I was your temporary lover while you were here. You never once let on that you cared beyond what we shared," she reminded him. "I knew that I would be forced continue on, just as I had to do after my husband was killed because Livia is the only person that I truly have. I did what was necessary to protect her and I would do the same again."

"If you loved me as much as you say, you would not have deceived me."

"Then maybe you never truly knew me."

"How could I have when you had not been honest?"

Her heart ached, but he was correct. She had been deceptive and it was her fault that she lost him. Maybe she had never really had him. He may claim love but he could not begin to understand her position—that she had to protect family—protect Livia and she could only do that by providing a safe home.

Caroline also could not accept that he loved her. He would not have flung accusations at her without first attempting to understand. Instead, he had turned cold, a heart of stone.

"I wish you a safe journey, Lord Wyndham. My family and I will await your decision as to what becomes of us."

"Very well." He offered a swift nod then turned and left her home.

Once he was gone, Caroline flung herself onto her bed and cried until exhaustion overtook her.

CHAPTER FORTY-SIX

S TERLING PACKED HIS belongings and had them delivered to the entry then asked that someone take him to the ship.

He had not slept last night but stood at his window and at times watched Caroline's window.

Her lights burned until the early morning hours before they were extinguished.

Did guilt keep her awake or fear?

He wanted to believe that she loved him, but she had not been honest and deceived him. How could he trust anything that she said?

Had it been something personal or private, he likely would not have minded. But the secrets she held affected the entirety of Wyndview Farm. In fact, every employee, including his mother, kept the truth from him—their loyalty to Caroline.

That he could not forgive, nor could he trust her, no matter how much he had fallen in love with her.

It had to be love, otherwise his heart would not ache with such intensity.

"You are leaving?" his mother asked as she came down the stairs.

"I have the information I came for and it is time."

"What of Caroline?"

"What of her?"

"I had thought…"

"It matters not."

"She did not lie to you," his mother insisted, just as Caroline had.

"She deceived me, which is the same."

"It is not. She had her reasons."

"She wanted to protect her father."

"And her daughter," his mother reminded. "Caroline would do anything for her daughter."

"Even lie to me."

"Any mother would deceive to protect their child to see that they were safe and secure."

Sterling arched an eyebrow and stared at his mother.

"I will admit that given Avery was only eleven that I should have returned, and it is a decision I will always regret. But he had four older brothers and your father. He was not left alone in the world to fend for himself."

"Neither is Livia."

"Her father was dead and all she has is her mother. She had not known her uncle until he arrived here and her grandfather only cared about grapes and has little to do with her. Livia's survival, having a home and food and her happiness rested on Caroline's shoulders alone. She would do anything to protect her."

"No matter who she angered or betrayed?"

"Yes."

"That is the answer I needed to hear." He picked up his valise and started for the door.

"What a person does out of love carries different consequences. She did not deceive you out of malice but to protect her family."

He knew that, but she should have trusted him with the truth. Maybe not at first, but later, after they had become close. Yet she hadn't, and he doubted that she had ever cared.

"She was dishonest. That is all I need to know." Sterling yanked open the front door. He could not stand there and argue with his mother any longer. His decision was made because Caroline had taken his heart and stomped on it just as she had the grapes. Except he bled red, not wine.

"If you walk out that door and sail away, you are no better than your father—stubborn with no room for forgiveness. Demanding and unyielding, no room for understanding. Expecting everyone to rise to an impossible standard that you have set then sending them away when they fail or leave them behind."

"This is different, Mother."

"It is not, Sterling, and for that I am sorry."

"Goodbye, Mother."

"What of Caroline and her family?" his mother called after he was seated in the wagon. "Who will be your estate manager?"

"William or Caroline, it does not matter. Let Hallaway be in charge of the grapes and wine for as long as he wants. I no longer care."

CAROLINE REMAINED IN her home, as did her father and brother. They were not certain what to do. She assumed that when the decision was made, Wyndham would come and tell them. A part of her wanted to start packing, believing it was inevitable that they would be asked to leave. Yet she couldn't bring herself to do so. Maybe it was because she was nearly paralyzed with fear. Where would they go and what would they do?

The anxiety also temporarily overrode the pain in her heart. That ache deep down that she had lost love.

The knock on the door startled her but she could not move. She looked at her father then William. Her father was only here because neither her nor William would allow him to go the vineyard until their fate was decided. William had paced and waited to learn their fate.

Caroline took a deep breath, crossed to the entry and opened the door only to find Lady Wyndham standing there.

"Did you need something Lady Wyndham?"

"No, Caroline, I came to see you."

Her heart sank. She was going to tell her that Sterling was gone. She should not be surprised because there was no longer a reason for him to remain, but it hurt deeply.

"What of our circumstances?" William asked.

"To quote my son after I asked who was to the estate manager, 'William or Caroline, it does not matter. Let Hallaway be in charge of the grapes and wine for as long as he wants. I no longer care.'"

Her brother let out a sigh of relief and part of her fear eased.

"Walk with me Caroline."

She did as Lady Wyndham asked and stepped outside onto the terrace.

"I am sorry things did not turn out better."

"We have our positions and we still have a home. I can assure you that we are very grateful."

"That is not what I meant."

She did not want to discuss Sterling, especially with his mother.

"I really thought he had changed. I thought he found happiness here. I wanted so much for the two of you, I hoped…Why else would I make certain you were with him every time I sent him away? The two of you were prefect for each other."

Caroline could only stare. First the manipulation so Sterling could remember where he came from. The second manipulation was because Caroline needed to take more time for herself. Now, to find out that there had been a third and that it was because his mother decided to be a matchmaker was too much. Had she not interfered, Caroline would never have come to know Sterling so well, nor become his lover, and she would not be hurting so badly right now.

Oh, she wanted to give Lady Wyndham a piece of her mind

but knew that it would not do any good.

"It was never meant to be, Lady Wyndham. And even if there had been a possibility, I destroyed any chance by my deception."

"He is as stubborn and hardhearted as his father."

He was not. No matter how he had treated her yesterday out of anger, she knew that he had changed, but it was likely only temporary and he would revert to who he had been once he was back in England. "Then perhaps it is best that it ended this way."

It was something that she would need to tell herself in the days to come, especially during the long nights alone in her bed.

"Perhaps," his mother agreed. "But I do not need to be happy about it." She forced a smile. "But, now that my son is gone, I expect you, along with your brother and father to join me for dinner tonight."

Caroline was fairly certain that she would have no appetite.

"I insist!"

"Yes, of course." Perhaps by the time the dinner hour arrived she might be in better spirits, but it was unlikely.

CHAPTER FORTY-SEVEN

WHEN STERLING HAD arrived at the ship and informed that captain that he was ready to leave, he was told that it would not be for another three days since supplies needed to be arranged and the sailors who had taken leave needed to be rounded up and brought back on the ship.

He had wanted to be gone—immediately. Instead, he was left to cool his heels and wait on others.

He certainly did not want to return to the estate until the ship was ready to sail. He could not risk coming face to face with Caroline again, nor did he want to be lectured by his mother any more than he already had been. He wanted to remain angry with Caroline. He wanted to hate her, but it was hard to hold onto those emotions when he'd been told to wait. It was like stomping out of a room and slamming a door to make a point only to be stopped by a wall and unable to vent his anger.

Instead, he had gotten settled into his cabin and when he could not stand to be on the ship any longer because he knew that he would be confined to it for the next two or three months, depending on currents and wind, he disembarked and walked along the docks, then into town and visited the shops and taverns that he had not taken time to explore previously.

At the last tavern, and after he had eaten a meal, Sterling proceeded to get drunk, so drunk that he had no idea how he made it back to the ship but he woke up in his bunk and immediately reached for the chamber pot as he tossed up his accounts.

Never had he drunk so much before, but he supposed that was what came from having a heart broken.

Not only broken but shattered by a woman who he thought he could trust.

He would be better off to return to London, find a bride of equal rank, and one who understood duty and would not expect an emotional attachment.

At least it wouldn't matter if she lied because she would not have the power to hurt him.

Sterling recalled that he may have said that to someone at the tavern, but the memory was not clear, and it could have been a dream, but he was fairly certain that person had called him an arse and he'd struck him.

He lay back on this bunk and pinched the bridge of his nose. It was a dream, or nightmare, brought one by the whisky and ale because the person who had confronted him had been his brother, Elliot, who was far away in Madeira, and who he planned on visiting before he returned home.

CAROLINE ROSE THE next day with determination to put Sterling behind her. Despite her duplicity, she and her family still had a home, her father had a position, and now William did as well. She would teach him what he did not already know about managing Wyndview Farm and then leave it in his capable hands. She would also encourage Lady Wyndham to hire a housekeeper and then Caroline would only take care of the home she lived in, her daughter, brother, and father. This was to be her lot in life.

Yes, she had enjoyed her time with Sterling and it was good to have been wanted again, loved even, but it had come to an end. She would also never again put herself in a position to risk her heart. It had been devastating when Peter had been killed and her heart now ached just as much by Sterling's rejection and Caroline knew that she could never suffer this way again.

However, that did not mean she would not take tea with bachelors—*eventually*. One day her brother would marry and she and Livia would need to find another place to live. Maybe one of the bachelors Lady Wyndham had been eager to introduce her to would be a good match. Not for love, and she certainly did not want to go through a courtship. No, she wanted an arrangement for the sake of security for herself and her daughter and in exchange, she would be an excellent wife, keep an exceptional home, and be a pleasant hostess if there was a need. However, he would need to have standing enough to employ a cook, because it was true that while she could prepare a meal, they were rarely of good quality.

There was no hurry and she certainly was in no rush, but Caroline needed to be prepared for the day her brother decided to marry and when she would need a home of her own. Fortunately, she had a lot of time since as far as she knew, William had not yet met anyone that he wished to court, but he would, one day, therefore, it was better to plan for that now, then rush and make a horrible mistake.

She wiped a tear from the corner of her eye then set out to find Lady Wyndham.

CHAPTER FORTY-EIGHT

A T A KNOCK on his cabin door, Sterling grumbled for them to enter and hoped that it was the captain telling him they were ready to sail. He didn't even open his eyes as the door creaked open.

"Good God, by the stench in here, someone should dump you in the ocean."

Sterling cracked his eyes open and squinted at the entrance to his cabin. Maybe it hadn't been a dream. "Where the bloody hell did you come from?"

"I told you last night, but I would not be surprised that you do not remember," Elliot answered.

Sterling pulled himself up then swung his legs over so that he was sitting on the side of the bunk. He then took deep breaths and hoped that he didn't need to reach for the chamber pot again.

"I have a vague recollection of you," he finally said.

"I should hope so," Elliot chuckled. "If you are going to give a man a blackened eye then you should certainly recall doing so and why."

"You called me arse…I think."

"I did and have not changed my opinion on that matter."

Sterling tilted his head and glared at his young brother. "Why are you here and not on our estate in Madeira?"

"Those questions will be answered, *again*, after you have washed, changed your clothing, and meet me on the deck because if I am forced to remain in this cabin with you a moment longer, I will be the one retching."

It was not so bad here, was it? Sterling sniffed then drew back. Even if he did change his clothing, he would still be offensive, as was the foul odor from the chamber pot. It filled the entire space of the small cabin. "Find me an inn and order a bath," he said, then slowly pulled himself from the bunk. "I will pack suitable clothing."

His head pounded and his stomach churned. He hoped that being off a ship that gently rose and fell with the current of the ocean waves would relieve one of his ailments, but he needed to locate Dover's Powder for the other. "And make sure there is a pitcher of water. I am parched." Not just thirsty but his mouth was as dry as cotton.

"I am not your bloody servant," Elliot retorted.

"Please," Sterling ground out.

Elliot left, closing the door behind him, but laughed his way down the corridor.

Oh, his brother would never let him forget today or last night. Except, Sterling barely recalled last night.

After he had managed to change his clothing, and pack a few sets of clothes and necessities, he made his way up to the deck only to wince when he encountered the bright sun made worse by the reflection of the ocean. He tilted his chin down and adjusted his hat, then made his way to the gangplank hoping that Elliot would soon return.

"Have you decided to remain?" the captain asked.

He had not, except, he had not seen Elliot in nearly five years and even though Sterling had intended to travel to Madeira, there was no point in doing so if the person he had intended to visit was here. "Yes, for now," he answered. "I wish to visit with my brother."

"Does that mean we will not be sailing to Madeira but back to England?"

"Does it make a difference?" Sterling's head pounded too

fiercely to have a conversation.

"It takes, at the most, up to eight weeks to sail to Madeira while sailing directly to England could take up to three months depending on the weather we encounter, therefore, I would need to plan for the proper provisions before we embarked."

The calculations, timing, sailing to different places was too much for his head. "I will speak with my brother and find out how long he intended to remain and will then make my decision, but it is likely we will be here another sennight," Sterling answered.

Had Elliot arrived before yesterday, he would have known because there was no other reason for his brother to be here, other than to visit their mother, therefore, it was unlikely he planned to sail back to Madeira anytime soon and Sterling would like to remain with Elliot.

It just wouldn't be at Wyndview Farm where Caroline resided.

"WOULD YOU LIKE to join me in touring the gardens today to help determine what work must be done?" Caroline asked Livia.

At the word *gardens*, her child had lost the rose hue in her cheeks.

Caroline understood the fear and wished that she could help Livia recover somehow, but she hadn't taken the opportunity. The harvest of the grapes had happened right after the incident with the cobra and Caroline had not realized how deeply her daughter feared encountering another, for which she could not blame her.

She had incorrectly assumed that Livia had realized that she had been safe and had done the right thing and therefore would remember for the future. She hadn't balked at going back outside and often went to the kitchens or to visit Lady Wyndham, except to do so, Livia only needed to cross a terrace, where there were no plants or anything that could hide a venomous snake and it was only after she'd seen Livia carefully look across the terrace before she left the house did Caroline realize how deeply her daughter still feared.

Maybe if she hadn't been so caught up with the harvest, and all that needed to be done at Wyndview Farm, her lies, and falling in love with Sterling while she carried on as his lover Caroline would have noticed that her daughter had not recovered from an earlier fright.

"Where is your walking stick?" she asked.

"In my chamber," Livia answered.

"Take that with you and stomp the ground with it then you will not need to worry."

Livia took in a shaky breath, then rushed up the stairs only to return with the stick her brother had carved for her.

"Are you ready?" Caroline stood by the open door.

Livia hesitated and looked out, then exited onto the terrace. They started to walk away from the house, toward the kitchen gardens but Livia stopped, shaking her head. "You go on, Mother." She then thrust the cane at Caroline.

"It is not important that we inspect the gardens today," Caroline returned. She could instruct a servant to do so.

"We should visit Lady Wyndham," Livia suggested.

"Why is that?"

"Because she must be sad, like you."

Caroline frowned. "Why are either of us sad?"

"Because the earl left." Livia blinked up with her innocent answer.

"Perhaps she is, but she has another visitor now," Caroline answered. She'd met Elliot Wynd last evening when they had arrived for dinner. Apparently, his ship had arrived after Sterling's had sailed, or so she assumed. It was a shame since Sterling was on his way to visit his brother before he returned home.

Then again, perhaps they'd seen the other at the docks and

Sterling was able to visit with Elliot and alter his plans before sailing.

Not that it mattered to her since Sterling was gone and she would likely never see him again.

"Is he like the earl?"

"How so?"

"Nice."

"Much nicer," Caroline answered. Elliot Wynd was very likeable and he was relaxed and laughed and shared stories from his childhood which made Lady Wyndham smile. Maybe his visit would help with her disappointment in Sterling leaving.

Again, none of that was her concern. The Wynd family had nothing to do with her. Her father and brother were employed by them and they were nothing more than servants even if Lady Wyndham tended to treat them more like family or friends.

"Then come along." Livia tugged on her hand.

"We should not intrude," Caroline insisted.

"But I want to meet him." Livia let go of Caroline's hand and rushed ahead and was inside before Caroline could catch up and stop her.

Livia darted into the sitting room then stopped and turned around.

"Are you looking for something, dear?" Lady Wyndham asked.

"I thought you had a visitor and I wanted to meet him."

"I am so sorry, Lady Wyndham. I will do better in teaching Livia about our different stations."

"Why start now?" Lady Wyndham chuckled. "She is as welcome here anytime she wishes, as are you, just as my sons are."

While it was a relief and comforting to hear those words, Caroline did need to remember her place. Maybe she would not have fallen in love with Sterling had she. Even if she had still been forced to accompany him to their various locations, she would have done better at guarding her heart.

"Where is he?" Livia asked.

"Do you mean my son, Elliot?"

"Mama did not tell me his name, but yes, him."

Lady Wyndham chuckled again. "He is not here. He has…he had matters to attend to in town."

The way Lady Wyndham hesitation made Caroline wonder if there wasn't something she was hiding. Then again, the reason for Elliot being gone could be as simple as it was not something a child would understand. Not that it mattered anyway because she was certain his absence had nothing to do with Sterling since he had sailed away yesterday.

With that thought, her heart painfully contracted and she looked way and blinked as tears stung her eyes.

How could she love someone so deeply, without even realizing how much until he was gone?

Oh, life was easier when one did not love.

Chapter Forty-Nine

STERLING SANK DOWN as far as he could, wishing the hipbath was large enough that the hot water could reach his shoulders. As it was, his knees were bent as far as his legs would allow and he wasn't at all comfortable, so he pulled himself up so that his back was supported and the water only reaching as far as his waist.

Elliot stirred Dover's Powder into a glass of water then handed it to Sterling. He forced himself to drink it despite the bitterness and hoped that it worked quickly to relieve the pounding in his head.

"Eat this" Elliot held out a slice of bread. "It could help settle your stomach."

Sterling took the offering but it only made him thirsty again. "Could you refill the water?"

Elliot did as asked and Sterling alternated between eating the bread and drinking the water as his steaming bath began to cool and some of the pain began to ease from his neck and shoulders.

When he couldn't eat anymore, he set both glass and bread aside, leaned back and closed his eyes.

"Coffee?" Elliot asked.

That was exactly what he needed. "How did you know?" Sterling asked without opening his eyes.

"I have been in the same condition and likely a lot more often than you."

Elliot had been the one to enjoy life to the fullest until he sailed to Maderia, as their father had insisted before he died. Though, he supposed his brother may still be enjoying ale, wine, and every variety of women God had created. It wasn't as if such vices were only limited to England.

Sterling leaned forward and washed his hair and body with the soap provided, then rose and wrapped himself in a towel, tucking the end at his waist.

With a sigh he turned to face Elliot who had made himself quite comfortable on his bed, pillows stacked behind his head and back, half sitting, booted feet crossed at the ankles, and his arms crossed over his middle wearing a devil-may-care grin that Sterling was certain his brother had been born with.

"What?" Sterling demanded.

"I am simply enjoying my eldest brother's loss of control for possibly the first time in your life."

"What is that supposed to mean?" Sterling grumbled.

"You were always the most like Father: disciplined, serious, never one to step out of line, and certainly never drank to excess because you had duties that you must attend to, yet, I found you bloody drunk last night." He grinned again. "Care to tell me why?"

"No, I do not." Sterling grabbed a pair of trousers.

"Then tell me about… what was her name? Ah, yes, Caroline."

Sterling glared at his brother. First, he hated Elliot's description of his personality. Or maybe he hated that his brother was correct. Second, he did not want to discuss Caroline.

"Why are you here?" Sterling countered instead of answering.

"I decided visit Mother."

"You could have visited Southampton if you wanted to travel."

"Yes, you have our brothers whereas I am without family as is Mother. Of course, I never even considered that you might be visiting as well and was rather shocked to realize that the ship I saw in the harbor, that I had assumed was here to collect barrels of wine, had actually delivered you. Of course, I did not know that until I spoke with the captain and learned that you would soon depart so I hurried to Wyndview Farm only to find out that you had left."

Sterling frowned. Had Elliot arrived after he had left the ship that led to him getting drunk? He must have since the captain only knew he left the ship, not where he had gone and likely assumed he'd returned to Wyndview Farm.

"How long do you intend to remain?" he asked.

"I do not know." He shrugged. "It was not until after dinner, after the guests had departed, that Mother fully explained why she warned me not to mention you and your ship until they were gone."

Sterling frowned. "What guests?"

"Mr. Hallaway and his son and Caroline, who is quite beautiful even though she was downhearted. Her brown eyes were puffy as if she had been crying," Elliot commented looking him in the eye.

"What exactly did Mother explain?" Sterling ground out.

"It was a tale of love and betrayal, secrets, lies, broken hearts, and an earl who was too quick to judge and not tolerant enough to listen."

Sterling snorted. His mother had clearly sided with Caroline, though he was not surprised since she had been in on the duplicity.

"After I heard the whole of it, I went looking for you. Since you weren't on the ship, I visited practically every tavern near the docks before I found you deep in your cups and barely able to stand, so I got you back to your ship where I left you to sleep it off."

Sterling groaned. "Did I say anything?" Did he want to know?

"Only that you loved Caroline and that she lies."

"Yes, well, she did."

"And that is the end of the matter?" Elliot asked.

"I cannot trust her," Sterling reminded Elliot or maybe he was trying to convince himself.

"Mother said that you arrived behaving just like father, but then relaxed, laughed and remembered what it was like to be happy, just like father before moving to England, and with one deception, you reverted to our father, where nobody was allowed a mistake and excuses were not to be tolerated."

That was exactly what he had done and Sterling hated himself for that. But it was too late now and even if Caroline forgave him, Sterling wasn't certain that she could ever be trusted.

"WHY MUST WE hire a housekeeper?" Lady Wyndham asked for what must have been the tenth time.

"Because I should no longer be in that position. It was never my place."

"If it is wages you want, we can arrange for them," she promised.

"It is not the wages." Though, perhaps she shouldn't disregard the option so quickly. She may not need funds now, but the day may come when she must make and home for herself and Livia somewhere else, if she didn't marry for convenience. "I will think on the manner," she finally said.

"Of course, you will and then you will accept and I will not be forced to endure interviews," Lady Wyndham decided, as if the matter was settled. "And I will also see that you are paid wages for being my companion."

"That is not necessary, Lady Wyndham. I enjoy visiting with you."

"Yes, and while I appreciate your words, I did take advantage of you."

"You did not," Caroline insisted. "My father was paid fully for duties he neglected. I did those duties and the wages went to the correct household."

Caroline placed her teacup in the saucer on the table then settled back against the settee. "Truthfully, I am happy that I no longer need to fear the truth being learned and soon William will be responsible for everything."

"Then we will put our attention to inviting bachelors to tea." She smiled as if Caroline still wasn't suffering from heartache.

Then again, she had no way of knowing what she and Sterling had shared. It wasn't as if they courted. There may have been whispers when they worked closely during the harvest, but there was no proof that they were anything other than close friends, and he always came to her after everyone had retired, so of course, Lady Wyndham would see no reason why Caroline would object to inviting bachelors to tea.

"In time," she said.

"Is it because my son broke your heart?"

Caroline blinked at her. "No...of course not...how...why would you assume such."

Lady Wyndham chuckled. "Caroline, it was obvious."

"Nothing was obvious," she argued.

"I saw how he looked at you." She grinned. "More importantly, I suffer from insomnia and I often saw my son cross the terrace to your chamber once he believed everyone was asleep."

Caroline wished that she could disappear. Sterling being her lover was to have always been a secret.

"I thought that since the two of you became lovers that love was included."

"You know that such an emotion is not necessary, Lady Wyndham"

"Unfortunately, it is not. That saddens me, Caroline, because I truly had hoped to have you as a daughter-in-law."

She would have liked that as well.

CHAPTER FIFTY

ELLIOT HAD SPENT a good portion of the day with Sterling, but he refused to talk about Caroline, and when it came time for dinner, insisted they return to their mother at Wyndview Farm to dine.

Sterling had wanted to, but he couldn't risk seeing Caroline. It would hurt him too much so he told Elliot to visit him tomorrow, if he could find the time.

But, what if, with Sterling out of the way, Elliot decided that he wanted to court Caroline?

He had said she was beautiful, which she was.

If not Elliot, then another man would call on her.

His stomach knotted with the very idea of any other man kissing Caroline.

Jealousy was an uncomfortable emotion and he did not like it very much.

With those thoughts, he opened the door to a tavern, entered, and found a table in a dark corner and ordered a meal.

When a pitcher of ale was placed on the table, Sterling almost rejected it, but instead, he poured himself a glass. He swore that he would not drink half as much as he had the night before.

He had just pushed his plate away when Elliot entered the tavern and took a seat across from him.

"What are you doing here?"

"Mother kicked me out. She said you needed me more than she did."

Sterling snorted. For a woman who liked to have her sons visit, she certainly sent them away often enough.

"She also encouraged me to bring you to your senses before it was too late and Caroline was lost to you for good and you were miserable for the rest of your life."

"I will not be miserable," he insisted, though he certainly felt that way now.

"Tell me about the ball," Elliot prompted.

"Why?"

"Because Mother said so." His brother grinned.

"It was a bloody ball at the Governor's home."

"You can do better than that, Sterling. Much better."

So, he told him what he remembered, and answered questions, but admitted nothing as to his opinion or feelings for Caroline.

Elliot then asked about their visit to Stellenbosch, their penguin watch, the climb to Table Mountain, and then the weeks of harvest. Each time, he asked more about Caroline than anything else, and Sterling found himself answering, knowing full well that their mother had instructed Elliot what to ask, to make Sterling remember again, just as she had manipulated him into remembering an earlier, happier time for their family.

"Do not be like Father, Sterling," Elliot said quietly. "If I were lucky enough to have found what you have, I would be fighting to win her back, even if it meant groveling and begging forgiveness."

Sterling stared into his tankard of ale and knew that Elliot was correct, but it wasn't so easy to return.

If he were to be honest, he was ashamed and afraid.

His mother's scolding still rang in his mind and he could not help but to ask himself how far he would go to protect those he loved most?

Sterling did not like the answer that echoed through his mind. He would do anything, legal or not, and deceive if necessary.

He had never experienced the kind of love a mother, or even

a father for that matter, would have for a child, but he was protective of his brothers.

And he remembered the panic when Livia stood before the cobra and he forced himself to remain calm as he instructed her on how to retreat, then the relief when she flung her little arms around his neck and cried.

Something had shifted inside him and he still could not identify what it had been, but it was a warmth and need to protect.

Sterling did not want to be like his father and he would argue that he was not.

"Do not be like Father and let pride and pain become your shield. The person who will suffer the most will be you."

As his father had done, they only knew when he was deep in his cups and went on about their mother and that he had been wrong. He had erred and had lost her and it was too late.

"It is not too late for you and Caroline," Elliot said almost as if he could read Sterling's mind.

Unlike his father, he was leaving Caroline behind because she had deceived him and he feared that he could not truly trust her.

Except, in his heart, he knew that he could. She had only kept her secrets to protect her family. To protect Livia.

But for me, and Livia, I need you to prepare for a meeting with Wyndham. If you do not, there is a very good chance that you will be sacked. If that happens, you will never be able to work with the grapes again. You will not be able to tend the vines that Mother cultivated. They will belong to another. We might even be forced to return to England and you will not be able to visit Mother any longer. Do you understand me? That was what Caroline had been saying to her father when he walked into her home.

It wasn't simply asking but begging him to do the right thing.

Her father had failed her.

If he sailed home without her, was he just as stubborn and idiotic as his father?

He did not want to turn into a bitter man. He did not want to make the same mistakes his father had. There was more to life than Trade Wynd and heirs.

Was it worth the risk?

Could there be forgiveness?

Could he trust again?

Did he want to live without Caroline?

"What if she is not honest with me again?"

"Do not put Caroline in a position that she must fear for the safety and security of her daughter and you will have no concerns," Elliot answered simply.

She had only protected Livia, then her father, and lastly herself. There had been nothing malicious in her deception, only fear because she had lost everything once before and was afraid of losing again.

He was a bloody, arrogant fool.

He also understood why she hadn't told him at first, and why it became difficult. If he'd had a secret that he held onto for so long…

He had. He knew that he was in love with her for two months before he told her. He had been too afraid because of rejection. She'd been too afraid because of what could be lost.

Maybe if he would have confessed what he was hiding, she might have as well.

Except, he would never know.

"It is your future, your happiness, and your trust," Elliot reminded him.

ALL WILL BE *well,* Caroline repeated to herself even if it wasn't said out loud.

She was grateful for what they had, especially in this moment as she sat on the terrace with Livia and enjoyed the biscuits that Cook had just taken from the oven.

They had a home, her brother would be the next estate manager after she finished training him, and her father would take care of his grapes and hold onto the memories of his wife.

She would be happy if her heart didn't ache so much and she would live with the regret of her poor choices for the rest of her life.

No, she was not going to think about Sterling because she might cry. Tears were for when she was alone and she did not want to explain to Livia.

She was too young to understand anyway.

"I thought he left, Mama?"

Caroline looked at her daughter. "Who, darling?

"The earl." Livia pointed to behind Caroline.

She slowly turned to find that Sterling was standing just outside the door of his home.

He should have already sailed. At least that was what she assumed. Had he seen his brother and decided to remain? It certainly was not because of her.

He likely thought to come outside but when he saw her, he was not certain what to do. There could be several reasons why he was standing there that had nothing to do with her.

Except, he was staring at her. Making Caroline nervous. Therefore, she stood and smoothed out her dress while simultaneously wiping her sweaty palms on her skirt.

"I am sorry."

He said three simple words that nearly caused her heart to stop.

He took a step in her direction. "I understand."

She was afraid to ask what it was he understood, and she did not dare hope.

"I, too, would go to great lengths to protect my family, especially if I had a young child. At least I like to think that I would."

Her hands started to shake. He kept walking until he stood before her.

"I do not want to be miserable like my father. I don't want to lose love because of pride. I don't want to become bitter because I rejected love and was too proud to forgive. Too proud to ask for forgiveness."

Tears sprang to her eyes.

"It is true that you make me a better man. Or, you had been responsible for until I was a complete and utter unforgiving arse to you. My only excuse was that it came from a place of more of pain and less of anger." He reached out and took her hands. "I love you, Caroline. I do not know when it began. I just know that I do, and I swear with everything that I am that I will never treat you poorly but will honor and cherish you every single day. I do not want to return to England without you. Please say that you will come with me."

All she could do was stare into his blue eyes, warm and sincere, and her pulse pounded as her heart melted. Could she trust that this was true?

"What about me?" Livia asked.

Caroline dropped her chin and tried not to laugh.

"I do not want to go back without you either, Livia," Sterling answered with a chuckle.

"Okay," her daughter answered happily.

"Caroline, I am asking you to be my wife, if you will have me."

"Yes," she said without even having to think. "I promise that I will never keep another secret from you and I will not even consider a deception. You will always know what is in my heart and what I am thinking. I never want to make that mistake again."

"I know you will not, and neither will I." He then placed his palms against her cheeks and kissed her.

It was the sweetest and most wonderful kiss she had ever received.

EPILOGUE

Six years later

CAROLINE HELD ON tightly and she leaned over the rail of the ship and tossed up her accounts. Sterling rubbed his hand up and down her back in a soothing manner.

"How soon will we get there?" She had been vomiting daily since a month into their trip.

"The captain says we will be there by today. We just need to watch for the port."

"It has happened again," Livia observed.

"What's happened?" her younger brother Joseph asked.

"We're going to have another sibling."

Caroline looked over her shoulder at her daughter, who was now eleven years old. How could she know? She was too young to know about these matters.

"She did the same before you came along, and before Lily," Livia answered.

Lily was barely two years old and she was down in the cabin napping with the nursery maid.

"It could be sickness from being at sea," Caroline said.

"Did that happen to you before?" Livia asked.

"No, it did not," Sterling answered for her.

"See, I told you."

"Is it better?" Sterling asked quietly.

Caroline nodded and he pulled her close so that she could rest her head on his chest.

"I promise that we will not leave until you are feeling better even if that means we have to wait until this child is born."

She tilted her head and looked up at him. "Lord Wyndham, does that mean that we will stay away from Trade Wynd for nearly nine months because this child will not arrive for six and then it is a three-month journey back?"

"I have before and I will again. I find the best things happen to me when I am away from Southampton longer than intended. Maybe we will stay away for an entire year."

"What do you think Damian would say?"

Damian was the brother who took care of the imports and exports leaving and arriving on ships and kept his offices near the warehouse.

"He will do well enough."

"So you say but he has been rather preoccupied of late as well."

"With the best of things," he said before he kissed the tip of her nose.

"Your father would not approve," she teased.

"And that is how I know that I am making the right decision." He grinned.

"There it is," Livia cried as she pointed. They both turned as the port came into view. Excitement built inside and Caroline could hardly contain herself as the ship drew closer until docked. She then grew impatient waiting for their luggage to be unloaded and then placed in a wagon.

Livia stood near and held tightly to her brother's hand, especially when he wanted to stray toward the tall grasses.

Caroline glanced down at her daughter with concern.

"There are some things I remember very well from when we lived here." She then shuddered.

She supposed that even though Livia had only been five that she would never forget coming face-to-face with a cobra.

When Sterling returned with the rented wagon, she helped the children after their luggage was loaded.

"Do you know what I want to do while we are here?" Sterling asked.

"What?"

"We need to take the children to Stellenbosch. It is their family and might be the very place where you stole my heart."

"If I recall correctly, what you wanted had nothing to do with my heart."

"In that, you are correct." He chuckled. "You have made me a very happy man indeed, Caroline."

She placed a palm against his cheek. "I love you."

He turned to kiss her hand. "Let us go introduce our children to their grandparents and uncle."

"You did tell them to expect us, did you not?" Caroline asked as Sterling helped her into the back of the wagon.

His blue eyes lit with mischief. "I may have neglected to do so," he offered casually. "I decided that it might be more fun to show up without notice and see what happens. It did work out well last time I did so."

"That is your opinion," Caroline laughed. "Thankfully we have their grandchildren with us so your mother should not be too cross."

"Nor your father." He laughed and joined her. "In fact, I would not be surprised if my mother kept sending us off together, but this time so she could spoil our children without our interference."

"You are likely correct." Caroline looked into his eyes, her heart swelling with love. "And I would not mind at all."

About the Author

USA Today bestselling author Jane Charles is a prolific writer of over fifty historical romance novels. Her love of research and history lends authenticity to her Regency romances, and her experience directing theatre productions helps her craft beautiful, touching stories that tug at the heartstrings. Jane is an upbeat and positive author dedicated to giving her characters happy-ever-afters and leaving the readers satisfied at the end of an emotional journey. She is a lifelong Cubs fan, loves wine tastings, and lives in Central Illinois with her two huskies and husband. She is currently writing her next book while planning her dream trip to Europe.

Facebook: Facebook.com/JaneACharles
Facebook Author Page: Facebook.com/JaneCharlesAuthor
Reader Group – Romance and Rosé:
Facebook.com/groups/romanceandrose
Instagram: janeacharles
TikTok: @janecharlesauthor